DRIFT

ROMAN HAWTHORNE

EDITED BY
PAM ELISE

COVER BY
NICOLE HOWER

PROLOGUE

THROUGH A MICROSCOPE, Victor Hart examined a chemical mixture that had blown up the compound to twenty times its size. Victor was beginning to suspect that his assistant, Chaitin Russell, had been correct in his analysis. The compound seemed too volatile. Filaments formed spontaneously and then disappeared, connecting the elements for fractions of a second, just long enough to change them in some way that was too discreet for the microscope to detect. The chemicals could never be used in an aging treatment. Bright greens and yellows flashed as lux operons activated under his eyes, forcing him to look away at times. An entire six-year project was dead if the chemical soup was so volatile that…but wait, he could test that.

He pulled a small sample from the petri dish using a sterile pipette, a finger-sized hollow tube that drew in fluid for transfer from one dish to another. A thought occurred to Victor mid-lift: he still had hamsters left. A dab might tell him if the chemical agent was as corrosive and deadly as it looked under twenty-time magnification.

Victor grumbled as he made the short trip across the lab to

where he'd stacked the four hamster cages atop one another. He pulled down the top one, in which a tiny white rodent hid behind a toy log. With practiced hands, Victor scooped out the hamster and, holding the pipette steady, shook a drop loose onto the creature's back before he placed it back into the cage.

Then he waited. Seconds passed, then minutes, and nothing happened. A slow grin crept onto Victor's face. This meant that he was wrong (thankfully). The agent seemed inert and only reacted with itself, giving the appearance of volatility under a microscope, but in fact, it might not have been as dangerous as Victor thought. He turned back to his work. Sure, there were more studies he'd have to finish before he could test on humans, but a stable solution held great promise to advance the field of aging. Completing his recent work would add one more success to his collection for the skin crème he'd already developed that reversed the appearance of aging by tightening the wrinkles around the eyes and the gel that could be used as a preventative against those pesky sleep bags. Victor used that one himself so that his long days and late nights wouldn't be obvious. In many ways, the new antiaging serum would be more of the same, but in one very specific way, it would be revolutionary.

If Victor turned out to be right, this mixture would repair specific DNA damage that happened to all human cells over time. Aggregated sun damage? Missing or damaged cytosines in the subject's DNA would be replaced or repaired with a one-time injection to take ten years off someone's body.

And how much for said treatment? Two-hundred thirty-seven thousand dollars each round, if Chaitin had calculated right. That would make them both billionaires in the first year *if* they could get the chemicals distributed.

His mobile buzzed, and he placed the pipette down on the counter and reached into his pocket.

"What's going on, Chaitin?" he asked.

"Are the samples ready?" Chaitin queried.

"Yeah, I guess," Victor said, then hung up and ran his hand across his head. In truth, he needed more time, but he'd asked Chaitin to ensure he didn't lose track of when the marketing demo was. Their first interview with a cosmetics supplier was later that afternoon. Victor scanned his lab to look for the baby hamsters his product had produced so far after months of applications. Two of six were still alive, so that was progress. He scooped both up and placed them in the cage with his latest experiment. Borderline Cosmetics would want to see a live demonstration, never mind that it really took several months for the treatment to work. The lag was by design, as DNA was a dangerous thing to manipulate quickly. Victor needed the time to identify and fix problems along the way. But Chaitin insisted on a demo, and smoke and mirrors would have to do the trick.

The petri dish began to glow, this time brightly enough to be seen without the microscopic lens. Puzzled, Victor left the hamsters and the cage on the counter, carefully fastening the wire door in place. He crossed the room to examine the petri dish. He pulled it out from under the microscope and shook his head at the bubbling liquid underneath. He didn't have time to retest it. Instead, he decided to store it for examination later. He cursed at himself for working so far from what he called the fridge, a flash freezer that took temperatures down to nearly absolute zero, which was low enough to stifle almost any chemical reaction. The dish would be safe in there until he had a chance to examine it more closely. Victor pushed the button on the refrigeration unit to unlatch. When the door opened, emitting a vapor hiss into the air, Victor stepped backward, sloshing the petri dish he carried. A droplet fell on his skin between his glove and his lab coat. He wiped it onto his pants without too much thought. It wasn't as though the serum would work without the activator, and he hadn't injected it, so there was no cause for alarm. And anyway, the hamster hadn't so much as whimpered.

He pushed the dish into the fridge and slammed the door shut. Victor's face began to burn, and his fingers tingled. He suddenly felt light and airy, as though he could float up to the sky. An itch started on his back just out of reach. Victor punched the button to lock the fridge and, at the same time, heard an animal cry out in pain. He turned to the table where the hamsters were.

Was it his imagination, or had the older hamster grown in size? And…

He staggered toward the cage, and his eyes shot wide. One of the two hamsters cowered in the corner on the far side. The other lay on its side, entrails exposed, while the older hamster, the one he'd dropped the fluid onto, chewed its way into the creature's stomach. Victor fell to his knees, and his head pounded. He reminded himself that it had been stupid to cage the hamsters together anyway because hamsters weren't exactly friendly and were highly territorial. It could still mean nothing.

His feet felt confined in his shoes, so he kicked them off while he was breathing lightly. Another animal scream sounded out. Victor looked toward the counter and saw that the other hamster had died too. Now there was only one, and at the rate that he chewed through even the bones, soon there would be nothing left of either. That part wasn't normal hamster behavior.

Victor's teeth bit into his lower lip. They weren't his teeth any longer. They were massive canines, and they drew blood. He spat out a mouthful and thought about the new information. The hamster was a mass of fleshy tentacles that smashed themselves against the glass. If Victor wasn't mistaken, the creature wanted him next.

Chaitin was on his way, Victor reminded himself. He

reviewed what he knew. The hamster was changing; that was undeniable. Victor had been wrong about the new treatment being inert. But the change wasn't necessarily permanent. Beads of sweat gathered on his forehead. Each thought took more and more time to parse. Maybe all Victor needed was a rest on a couch. And to get rid of the evidence. If the cosmetic company got wind of the fact that the chemicals could be dangerous in the body then those risk-averse types would never buy in.

He realized as he stumbled that his feet had grown broader and flatter and, from the feel of them, had developed webbing between his toes. That was alarming, sure, but again, there wasn't much of the mixture on his skin, so the changes must stop soon. He grabbed the hamster cage and wandered aimlessly through the room. Victor had been doing something, but he couldn't quite recall. The doorbell rang, and he ignored it. Making his way back toward his bedroom was his only goal. He was so tired. Victor tried to remember if he'd left the old formula samples on the counter or the dangerous new one. They both used similar delivery mechanisms and looked almost exactly the same. He *thought* it was the old one and that he'd put the new one he'd been testing away. His breathing grew labored as he passed through the door to his room. Victor had the wherewithal to shut and lock the door to his bedroom. He placed the cage, now with only one confined hamster, on his dresser and collapsed into his bed.

Chaitin Russell glowered. He'd done his best to do the presentation solo, but nobody seemed convinced that the new serum was as revolutionary as he'd claimed. Trying to find Victor earlier that day had been fruitless, so he'd grabbed the samples from the counter and tried to give the presentation, but he was a researcher. Chaitin didn't have Victor's gift for convincing others, and it showed in the nonplussed faces of the six-member board of Borderline Cosmetics who seemed more interested in the fact that the serum glowed than whether it was effective at treatment. When he'd tried to steer the conversation back to antiaging, they'd each gotten that bored here-we-go-again look on their faces, and all sat in an uncomfortable silence now that the presentation was over. Chaitin smacked his lips together just to have something to hear.

"Mr. Russell," one of the board members finally said. "I'll be honest with you. If this is as effective an antiaging serum as you say, it will knock out half of our products. We can't possibly charge enough to recover the cost, and just knowing that something like this exists would shrink our current markets."

"But you wanted this demo," Chaitin inelegantly argued. "This is exactly what we're here for."

"Tell me about the glow," the board member said. "That's interesting. Why does it do that?"

"Whenever the marker comes in contact with a specific DNA sequence, it glows."

"But you have two different colors glowing in there: red and blue."

"So if you have different DNA in there with this, then it's going to glow different colors?" another asked.

"Possibly. We use that for marking DNA to see what survives the reactions."

"And different bonds being made and broken are what's making the colors change?"

"That's right. But it's not important. What is important is—"

The woman raised her hand for him to stop. She turned to whisper something to one of the other board members, who nodded and replied with something Chaitin couldn't hear. Then, the woman turned her head toward him.

"We'll take all you've got. And then whatever more you can produce," she said. Chaitin's jaw dropped.

"It didn't seem like you wanted an antiaging serum," he said.

"Oh, we don't," the woman said. "What we like is the color changing with DNA. We see a gift market for it. Imagine: get your own unique vial of perpetual color-changing DNA specific to you and the love of your life. And because it's so much a luxury market item, we can sell it for almost twice what the premier antiaging crème goes for. You decide what you want to do, Mr. Russell. The choice is yours: make an anti-aging serum or millions of dollars."

With that kind of money, he could start another lab. Another stab at aging, working out whatever kinks in his *own* lab so he didn't have to rely on the unpredictable Victor, to whose coattails he'd affixed himself for better or worse (and lately, worse was winning). And, as a novelty gift, they wouldn't have to wait five more years for the gold standard study to prove their stuff worked. They could ship it almost immediately.

"Okay," he said, nodding. He'd make the decision. If Victor wanted to make the decision, he should have been there. "Okay, where do I sign?"

"Imagine. It's a one-of-a-kind gift for lovers. Men will buy these for their wives and girlfriends. I can already see them flying off the shelves," replied one of the members.

"We'll get you the paperwork," the woman who'd been doing most of the talking said, then turned to her board member partner. "We can get started immediately. We already have the formula. This is just legal formality now. How fast can we get this out?"

"A couple of months, through our gift program," the other board member said. "Shouldn't be a problem."

"Good," she said. "Shall we go ahead and cut the check?"

Chaitin couldn't keep the smile from his face. He'd give Victor half the money, of course. But him being the one to sign meant that was *his* choice. And when he got around to telling Victor that Chaitin wanted to start up his own lab…the look on Victor's face…assuming he could even find Victor.

———

Victor crunched on the bones of the tentacled hamster with his teeth. The hamster had put up a good fight. The tentacles had even given it a bit of an advantage but so had Victor's arms, the span of which had increased to almost reach thirteen feet. He crouched in the corner, delighting in his feast as the tentacles squished and crunched in his mouth. So far, it had been a week, and the effect hadn't worn off, which was both good and bad. It meant that his formula had staying power, which he'd wondered about. The hunger he could have done without. Even while relishing the delicious iron flavor of the rodent's insides, a kernel of self-disgust rooted itself in his gut. Nothing else but the blood did the job.

His doorbell rang, and that caused his stomach to growl and his mouth to water. The rodent was one thing, but something larger awaited. This something might sate him long enough to get some science done. Victor scrambled across the house, crashing through the door to his bedroom as though it wasn't there.

"Victor," came the voice he knew too well, stopping him in his tracks. He couldn't, could he? He licked his lips, carefully working his reptilian tongue around his pointed teeth. The doorbell rang again. Victor ran his hands through his cordlike hair and straightened the tattered remains of his lab coat. Best to look presentable, after all. He shuffled and dragged his legs to the front door, careful to keep his rasping breaths as quiet as possible. The doorbell rang a third time, and he could see Chaitin's outline through the frosted glass.

"Victor," Chaitin said. "We're rich. Here, I'm sliding your check under the door."

Victor saw an envelope slide beneath.

"I know you're in there. Open up. We have a lot to talk about."

With his tenuous fingers, Victor grasped the door handle and slowly pulled it open...

CHAPTER 1

CONSPIRACY THEORY NONSENSE

KATIE TAPPED four slender fingers against the monochrome gray surface that was allegedly a desk. Her other hand rubbed at the vertebrae just above her shoulder blades, working at a tightness in her neck from staring downward. Her eyes blurred at the somehow both drab and polychromatic cubicle walls—overall, trending blue—that made her prison. Sometimes, if she stared just right, she could see shapes in the endless multicolored dots. No such luck today. The only potential antidote for hours of boredom ahead lay across her desk in the form of two likely embellished reports of tentacled creatures, toxic fumes, and people turning to jelly.

More conspiracy theory nonsense that her mother would lap up like a kitten on milk. *Would have* lapped up, she reminded herself. She was the type of woman who skipped vaccines because she "don't want the government tracking me. Mark my words, they'll be onto you next." It didn't matter that the woman's daughter was responsible for contact tracing during communicable disease outbreaks. If "the government" had really wanted to track Katie's mother (and why would they?), they only had to ask Katie. And Katie would tell because there were only two possibilities for her mother's whereabouts: laying mahjong tiles down on Fifth Street or watching her "news" programs from the couch of the same single-family home Katie had grown up in. Katie gritted her teeth and launched a thumbtack at the cubicle wall to see if it would stick. Too much time on her hands and not enough to think about if she was obsessing about her dead mother again.

Katie shook the mouse and brought up her spreadsheet for the day to begin the analyst part of her job, something she'd thought she would avoid technically being a field agent. She pulled up a spreadsheet labeled "2022 COVID-19 Contact Tracing Report—Midwest Region" and scanned down the rows. There were always gaps in the data. Cities and towns in the Midwest were just too far apart for the few field offices to find every contact. Field agents often found they were up against flat-out lies about who had been at the latest birthday or impromptu celebration too. She couldn't do much about the lies, but the missing data she fixed using the mind-numbing work of averaging and updating. It didn't take long for the numbers to run together in her head, a sure sign that she needed a break, which came in the form of more coffee, of which she'd already had three cups and it was barely ten, or a cigarette, which she'd allegedly given up as of…well, the day before. Once the idea of a cigarette was planted in her mind, it clung there like a weed and sucked at her attention. Katie pulled on the drawer at the bottom of her desk, and there, like a lifelong friend who would try to kill you every day of your life, sat her light-blue box of cigarettes and the third disposable lighter she'd bought after she threw away the Zippo that her mother had given her on her eighteenth birthday.

Her fingers crept toward the box, and she could already feel the smoke gathering in her lungs. The lightheaded feeling imagined itself into existence as her limbs tingled from the hazy air collecting inside. She quickly wrapped the outside of the box with her fingertips and then, with a snort of disgust, shoved the box farther back in the drawer and slammed it shut with a loud bang. The craving didn't go away.

"Good choice," came Neko's patronizing thick voice, full of gravel and needlessly supporting her for not caving to her nicotine habit. He meant well, though, so she swiveled, nodded, and grinned.

"Wasn't even a contest," she lied, biting back the craving. "What's up, Neko?"

Neko was tall. He wasn't as tall as her, but few people were over her six feet. He was a healthy five-eight and had black hair that hung limply down both sides of his round face, and somewhat less of it on the top of his skull. She'd always joked that he looked like a jack-o-lantern when he grinned, as he did now. That was partially due to the spacing of his false teeth, one gold and one silver with a couple of white ones in between.

"Got another one," Neko said, his grin going wider, displaying gaps among his molars. "This one in your old stomping grounds."

"Atlanta?"

"Older. Arlington, Virginia. Someone saw something they said was a 'freakishly large woman with scales and a five-foot tongue that whipped around like a wacky inflatable tube man.'"

Katie rolled her eyes and couldn't stifle a chuckle. Her mother would *die* for this one, if she were still alive. She shook her head.

"We better get right on that, Neko. Got to watch out for those monsters before they eat everybody up," she said, mimicking her mother's Midwestern accent the best she could, having been gone for half of her life.

"Yeah, well, you know the routine. Three makes a trend," Neko said.

"It'd be better than sitting in here, I guess," she said. Katie flicked another thumbtack and watched it effortlessly jab into the cubicle wall. Then, she played off her success with a shrug.

"Can't the FBI look into it, though? I mean, monsters aren't exactly a disease."

"Ah, you haven't even read the reports, have you?"

"Skimmed them," she said, though the folders were very obviously in the same place they'd been all morning.

"If you *read* them, you'll notice on line one of the first report, the subject starts out normal, then sprouts eight new appendages and bounds around like some messed up spider."

"And we're taking this seriously?"

Neko grinned again. "Come on, Katie. Free trip to Arlington. Morton's Steakhouse? Legal Seafood? Smithsonian? It'll be fun."

"I've already done all those things."

"But have you done it for *free* and with your lovable teammates?"

Katie tapped her fingers on the desk. People had overactive imaginations. Probably, what they really saw in Arlington was a shadow on a back-alley wall, or maybe they were on hallucinogens or delirious or something. There was usually an explanation, and conspiracy theories were, in her opinion, a serious waste of time and government resources. But the government had to issue an official report *denying* the existence of monsters, which didn't convince anyone who wanted to believe.

When it came down to it, it was Katie's task force. She got to decide what was worth investigating and what wasn't. But with the alternative being pruning through the list of COVID-19 contacts in—she reshuffled the mouse and swiveled back to her computer—Bristol, Wyoming, Arlington might be a welcome change.

"What did she say, Neko?"

Katie pushed backward with her feet against the cubicle wall beneath her desk. She stopped a second later and swiveled again. Blond curls that somehow held their body, even after removing field gear, entered Katie's field of vision.

"Hi, Viv," she said, offering a smile. Viv was her favorite, though Viv could get dark sometimes. And someday Katie would solve the mystery of the resilient bounce that Viv worked into her hair. Viv's eyes glowed in the halogen lights, picking up a hint of yellow but otherwise hazelnut brown. Unlike Neko, Viv had all of her teeth and, if one judged by her smile, a few extra. She was the only other member of the task force who smiled as often as Katie did, although for Katie it was a defense mechanism that sometimes looked strained, whereas Viv wore smiles naturally.

"Katie Batie," Viv said, making up unsolicited rhymes again. Usually entertaining, sometimes annoying. This morning, anything that distracted Katie from her spreadsheet work was welcome.

"You think we should go too?"

"I have *the perfect* dress for *Morton's*. Sequin-ny and fun, and some new platforms. I know what's on that spreadsheet, and I can tell you I have *no good outfits* for *Bristol*."

"And that's your professional opinion? Flights from Clarksburg to Bristol are going to be a hell of a lot cheaper than into DC."

Viv's smile turned down briefly in a look of mock hurt, but she could never keep it there. It bounced back up and lifted her bright eyes with it.

"But you *know* how it's going to go in Bristol. The same way as Kelin. Nobody will want to talk to us because we're federal agents. Some will lie, and some will actively hide from us. If we're *very* lucky, we'll avoid a death threat or two. Why? Why do that to ourselves when this *opportunity* presents itself."

"You know there's no monster, right?"

Viv was a lot like Katie's mother, who learned everything she needed to know from mirroring David Duchovny's character in *The X-Files* almost two decades before. "I want to believe" was Viv's mantra too. Anything that Viv could convince herself was true... *was* true. But unlike Katie's mother, Viv was *alive* and also curious, making her beliefs way more fun. Sure, ancient aliens were here and jump-started human civilization, but did you also know that the dinosaurs ate them before they could do it? Viv was full of contradictions like that.

"No monster. Got it. But I think with three cases, they *might* spring for hotel rooms, right? We haven't used any travel money all year."

So that was how badly Viv wanted to go to Arlington. That part of the conversation should have been a lot harder. Katie blinked once, turned her head back to the screen, and then back toward the two of them.

"What does Darius—"

Darius handled the travel budget. Viv decided where to investigate, while Darius was responsible for how they get there.

"He said he'll approve," Neko interrupted.

"Or, and I quote," Viv added, "'It's a goddamn waste of time, but so is this fucking contact tracing for people who don't give a damn. If you're going to waste your time, at least you can do it with a raw steak and a martini.'"

Katie liked Darius King. He was a double-edged sword at times, but if you asked him a question, you got an answer: no frills, no hedging, and no double-speak. Granted, Katie had already run into several situations where she didn't exactly *like* the answers, but she respected him for it. And from what she could tell, she'd earned his respect by telling him exactly what he could do with the answers that she didn't like. They had an understanding.

She took a deep breath and let it out. Her grin widened.

"Well, pack up, I guess. But the spreadsheet work still happens in Arlington. This isn't a vacation."

"Eep," exclaimed Viv, clapping her hands together and bouncing a little too excitedly to remember that the undershirt she wore didn't exactly provide a lot of support. Katie flashed a glance at Neko, and he immediately diverted his eyes back to meet Katie's instead of watching the bouncing Viv show. Katie cocked one eyebrow, and Neko showed a few more teeth and then sealed his mouth into a straight line. Katie shook her head.

Katie was only a few years older than the pair of them, being twenty-seven to Neko's twenty-five and Viv's twenty-four. She wasn't surprised at what went on between Neko and Viv. But her one insistence was that they keep it out of the office, which they managed to do—mostly. Every now and then, they would be a little too slow to respond to her calls, or Darius would come in with a complaint, but they were young and *in love*. She thought it was sweet when it wasn't annoying.

"Finish out today," she said, stressing the last part, "And tonight, pack bags. I'll let Cassie know that we need tickets."

"First class?" Neko added, gold tooth flashing as he opened his mouth again.

"You paying?"

"Coach. Got it."

———————

The searing heat hit Katie in the face as she left the plane, dragging the only designer anything she owned, which was Vera Wang luggage covered in metallic pink canvas on the top and light silver on the bottom, the two colors separated by a thin red line that seemed bright enough to shine. She hated the bag, but it had been the last gift from her mother, and the last of her mother's desperate attempts to feminize her. It didn't work, but as many times as she'd tried to get rid of the thing, she could never bring herself to do it. So now it announced to the world a host of assumptions about who she was, while her close-cropped hair, mirror-black sunglasses, and crisp business suit told a completely different story.

Unlike her, Neko, and his not-quite-cojoined girlfriend Viv, were nothing but what they seemed to be. He was a prematurely balding man with just enough hair to still be mildly attractive, or at least that's what Katie told Vivian. Really with his gap-filled teeth and the snarling way he smiled, Katie thought he always looked like he was extra-skeevy. He apparently was just the right amount of skeevy for Viv, who now hung on him as he pulled his-and-hers luggage over the tarmac. Katie couldn't imagine how the two clung so closely together. She could barely lower her arms to her sides because of the sweat that accumulated under her arms, aggravating fresh razor burns. She cast a glance over her shoulder.

"It's toooo hot," Vivian said, her smile turning into a grimace. "Who decided that was a good idea to build a city on swampland?"

"It was a compromise, Viv. For the last time, hopefully this entire trip, it was Jefferson and Hamilton fighting that put the capital there," Katie said. "Where should we go first? Any opinions?" she asked Vivian, just before they crested the sliding doors ushering them to the baggage claim area. A wall of cool washed over her, almost making her cry.

"Interviews," Viv said, wiping her brow. "Over in Alexandria near Adams Morgan, and then another down in Old Town. Arlington too."

With a quick pivot, Katie swung left toward the exit. She took a deep breath. "Okay, let's get our bags. We'll drop them at the hotel, and then straight to Old Town Alexandria."

"I don't want to go to Old Town first," Viv said. "I want to go to the hotel. Then, I want to check out Arlington. They have the Arlington Cinema Draft House where you can get beer while you watch movies." She lowered her voice ever so slightly. "They're showing *Bridesmaids*."

"After we check at least one of these off of our list. It's too early not to."

"Fine. But then you're watching *Bridesmaids* with us."

Katie rolled her eyes. "It's not a negotiation. I'm in charge."

"I want to see *Bridesmaids* too," Niko said.

Katie turned and stared at him. "I thought you liked shoot 'em ups?"

"I'm complicated."

That brought a thin smile to her lips, and she nodded.

"Okay. If we're all going, then it counts as teambuilding, so I'll pick up the tab. But first, to the hotel, then we have to go to Arlington Boulevard to check the one from last week. That one they said they had proof of when they called."

"Do they?" asked Neko, cocking one eyebrow. "The last time someone had proof they were wearing a tin foil hat and claiming the Earth was being taken over by lizard people."

"I'm skeptical too," Katie replied. "We still have to check it out, though."

It was over an hour before they made it to the hotel off the interstate through afternoon traffic and then back out to the mall. What time wasn't spent speeding up and then braking in the sea of cars was eaten up at the hotel. Katie made it down to the hotel lobby in just under ten minutes. It took another twenty before red-faced Viv and grinning-too-broadly Neko made it down from their hotel room. Katie glared.

"We have work to do," she reminded them. Viv only giggled and tucked the tail of her sleeveless shirt into her cut-off shorts.

Katie scanned her. "Professional jobs to do."

"It's hot," Viv complained and made no move to go back to

her room and change into light cotton dress skirt and a collared shirt like Katie wore. "A girl's got to keep cool."

"And that's what you brought? No skirts or at least khaki shorts?"

Arlington was the first sign that something strange truly was happening. Katie's first signal was the double-wide entrance gate into the Cypress Street home that she could easily fit two of her single-family rental homes inside of. The normally imposing black sport utility vehicle that Katie liked to rent, mainly because people tended to talk more when they might be whisked away, pulled through the gate slowly. Next to the house, it looked like a child's toy. In her experience, people who lived in homes as expensive as that one didn't truck with conspiracy theories. They weren't better or smarter, just too focused on making money to spend time on anything that didn't smack them in the face.

The man who answered was exactly who she expected him to be, tallish with an easy but guarded smile and white hair with gray-blue irises hiding behind wireframe glasses. He wore a cardigan with leather patches on the elbows, sporting a look that might have been completed by a gourd pipe, but he didn't have one of those.

"Come in, come in," he said, eyeing first Viv with her cut-off shorts with a look of disdain, then Neko, before finally settling on Katie. He seemed to ponder for a second before he seemed to decide that she must be in charge and lingered his eyes on hers as he turned. She followed.

The door was easily eight feet tall. When Katie passed through it, she saw why. On the other side was a grand entry hall stretching up at least twenty feet into the sky. White wood shone like marble and uninterrupted vertical lines practically forced her eyes toward the massive chandelier suspended above their heads.

"You said you had proof on the call, right?" she asked, struggling to match the man's quick, wide steps.

"I do," he said. "I can't explain it. One moment she was here, then I went out for the mail." He pointed back into the house toward from where they'd come. "I came back, and my Jezel was gone. Disappeared. And this monstrosity was…"

The man seemed to stiffen as he said the words. It was as though he struggled to hear himself say them.

"You…don't believe in monsters?"

"Didn't. I didn't until last week. Down here."

The man turned to a hidden door just before the elevator—an elevator in a private home—and pushed a button in the wall that popped the door out. Katie looked back over at her team quickly and nodded at each one in turn. Before going into the basement of this guy's house, she wanted to make sure they were all paying attention. Anything could be down there.

What was down there challenged even her cynical mind. The stench caused her to gag and pinch her nose closed as they descended steps that seemed to circle forever. A cross between rotting eggs and diesel exhaust assaulted her, and her eyes watered from the smell. She persisted. When they came around the final twist in the spiral staircase, she had to blink three times. There, splayed across the couch, she saw what at first looked like a deflated giant tent balloon. As she got closer, through peeks around the man in front of her, she saw that the tent balloon had definition.

On one end of a large couch was what could have been a head, pointy and lumpy and nearly touching the floor from where its point draped over the couch's arm. Toward the other end was an amalgamation of assorted limbs. Only, as Katie looked closer, she realized they weren't limbs. There were far too many of them, for one thing. For another, some had what appeared to be snake heads on the ends, and others had suction cups like octopuses. Fourteen of them altogether, she counted, and a weird flesh-toned section separating the top and bottom looked oddly like a...human abdomen?

"What is that?"

"I was hoping you could tell me," the man replied. "I found it lurking in the study as I was looking for my wife. It must have...have..."

"Have what?"

"I didn't think about it until after I...I mean, I had to kill it, right? Look at it?"

Katie felt a confession coming, but she wasn't sure what the man had to confess about. She stepped toward the creature and then moved to the right so that others on her team could see. She heard gasps fill the air.

"I think it might be her," he said, his voice choking. "I...I think I killed my wife."

"That thing?" Neko asked, pointing. "That used to be a person?"

The man clamped his mouth shut and pointed to the midsection between the floppy squid-like head and the tentacles and snake heads.

"Look at that," he said, pointing to what looked like a bunch of squiggle lines just beneath what might have at one time been a navel. "Tattoo from when she was in college. It used to be a butterfly."

Katie didn't see a butterfly in it. Nor did she see a monster. If it hadn't been for the stench, she would have thought it was an elaborate ploy to cover up for the fact that the guy had simply murdered his wife. The poor woman was somewhere in the backyard, probably, buried under some azaleas or something. Katie saw a clever and expensive smokescreen. She nodded to Neko.

"Take some pictures," she said and then to Viv: "You get some blood samples if it has any. We need to know what we're dealing with."

He nodded, and all three of them got to work. Despite Viv's too-casual look, she pulled her hair back, donned a pair of latex gloves, produced her kit from the bag that Neko slammed to the ground, and got the samples. Meanwhile, Katie interviewed the man.

The incident had taken place earlier that morning. According to him, it was their anniversary, and he'd given his wife her present: a glowing pendant from the Home Sweet Awakenings section of Thomas's Jewelers. It had set him back nearly twenty grand. He'd left her admiring it and trying on clothes for the brunch they were going to have the morning before their flight to Paris later that day. He'd only stepped out for a few minutes, not long at all, and had come back to find the bedroom disheveled and destroyed.

"My first thought was that someone had broken in," he muttered between his fingers. "I'd turned off the alarm to go out, and that would have been the perfect opportunity. I was frantic as I searched the entire house."

"No servants?"

He shook his head. "We don't believe in living like that. If we own the house, we take care of it ourselves."

She wasn't sure she believed that he and whoever his wife had been could take care of a property that size without help, but she let it go.

"And when you go to the study?"

"I saw this thing stumbling around, slamming into things. I grabbed the poker from the fireplace over there and swung. I hit it three times before it went down, and then I hit it again until it stopped moving. That's when I saw the tattoo."

"And you realized it was your wife?" she asked, mainly to gage his reaction.

His face blanched, and he squeezed his eyes shut as he nodded. That seemed unusually authentic to her, and she couldn't tell if he was lying. She was about to ask another question when she felt something touch her elbow. Katie hadn't realized how jumpy the whole thing had made her until she stopped herself from kicking Viv in the shins.

"Look at this," Viv said, holding a sample vial up between two blue-latex-covered fingers. Katie examined the tube and saw swirls of red in orange translucent liquid that seemed viscous as Viv slowly wagged it back and forth. A droplet glowed on the tip of her gloved hand. "I...I think this might be real."

But it was Viv. *She wanted to believe*, Katie reminded herself. If Neko agreed though, that would mean something. She turned her eyes toward him to find that he was already looking at her.

He wasn't smiling.

Neko's narrowed eyes said it all. Nobody would be going to Arlington Cinema Drafthouse that evening. Katie gave him a shallow nod and turned to the man.

"Leave this room to us," she said. "Don't leave the house, though. I'll have more questions."

A stray thought penetrated her mind. Whatever this was, it was easily bigger than she was. If it could actually use those tentacles, then it wasn't hard to see it as potentially dangerous. In her mind, the man had gotten lucky when he'd struck down whatever it was. That situation could easily have been reversed. She turned to Neko.

"Did you pack our swarm gear?" she asked. Katie called it swarm gear, but really it was just police riot gear with protective masks installed that had been rebranded with the Bioengineering Task Force logo. Neko was generally always ready for anything. He nodded.

"In my blue bag, back at the hotel."

She nodded back. "We're getting it before the next stop."

CHAPTER 2
LEAVE, INTERRUPTED

A TRAVEL BUS bumped and churned its way south on I-95, bouncing the woman's head uncomfortably against Aristide's full bladder. The first thirty minutes, which had gotten him from the only bus stop near USMC Quantico about as far as Fredericksburg. The coffee he'd shared with her there had worked its way through his body and was very nearly prepared to come out. Another bump, and he shook her gently awake. Her groggy eyes stared up at him for a second. She smiled quickly before nestling her head back down, digging even harder into his bladder and making him wince. He gave her another shove.

"Stop it," she muttered, "I'm not moving."

"Hey," he whispered and ran his fingers through her dirty-blonde hair while wishing to God he had a better memory for names. "I've got to go to the bathroom."

"Eviana," she whispered back. "Or Evian, like the water. You pick." She smiled up at him as the spark of recognition fired behind his eyes.

"Sorry. Okay then, *Evian*, I have to go to the bathroom, or we're going to get a lot more familiar than we already are."

She lifted her head too slowly and shifted her green eyes toward his brown ones.

"Want company? Or…are you being serious?"

Another bump. Another wince.

"No, for real."

He eyed his drab olive-green sea bag overhead across the aisle as he stood. Aristide did the mental math to determine how much he trusted a woman he'd just met and whose name he could barely remember not to rifle through his stuff. When it came to it, he supposed if she did, there wasn't another bus stop until Richmond anyway. He could deal with the situation. Aristide twisted past her and took the four steps to the bathroom door before he noticed the green light had turned red.

Shit. Occupied.

Someone had beaten him to it. Aristide heard a giggle and turned his head to see Evian—yeah, he had the name now—trying to stifle her giggle with a hand in front of her face. He shifted uncomfortably from one leg to the other. Sure, he could have called on his military bearing and pretended not to be bothered by the pain, but he was on leave now and would be damned if he was going to be anything but an ordinary civilian.

Besides, if he didn't shuffle, he was afraid that he might wet his pants. Aristide wondered if Evian would still be laughing when he had urine dripping down his legs, staining the front of his pressed jeans. But thinking about urine didn't help, so he scrambled to find another thought. His mind landed on the idea that when he made his return trip to the barracks at Quantico, he already had a hell of a story to tell. Met a girl at the bus stop and used his gift of gab to strike up a conversation. She'd turned out to be a military brat taking a semester break after a less-than-stellar first year of college, so they found a lot to talk about. They ted in the terminal, in line for the bus, and naturally ended up sitting together because they weren't done talking yet.

Fifteen minutes into the ride, she divulged that she always slept in moving vehicles and had asked if it was okay if she leaned on his shoulder, which turned into his lap.

He'd have to embellish that part of the story to be more impressive. Might even add some detail to what they were doing on the bus and definitely *would not* tell anyone that he'd turned down her request for "company" in the bathroom because he had to piss too badly.

Then, he shifted his weight again.

It all came back to urine.

And the light was still red.

And...there was a strange sound coming from within. A cross between a groan and a whimper, like maybe somebody snuck a dog on the bus somehow. Except it didn't sound like a dog. It sounded like a human, whimpering like a dog. He sighed loudly, danced for a second, then rapped three times quickly on the door.

"You okay in there?"

The only response he got was silence, but it was a response. The groaning stopped.

Aristide rapped again and gave himself an internal eye roll at what he was about to do.

"I'm a Marine. I can help."

Evian giggled again, and Aristide looked at her and gave her a sheepish grin with a shrug. The groan came back louder this time. There was something wet to it, like a gurgling brook trying to talk. And, if he wasn't mistaken, a woman's tenor hiding underneath. His eyes furrowed as he struggled to hear more.

"No, no, no, no," whispered the woman's voice. "No, no."

"Ma'am, are you okay? I can help," he said, raising his voice and doing his best authoritative impression. Evian slipped out of their seat and came to stand beside him, rocking gently with the motion of the bus.

"What's going on? People are staring at you."

"Listen," he said, pointing to the door. Evian lowered her ear to it, and her green eyes went wide. He loved those eyes. And her button nose and angular chin. It was a shame that they would be parting ways somewhere around Shreveport, Louisiana, as she branched off northbound toward Natchitoches.

"I *said* it really does sound like someone's in trouble in there," Evian said, repeating what he'd obviously missed the first time.

"Should I try to get in? Tell the driver?"

"I don't know. Yeah, maybe. Maybe tell the driver."

The gurgling got louder then, and in Aristide's mind, he might have been losing precious time. If the person was dying, he'd at least been certified in cardio-pulmonary resuscitation and could help. Making it to the front of the packed bus seemed like it might take too long.

"You go," he said. "I'm going to try to get in."

Evian turned away from him, following his instructions, probably because he was a Marine. He didn't know what he was doing any more than anyone else, but he had noticed that telling people he was a Marine seemed to make him the de facto leader. Once he'd come across a man who slipped in a brook in the woods and broken his wrist. The man's entire party had turned to Aristide, and he'd offered the apparent solution they needed to call an emergency rescue team...after putting together a makeshift splint from two pieces of wood. That wasn't Marine Corps training, but a lifetime as a Boy Scout that taught him how to do that. Still, he guessed maybe he'd been the right person to be in charge in that situation. Possibly this situation would be similar. He put his shoulder against the door and shoved.

The door shoved back.

Hard.

Aristide flew across the laps of three teenage boys, who promptly forced him up and away from them, back toward the buckling door.

"Weirdo," the one with the hat said as Aristide flew toward him. Whatever had buckled the door was still there, and now he could hear the "no, no, no, no" issuing rapidly through the opening like a machine gun report.

Something slick and oozing that looked like an extended human arm stretched to distortion, gray and covered in black splotches, spilled onto the space toward him rapidly. It had almost collided with his chest when something clawlike yanked him away from the oncoming projectile. He heard the crunching of bones and flesh as the appendage impaled one of the boys—at least one and judging by the high-pitched screams, possibly all three.

Aristide didn't look. His eyes darted toward his seabag up in the shelf over where the boys had been sitting before he dismissed the idea just as quickly. Somewhere in there was his Glock 19 revolver. And somewhere *else* in there were bullets, not loaded or even in a magazine.

And whatever had come through the door moved fast. Not as fast as Evian, who was now wide awake and still pulling him off-balance toward the front. He tried to catch his feet, but every time, she yanked harder.

"Don't stop," she said. "Whatever you do, don't stop. As soon as they get an idea of what's back here, we won't be able to get to the front of the bus."

A short blonde girl in a sleeveless paisley shirt seemed to have overheard her and turned, then screamed after her eyes, like Evian's, went saucer-wide. Aristide still didn't know what sort of creature had come from the bathroom, but the sounds of bones crunching behind him told him that it hadn't stopped. It *had* slowed, almost like it was feasting on whatever was back there and dragging whatever it had managed to catch along with it for a snack, probably what was left of the boys since the screaming had stopped.

But that ended their forward progress. Suddenly, everyone who had been sitting in front of them stood at the exact same time, including the nearly three-hundred-pound man in a camouflage shirt who had tried to make conversation with them in the terminal as well once he found out Aristide was a Marine. That man turned and stared at Aristide for a second before his eyes shifted up and gaze seemed to fall beyond Aristide and upon the crowd forming behind. Then the man's mouth dropped open. He screamed higher-pitched than any of the unfortunate boys.

The fortunate thing about the bus finally coming to a stop then was that Aristide finally gained full footing. The unfortunate thing was that whatever was behind them hadn't slowed with the bus. Evian's look transformed from alarm to abject fear as Aristide gave up on the aisle, moved up onto a seat, and tried a window, stepping on two unsuspecting men with questionable facial hair in the process. One of them tried to push him back, but Aristide was prepared this time. He shoved back offered a glare. Boot camp and combat training had melted most of the fat away from his one-hundred-and-fifty-pound body and exposed rippling muscles beneath. Then, the same had built those muscles up so now, he weighed nearly a hundred and sixty, but all of it was muscle, so when he wanted to stay put, he stayed put. Aristide did the one courtesy of glaring at the man with maybe a fu-Manchu mustache if that also included a soul-patch and communicated with what was supposed to be a quick glance backward.

He froze. Now Aristide had a full view of what was chasing them. Strips of a red sequined party dress hung off of its shoulders and told him that maybe it had eaten a stripper. The arms seemed to have no clear definition, the dragging ends changing from hands to claws to tentacles to what looked like jellyfish strands. Through all the changes, it somehow managed to hang on to the half-torso of the boy who had shoved Aristide and called him a weirdo. Seeing that broke Aristide out of his hypnosis and reinvigorated him to yank at the window. When he got the window down, the flaw in his plan became apparent. The driver had not yet seen fit to *fully* stop the bus, as he'd thought he would. The bus only slowed to about twenty, if Aristide had to guess.

Aristide had mixed feelings about whether he wanted the bus stopped. He looked back at Evian and then out the window again. Stopping the bus meant hurling the creature forward into them. What happened after that was anyone's guess, but Aristide was pretty sure that he was the only Marine on board and that the steroid-amped bodybuilders would scream like little girls instead of put up a fight.

He shared this information through an eye-connecting glance with Evian, who nodded. Aristide bit his lip and mentally prepared for pain as he kicked out the window.

"What the…"

The man with the fu-manchu thing seemed to finally figure out what was going on. He grabbed at Aristide and then at Evian once Aristide slapped him away. With a grunt, Aristide grabbed Evian by the arm and yanked her forward to him. She landed against him, and from the look of excruciating pain on fu-Manchu's face, also planted a foot in the man's crotch. The no-no-noes got closer. Evian went through first, helped by a shove from him. He didn't wait for her to land before following suit.

A tree caught them both.

Not a comfortable landing, since it wasn't one tree, more like three or four. But the bus happened to be starting up an overpass, and it happened to be late spring, and the trees were not only full of leaves but flowers, so a few failed attempts at stopping later, and what Aristide was certain were gashes in his arms, legs, and bruises everywhere else, they'd managed to land alive and breathing but not moving. He lay in the shade of a short cherry blossom tree watching the pink-purple petals falling around them. Farther ahead, also in the dirt, lay Evian, her chest rising and falling and petals stuck in her hair. She sat up almost immediately, not looking at him but looking in the direction that the bus was going. As sure as he'd guessed, the brake lights had been lit about two-hundred feet up the road, and screams echoed down to the valley they were in down from the full overpass.

Aristide staggered to his feet and limped over toward where Evian lay before offering her a hand. She accepted and to his surprise threw both arms around his neck and squeezed him tightly to her. Only then did he realize that in the excitement, he'd lost bladder control and smelled like a port-a-john. She didn't seem to care and only pulled him tighter and tighter toward her.

He eyed the bus and considered for a second whether to go back for his bag and his gun. A violent shake of the entire vehicle made his mind up for him.

"We have to go," he said.

"Where?"

He looked around. On the particular stretch of I-95 that loomed over their heads, there wasn't so much as a sign stating whether the ubiquitous Starbucks might be nearby. Instead, it was all mile marker this and exit that, with nothing on the signs indicating civilization as far as he could see.

"Somewhere," he answered, limping. His leg didn't feel broken that he could tell, but it definitely was going to take a while to repair. "Once that thing gets bored up there, it might come to look for the ones that got away."

"That thing? You know what that was, right?"

"No. I have no fucking clue what that was. If you're trying to tell me something, you're going to have to remember that I'm a Marine. We break things good, but we're not that smart," he said, grinning for effect and then wincing at the bruising around his mouth.

"The red dress? Don't tell me you didn't notice her in the terminal."

"Oh shit," he said as it dawned on him. "The newlyweds. That was the *bride*."

"Bridesmaid," Evian corrected. "The bride didn't get on the bus. They loaded up into a limo."

"It ate the bride first?" Something about that seemed off.

"Marines really aren't that bright, are they?" she asked as she took his hand and picked a direction to drag him forward. "No, that was the bridesmaid. She turned into that thing."

"The fuck…"

"Exactly. Now you get it. Now we get to wonder if she picked up whatever the fuck that was that did that to her at the bus station and whether or not *we* got it too."

"Fuck."

That ended the conversation. He plodded after her, hand in hand, in the direction she chose—the opposite way from which the bus was headed. They were moving back toward Triangle, but it would be a long way on foot.

"Phone?"

"Purse," she replied, shaking her head no. Still on the bus. And one thing was for damn sure. Neither of them was planning to go back and get it any time soon. "No money either. What the hell are we supposed to do now?"

"Walk, I guess," Aristide said, running his hand through his short black wavy hair. Just to be safe, he ran a hand over his wallet and was relieved to find it still there. "I've got money. We'll be okay."

The idea that they would be okay was premature. The air was so thick that every breath felt like biting down on stale cake. Aristide put one foot in front of the other, modeling his stride on his Marine Corps forced marches—head down, one step, then another. Evian kept up with short strides and the occasional run, impressive for the thirty minutes it took them to get from the intersection of Route 1 and Route 3 to JJs Southern Pub, a solitary place along the side of the road tucked back between some trees. The walls to JJs were solid brick, and the windows were tinted dark black as though it used to be a strip club or some other nefarious thing. Given the location was so far from anything else, Aristide guessed that was probably exactly what it had been. Nothing else would draw people this far, and at first, he had the niggling suspicion that when they tried the door, it wouldn't open, despite the cluster of four-by-four pickups in the far corner.

Aristide rubbed the back of his neck as he came to a slow stop outside a door that seemed to be made up of two-by-six planks.

"Are you sure you want to go in there?"

Aristide smiled weakly at Evian.

"No worse than the bars on base in USMC Quantico," he said. He squeezed the sweat out of his eyes. "And we haven't seen anything else remotely resembling civilization."

Not entirely true. They had passed a series of closed-up strip malls that looked like they'd been "it" places once upon a time. One even had a shuttered skating rink attached. They were echoes of what civilization had once been there. Now, there was only the pub. He shoved on the door. It creaked slowly inward, blasting him with the chill of an overworked air conditioner. Evian scooted in behind him and kept most of her body behind his, away from the scrutiny of the leather-clad bartender and baseball-cap wearing clientele. Four gentlemen crowded around one end of the bar. Every eye was on the pair of them as they sidled up to the far end, careful to avoid the occupied territory. One man spit into a soda bottle that seemed still to be half-full.

The bartender in his sleeveless leather vest floated down the bar toward the pair.

"What'll you have?"

"Do you have a phone?" Aristide asked quietly to keep the overly eager eavesdroppers at the end of the bar, whose entire attention was still directed at him and Evian, from overhearing.

"Strange request. It's a pub, right? I should be more specific. What'll you have to drink?"

Aristide eyed the bar shelf behind the man. Top shelf in here was Cuervo or Smirnoff. He shook his head.

"Bourbon and Coke," said Evian, finally peeking around Aristide to converse with the bartender. This brought a broken-toothed grin to the bartender's face.

"For the lady," he announced and pivoted around to make the drink.

"And a phone?"

"Paying customers only," the bartender said.

"I'm the one paying for that drink," Aristide told him.

"Says you."

"He is," confirmed Evian. "And please, we really need a phone."

"Anything for a customer," the bartender said and reached under the bar to retrieve what had to have been the last rotary-dial phone in existence. He plopped it down before her.

"Dial nine to get out," he said.

"Like a hotel," Aristide commented.

"Exactly. It was a package plan," the bartender said. "Came with the internet."

As Evian dialed out, Aristide locked eyes with the bartender.

"Seen anything unusual around here?" he asked.

"Other than the pair of you?"

"I have," came a voice from the far end of the bar. The curly haired man in the John Deere ball cap who had been staring, along with his neighbors, chimed in a husky voice. "But I guess it depends. What kind of weird? Three home runs in the top of the ninth weird, or are we talking aliens?"

One of the men, shorter with straight orange hair falling out from beneath his Oakland A's cap, snorted with derisive laughter. Another chuckled, but John Deere didn't laugh. His face, from what Aristide could tell, was dead serious.

"More the aliens kind of weird," Aristide said.

"Here we go," said Oakland. "Now you got him started."

John Deere punched Oakland in the arm and cleared his throat.

"I'll tell you what I saw if you tell me what you saw," he said.

Evian grabbed at his sleeve.

"They want to know where we are," she said. "Did you see the name of this place?"

"JJs," the bartender offered kindly. "On Route 3. Well, the only one. Is that Jim you're talking to?"

Evian tilted her head as she listened to something on the phone and cracked a smile.

"It is," she said, turning her eyes up to the bartender. "He said tell your sister he says hi."

That elicited another chuckle from Oakland, which the bartender professionally ignored.

"Say the same to his mother," he said.

Aristide glanced at her.

"Are they going to come get us? Do they know about that thing that we saw?"

She slowly shook her head while still listening in.

"No, we'll stay here. I plan to get good and plastered. No, not too plastered to give my statement. Yes, officer."

"What did you see?" prodded John Deere.

"It's hard to describe," Aristide said, realizing suddenly that he had seen very little, having been so busy running for his life. He'd heard a great deal and had witnessed a tentacle drill through someone's stomach. The rest all jumbled together in his head. "I remember a red dress and tentacles."

"Are you listening to this guy?" Oakland added.

"Shut up, Finn," John Deere said, smacking him on the arm again. "This shit is real, whether you want to admit it or not."

"Your wife ran off," Finn replied. "That's what happened. She didn't change into a lizard person. Telling that story again ain't going to make it true, Greg."

"It happened," Greg replied, motioning to the bartender for another drink. Aristide noticed the drink was a shot of Jameson and a Budweiser. The man took the shot, grimaced, and then took a swig of beer and grimaced again.

"It's shit beer," he explained, "but it's cheap."

He wiped his mouth on the back of his hand.

"It was about a week ago. My wife came home late. She has choir practice on Wednesdays and sometimes the girls go out," the man began, talking in a slow drawl. "She came home. Of course, they'd been drinking again, and she smelled like bourbon, so I made her sleep on the couch."

"Sure. The girls were out at choir practice getting sloshed," Finn said. "And she definitely wasn't cheating on you or anything."

"You don't know a damn thing, Finn. She wouldn't do that."

"So who gave her that necklace, then?"

"I don't know. Maybe Teresa?"

Finn laughed.

"Doesn't matter, does it? Next thing I know, I hear the sound of crying from the living room. It was more like a whimpering than crying. For a second there, I thought maybe she'd brought a dog back. She does like to pick up strays. I come out to check on the situation, and I swear to God there was this lizard person wearing my wife's summer dress."

"What did she look like?" Evian asked.

"Like a lizard-woman. I mean she had claws instead of hands, scales all over. Her face had kind of morphed out. But here's the thing—she was still changing in front of my face. Her nose stretched out and fangs stuck out of her mouth. But the worst part was her eyes," he said. "I could see her eyes, and they were *her* eyes. Blue like the ocean that one time we could afford a real Cancun vacation. Blue like that all through the change until the very end. Then, one or two blinks, and even that was gone. That's when she—"

"Sure, if you buy that," Finn interrupted. "There's no telling what actually happened. My guess is she went off with her choir instructor." Finn's lips parted in a cruel grin that Aristide wanted to punch off, but he reminded himself that to be this comfortable with each other, these were all probably friends here. Even if Finn was an asshole, it would take more than cruelty for them to justify them letting a complete stranger clock Finn in the teeth.

"That's where I got this," Greg said. He slapped his beer down on the counter and broke away from the group to approach Aristide and Evian. En route, he rolled up his sleeve to reveal four deep, parallel gashes running across his forearm. "That wasn't from no choir director. That was her not recognizing me. That necklace was smashed up on the floor—fell off during the change I guess."

"And yet somehow when Jim looked all over your place, he didn't see anything that told him a *lizard-woman* was there."

"I wouldn'ta believed it either except I was there and that's what I saw. What about you?"

He motioned over to Aristide, who looked in turn to Evian.

"I was busy running," Aristide said. "Did you see anything, Evian?"

Evian had. She relayed the transformation and described the woman as being half a foot taller than Aristide, who was by no means a small man, and having tentacles for arms, along with four or five others fanning out around her midsection like a slime-coated skirt. Aristide was right about the red dress, but only the remains of a dress clung to her body, having obviously swollen to at least twice her normal size.

"Three times," Aristide said. "At least three. You think it was a bridesmaid, right? From the bus station?"

"Which station?" Greg asked.

"I do," Evian said to Aristide, then turned to Greg. "Triangle. They were having a wedding or something, and there was an entire bridal party on the bus."

"Well shit," the bartender said.

Evian turned to look at him, but Aristide had seen him turn to the television and followed his gaze. There was a picture of the bus, overturned with a massive gaping hole ripped out the top of it.

"That you?"

"That's our bus, yeah."

"Well, look at that. That's Carl," the bartender said. "Looks like Jim's there now too. It may be a while if you're expecting him to come this way."

"We were on that bus. Should we go back?" Evian asked.

"I don't think that would be a good idea. Did you tell him what happened? Why are they so close to the bus?" Aristide asked, not really expecting an answer, but he got one.

"They probably didn't believe you," Greg offered. "Didn't

believe me neither. Something like that you really do have to see to believe."

"So what do you want to do?" Evian asked Aristide, as though he had anything resembling an idea.

"Have some more drinks. On the house, given all you been through," the bartender said. Aristide signaled for one more shot, but only one.

"I'm not staying," he said when the bartender poured him a shot of Jameson. "There's that creature out there, and it's going to kill again. And you have a lizard-woman too? No thanks."

He turned his attention to Evian and downed the shot.

"What do you think? Keep going? We can rent a car or something."

"After we give our police statement. I'm pretty sure it's illegal not to report a crime."

"The longer we wait, the more likely that thing is going to find us."

"Betsy never came back," Greg volunteered. "Been a week and she didn't come back once."

"She didn't?"

He shook his head. "I don't think she's likely to. Don't know where she went, or why, but she's gone now."

"So you don't think that she'll follow us here?" Aristide asked.

"Do you?"

Aristide went through the actions from before. As personal as it had been to him, fleeing for his life, the creature hadn't exactly been chasing him. It had been heading toward the front of the bus, and people kept getting in its way. The typical response it had taken to that was to kill or decapitate them, but it wasn't as though it was gunning for them or anything.

"Guess not," he said. "Still, there are people waiting for us."

"Always in a rush. That's the way it is here. A few folks live here, and then everyone else is just passing through," said the bartender, his eyes scrunched together. He paused for a second, then continued, waving his arm to the right. "There's a car rental place up the road about three blocks."

"We should go back," Evian said suddenly. Aristide's head bolted to the left, where Evian just finished up a shot that he hadn't seen her ask for.

"No," he said. "I'm not going back there."

"It's only half an hour," she replied. "Or I'm sure one of these men will give us a ride."

"I'll give you a ride," said Finn, grinning widely. Aristide glared straight into his eyes until the grin evaporated from the man's face. "Just a joke, buddy. Lighten up."

"You can ride along in my truck," Greg said. "Maybe if you tell them what you saw they'll take me for serious."

"I'm not doing it," Aristide protested. He turned toward Evian. "I'm going to Texas, remember? This has nothing to do with me. I didn't turn into a giant squid woman or a lizard-woman or anything like that. I didn't kill a bus full of people."

"But other people will *die*, Aristide. They don't know what they're dealing with."

Aristide motioned around the room. "We just told all of these folks. They know the police. You guys are going to tell them what we told you, right?"

Finn didn't answer. Greg indicated that he would, which didn't help since the locals already seemed to think he was off his gourd. The other two men who hadn't even bothered to introduce themselves just looked around like they'd only now arrived. Aristide felt his lips clamp down together.

"Seriously? None of you?"

"No offense," Finn said. "Right now, you sound about as off it as Greg. Just cause two crazies tell crazy stories don't mean that you're sane. Women don't change into monsters. Not that kind of monster anyway. The soul-sucking cheating kind, maybe. Interesting story and not a bad way to pass time in a bar, but there's no way in hell I'm telling anyone that story without a healthy caveat and maybe a couple of shots first."

"See?" Evian said. "We have to do it ourselves."

"I...can't," Aristide said. He nodded to the bartender and turned toward the exit. He could feel Evian's blue eyes piercing his back but didn't stop. He'd miss her and her long brown hair, the way she'd looked up at him from his lap in the back of the bus before this insanity began. He stopped and turned and stared at her then to the five men in the bar. He shook his head and walked back. He couldn't leave her here. Not with these people, and especially not near Finn. "You need to come too."

"I can look out for myself," she retorted. Her eyebrows had scrunched down and the corners of her lips arched up. "Have fun in Texas."

He glanced toward Finn again and swallowed, perhaps a little too hard because Finn took the opportunity to mock him.

"Go on, boy. We'll take care of your girl here."

Aristide met Evian's eyes and saw them quiver for only a second before recommitting to her glare. He let out a big sigh.

"What are you driving, Greg?"

"F-150, extended cab," Greg replied. "Plenty of room, just got to move my guns first, that's all."

"Let's go."

CHAPTER 3
ANEMONE

TAMITHA VEGA SETTLED into her seat, sliding cozily against the wall and out of sight, hidden away from easy viewing by the rest of the restaurant-goers. Charlotte, North Carolina, boasted a number of fine-dining establishments from Italian to Fusion to Americana, and her Tinder date had chosen barbecue. She slinked down into her seat and covered her face with her hand while she took a deep breath.

It didn't have to be a warning sign. She liked barbecue, just it was a little banal, given the other options. Even a cute gyro shop down on the water would have been a better choice for a first date, if followed by a walk along the promenade. And maybe, in her imagination, if the man showed up with flowers, that might be something.

But who was she kidding. It was already half-past eight and the man hadn't so much as texted her. This was going to be another no-show, just like the last three. The one before that, once he learned that she was an auto mechanic, had suddenly decided to travel to India. And here she was. Waiting for—

"Excuse me?" a man's voice interrupted her self-deprecating rumination. She snapped her head up and her eyes focused in on a man straight from the cover of a romance novel. His close-cut, neat cropped black hair didn't even move as he smiled down at her.

"Jason?"

"Tami Vega, right? I thought it was you," he said. Then he frowned. "You don't look much like your picture."

Tam felt her cheeks heat up and go flush.

"No, no," he corrected. "I mean that in a good way. Sorry I'm late. Just, well, I had to work late and I lost track of time."

She reminded herself that however delicious he might look, he was still over half an hour late for their tête-à-tête.

"Tam," she said and held out her hand in an intentionally stiff and awkward way. She glowered up at him.

"I guess I deserve that," he said as his frown twisted up into a full-toothed grin. "How about I buy dinner?"

Her mind stumbled over whatever else it was that she had to say. He was offering to buy her dinner as though they weren't out on a date, where he should have been picking up the check anyway. One of her hands worked its way back up to the bridge of her nose. She rubbed at the pressure collecting near her eyes.

"Oh, I didn't mean…that was supposed to be a joke," he said. It was kind of cute how he was cornered now, and obviously on the back foot. She let him stew for another thirty seconds before motioning for him to sit.

"Wine," she said. "Red. And good. Nothing ending in a 't'."

In about ten minutes and half a glass of Chianti later, Tam was finally ready to have a conversation that was deeper than the inevitable comments on how this month was unusually warm.

"What do you do, Jason? On your profile, it says medical work. What are you a doctor or something?"

"Surgeon, actually," he said. "That's why I couldn't get away. Surgery went long and, well…"

"Well?"

He held up his hand as if to stop her.

"The patient is fine," he assured her. "Just needed some time to make a quick stop on the way over."

There was honesty in his tone. When he smiled at her, his eyes seemed to glow and lock onto hers as though she were the only other person in the world. He reminded her of a puppy that she'd kicked around when she used to be a tomboy in the country. Tam casually wondered if she kicked him, whether he would come back the same way that dog always had. Always ready for another beating. She gulped down her glass and filled it again, brushing his hand away when he tried to do it for her.

The man was what her father would have called weak. Some women might consider him a catch, but she wasn't some women. And he wasn't her first. Sure, she could hang out with him, laugh at his dull jokes, but the end of the night was when she would have her fun. The time between now and her glory would be nearly as intolerable as waiting there alone with the eyes of every other woman in the restaurant deeming her unfit without a man at her side. In fact, she didn't know if she did have the tolerance for it after the afternoon of waiting.

"Jesus, Jason. What do you say we get out of here?"

"I…uh…I guess. Don't you want to know what I stopped for?"

"I guess. What?"

He reached into his sport coat pocket, the one by the side and not the inside one, and retrieved a small black box. This he placed carefully on the table and slid toward her.

"I didn't have your DNA, of course. I mean, I'd basically be a stalker if I did, right?" He laughed and showed a few too many teeth. "But I thought you'd like it anyway. Just mine is all that's in there. Think of it like a very fancy lock of hair."

Strange for a first date. But whatever it was, she'd pretend to be excited about it. She couldn't add to her collection if this man became the least bit suspicious. She sized him up with the same look that she hoped projected gratification as she reached for the box. He had to have been about six feet tall. If she moved some things around, the deep freezer would have enough room without needing to saw much of anything.

Her hand closed around the box, and she pulled it to her. Trophy keys of former lovers jingled in her purse as she leaned in. She flipped the lid open and saw for the first time a small triangular bottle with no labels. Inside a swirl of fluids spun around and around. There was something mesmerizing about the blue-green swirls in what looked like a pink mist.

"For me?" she asked, carefully examining the pendant attached to a thin silver chain.

"Of course," he said. "Would you like me to put it on for you?"

Once again, she batted his hand away, though somewhat more gently than the time before…and she batted her eyes for good measure.

"I've got it," she said. Tam undid the clasp and wrapped it around her neck. Fumbling blindly, it took her about three seconds to fit the clasp together. When she brought her hand back to the front, the glass container slid just between her clavicle.

"It's beautiful on you," he said. She did blush then, though she'd promised herself she wouldn't. "Do you still want to leave? We could order some—"

She leaned forward and planted a deep kiss across his lips. He tasted like hospital, as she'd thought he would. Tam stomached the taste for a good five seconds before pulling herself away.

"Yes," she purred. "My place."

. . .

Tam almost lost him at her front door. It was her own fault for being sloppy. The last man's hat was still hanging on one of the hooks.

"Oh," Jason said. "I didn't realize—"

"My brother's," she lied as she grabbed it and tossed it haphazardly into the closet. "He doesn't live here. Don't worry. Just was visiting last week."

Just as he was about to say something else, she turned her back toward him.

"Help a girl out?"

That usually shut them up, and it worked this time too. He pulled on the zipper of her form-fitting dress as she shrugged one shoulder through. Then, he sort of hesitated, and she tried to force her shoulder through the opening.

"Hold on a second," he said and muttered something she didn't get as he struggled with the zipper. A second later, something gave and her shoulder pushed through. She thought she heard something snap, but that couldn't have been the dress. She pulled her other shoulder through while stepping free of her heels. Aching calf muscles found relief when she settled her feet down onto the flat apartment floor—and into something damp.

"Shit," he said to her, looking down. "Already. That was fucking expensive."

Tam looked down to see the bottle had cracked. It wasn't much of a crack, but the ooze inside had dripped onto the floor and she'd stepped right into the middle of it.

"I can take it back. Hold on. Let me get it."

Jason bent over and knelt on the ground. If she'd had her awl available, she could have ended it right then. One swift blow to the back of the head would have done it and with very little mess at that angle. Her body tingled in anticipation. One more act of atonement for what she'd gone through as barely more than a child would have been added to the keyring in her purse. Still, she couldn't forget to breathe as he sopped the goop up with a handkerchief (who wears a handkerchief in a casual blazer?).

He mopped furiously at first. Tam could tell from the beet-red back of his neck that he was embarrassed. She ran a cool finger over the hot skin, imagining plunging her awl right through that same spot.

Tam's back itched.

Jason stopped cleaning. He stopped moving altogether. The patch of skin on the back of his neck sprouted hair more quickly than it ever should have. For half-a second, Tam believed in werewolves, and even more so when he spun up in a circle and knocked her across the room.

Her back itched dreadfully.

The awl was tucked safely away in a safe in the back of her closet, and so was no good against the man before her. Or… he'd been a man a second ago. Now his incisors pierced through his lips, and he came at her with a guttural growl. She was certain that he meant to kill her, and the irony in that would have made her laugh had it not been for the fiery itching across her back. She turned and sprinted toward the door, then through. In less than a second, she made it to her apartment stairs and in about five more managed to tumble down them without killing herself. Jason, the wolf-man, simply leapt over the balcony and was nearly on top of her in seconds.

Her garage was close. More tools were there, and now that she was being chased by a wolf, it was pretty open-shut self-defense. Shoeless, she crossed the busy highway, flicking off cars as they swerved to miss her at the last minute. She punched in the code to open the garage and then waited, listening, while the footsteps gained. Tam decided to give up on waiting when the garage door was about knee-height and she rolled underneath. From there, she looked to her right, where the tools were, and to her left, where a car undergoing a transmission change was lifted above the inspection pit. About fifty feet to the tools, about ten to the pit, and the footsteps were coming faster. Tam duck-rolled toward the pit and plopped down over the edge.

Her breath came in gasps as she lay at the bottom. As she did, she listened for the footsteps, which faded back the way they came. Seconds later, she was in total darkness.

Total darkness. The lights had gone out and the ascending ladder that she would have used to lift herself out of the pit was not operational. Tam was stuck. And worse than that, her back itched in places that she couldn't reach with her fingers. She backed against the side of the pit and rubbed her back against the rough wall. To her surprise, she felt something push her back away from the wall. Two exploratory tube-shaped appendages lifted up over her shoulders. Tam instinctually reached for one and yanked on it, then grimaced in pain. In immediate response, a bony dart shot out past her face and sank an eighth of an inch deep into the cement wall.

Her lips curled up into a smile.

Three more darts followed, this time intentionally. Then a fourth. She might be trapped in the pit, but sooner or later they'd be by to open the garage. And then, her work would continue. But, she suspected, if the man could turn into a werewolf, and this strange thing was happening to her could turn out to be the best thing to happen to her. The bodies would fall faster now. She would help them along. And then...the sky really was the limit.

In the distance, she heard a wolf-like howl. She'd track him down eventually and put him out of his misery. Or maybe, she giggled to herself, maybe she just might tame him. It might be fun to have a werewolf pet...unless something better came along.

CHAPTER 4
DANCING PRINCESSES

THADDEUS VLISSIDES SCRAPED a fingernail across a placemat bearing the dancing pictures of imaginary princesses —princesses who could no doubt count on their Prince Charmings to be faithful until the end. Each princess wore a careful close-mouthed smile beneath eyelashes at least a quarter-inch long and drenched in mascara. It was impossible to see the scars of poison offered in the form of a lush apple, the betrayal of a huntsman, or the cruelty of abusive captivity that hid beneath those oversized childlike eyes. The princesses were Teflon and demure. Untouchable by tragedy and resilient.

All except one.

That one wore a carelessly exuberant, wide-mouthed smile as though all of the joy in the world would be hers. An entire globe of adventure and excitement loomed before her based on that smile. But he looked into her eyes, and those told the truth that he knew about the world. Furrowed just a bit too much, Thaddeus Vlissides recognized the barely concealed pain they shared. It leaked out around the edges of her lightly done makeup. Combined with the wide twirl in which she'd been captured, she projected an appearance of madness. The mad and elegant dance was as much a denial of her angst as was his overindulgence in macaroons.

Thaddeus shifted his impressive weight to ease the tingling in his left hip, a byproduct of obesity-induced circulatory problems. Across from him was empty space. A jagged hole had been cut into his ceiling by some unknown projectile or...he had no other ideas. Chilling December air and snowflakes pushed into his apartment in a breeze that couldn't budge the rubberized placemat he examined like a priceless Roman sculpture. Thaddeus himself was more still than even that oversized wishful piece of mahogany furniture that passed for their dinner table. Icy needles grazed against one exposed knee, triggering a response that brought his foot up to kick at shards of glass that decorated the floor.

She'd been preparing for their evening together. Not the princess, but his wife, Julep. A tear worked from his eye down his cheek and flung itself mercilessly toward the princesses below. Six months of basting wands, fertility timings, and countless visits had culminated in one fewer person in his life instead of one more. Julep had been in denial about her own lack of fertility. Her eyes, like Thaddeus's and like the swirling princess's, had expressed the same madness. Like the princess's gyrations, Julep's preparations, including the rubberized mat that caught his tear, were acts of defiance. She would have a child, no matter the cost or what the doctors said.

Another tear followed that one and dropped, forming a puddle with the prior, diluting a smear of reddish brown that may have been blood or leftover barbecue sauce. Finally breaking solidarity with the princess, Thaddeus raised his gaze toward the wall, settling there on a lavender and cherry-colored smear.

A faint ringing sound filled Thaddeus's ears. Shaken from his stupor, he reached with his thick fingers into a blazer pocket and retrieved his phone. Without thinking, he slid his thumb over the biometric sensor.

"Thaddeus. Thaddeus, are you there?"

For a distracted second, Thaddeus recognized Julep's tenor in the question. But there was a smokiness to it that Julep's voice didn't have. The downdraft at the end could only have been Margie. His eyes drifted back up to where the shattered pendant had collided with the wall.

"Thaddeus, I think she knows. Thaddeus, are you there? I think she knows, Thaddeus."

He gulped back a lump as he tried to imagine what had happened after the pendant smashed. It made no sense. Smashed pendant, shattered glass—too much for just the pendant...there was something he didn't see.

"She knows," he finally creaked through his dry lips.

Silence. Then.

"Everything?"

"Every..."

But he stopped. No, not everything. She hadn't let him tell her *everything*. No sooner had he ejected the words "Margie and I" in a fool's errand to come clean and re-baseline their relationship trust than she'd hurled the projectile toward his head. He'd felt the chain whip by, almost catching him in the eye. No, she didn't know everything. She didn't know about the child.

"Why are you so quiet, Thaddeus?" Then, she gasped. "Is she there?"

"N...no," he said, dragging his eyes back up to the gargantuan missing chunk in the wall. "She's not here."

"I'm coming over," Margie said. "Stay there."

Where would he go? He hung up the phone and took another longing look at the hole. Had she gone through that hole? If so, how? They were seven stories up. In the city. Over a hillside. Someone would have noticed if she'd climbed out into the world, destroying their apartment wall. The building was old enough to be solid brick, and now it had a massive hole in it.

Thaddeus stood with shattered glass crunching beneath his black boots. The glass was from the skylight overhead; it had to be. The brick didn't have glass in it. He drew his eyes up, but the skylight was pristine and unbroken.

Nothing was there to indicate what had happened. Just a huge hole and a missing wife. He retook his seat, wishing he hadn't eaten the last of the macaroons when he'd taken them with him to escape her wrath earlier. Thaddeus lowered his head to rest sideways against the top of the table and stared at the unbroken wall to his right. Then, he pulled his hands up around his head and let the sobs flow from between his heaving shoulders.

Less than ten minutes passed before the jangle of keys awoke him from his stupor, and his heart leapt at the possibility that his wife, in all of her rage, might have returned to him. He stood too quickly, forgetting his borderline diabetes, and wobbled on unstable legs. He willed himself not to fall, his gaze locked on the door as it swung slowly inward. The first thing he saw was a leg push through, followed by the curve of a hip and waist—curves he recognized, only to realize he was deceived yet again as his comfort gave way to despair. Thaddeus wiped his tears away and bit his lip to keep it from trembling.

"Jesus," Margie said when she breached the door. "What the hell happened here?"

"I don't know. I came in, and the wall was missing. Julep too. I've been calling her—"

"I missed a call from her earlier," Margie interrupted, red creeping into her cheeks. Thaddeus wondered briefly whether the cold was responsible for that or if it was another side effect of hormones that fluctuated wildly due to a pregnancy they rarely talked about. A pregnancy that Thaddeus had claimed to be a lie until it had gotten so far along that the undeniable six-month bump protruded from Margie's belly.

His mind switched back to the missing wall.

A *missing wall*. That type of stuff doesn't just happen. Even in home invasions, it's not like walls destroyed themselves. A fifty-caliber rifle might have done it. A standard one couldn't punch a hole that big, but one with the right kind of round would do it. It would have to have been modified to increase the output velocity, and there were kits to do that. The problem with the notion was that the hole had some definite characteristics about it. The entire thing *looked* roughly the shape of a human being.

"What's that?" Margie asked, pointing to the ground where tiny fragments of the apology vial he'd gotten Julep lay on the ground. Some of the purple sheen of fluid inside had lined one of the shards. Margie squatted slowly, her left hand holding her back, and her hand closed around the shard. As she stood up, she must have clamped her hand down harder because Thaddeus saw a droplet of blood when she opened her hand to show it to him. The pink sheen seemed to glow, then a dark crimson-purple.

"Nothing. Just something I got for Julep."

"For Julep? Wait…I recognize this. Wait a minute," Margie said, her light-brown irises floating in a sea of white beneath narrowed eyes. "*That's* a splice vial, isn't it?"

The slit of her eyes narrowed even more as she drilled into his head.

"You were trying to get back together with her, weren't you? Did you never even intend to tell her?"

"She's my wife, and *your* sister, Margie. We owe her—"

"I don't owe her a damn thing," Margie insisted. Then, her voice softened. "You know what she's like—controlling, manipulative. Imagine having to *grow up* with that."

"It was a long time ago, Margie. She's not like that anymore."

"Do you have any idea why *my* husband *left* me?"

Thaddeus was certain some argument had gotten out of hand, and if it was the usual between Margie and Julep, then it meant that they'd both traded blows, and probably Chris, Margie's ex, had more sense than Thaddeus and had left. But before Margie could begin her explanation, her eyes began to bulge.

Her hair glistened. At first, Thaddeus thought he was imagining things. After he blinked twice, he realized he wasn't creative enough to imagine what he was seeing. The strands of her hair twisted in small clumps that merged into blue-green tentacles. Ridges pushed up through the flesh in her shoulders, revealing sharpened wedges that sliced through her camisole top. As it fell away, Thaddeus turned his head for modesty. It was an impulse almost immediately corrected as he swiveled back in time to see the ridges on her back spread and merge to cover her shoulders and arms with seaweed-thick strands that ran down her back and sides. Her chest turned colors, going from rosy-pink to gray-green, and the hair over her head flopped down in front of her face.

Once her body freed itself of its remaining clothing that dropped into a shredded pile beneath her, the bump in her belly began to writhe. Protrusions pushed outward as though something were trying to escape. In seconds, her belly—as blue-green as her shoulders and breasts—pushed outward in one prolonged shove, and he watched in horror as the flesh tore and octopus-like tentacles shoved through her skin. With a push, the table went down, and Thaddeus flew over it.

"You wanted her *back*?" screamed Margie, or the monster who used to be Margie. Thaddeus didn't respond. "You…her…"

The words seemed more belabored every time she opened

her mouth until there were no more words but only guttural noises and screams. From a crack between the table and the floor, Thaddeus watched the last remnants of his soon-to-be-sister-in-law's clothes ripped away. Her shoes split at the ends as blue-green, scaly-clawed feet pushed their way out.

His eyes went from the creature before him to the humanoid-shaped hole in the bricks behind her. Wheels were turning, and even his reluctant mind connected the vial's contents, the droplet of blood, and the gap in the wall. It was something that he'd never have expected. His wife and her sister, with his child (if it *was* his), had morphed into monsters, and only Thaddeus knew it. All of them had reasons to hate Thaddeus. With a gulp, Thaddeus stood slowly, holding his hands out in the universal "I mean no harm" position.

"Margie, you're not yourself," he said, understating by a mile the extent of what had just happened. Her head tilted sideways, and he thought he caught the glisten of a brown eye through the veil of seaweed-like hair. Margie didn't say anything. The four tentacles protruding from her stomach (and defying any laws of gravity) hovered before him and pointed at him as though the creature were considering whether to eat Thaddeus or perhaps give him a life-crushing hug.

"Argnnnnveeff," she said, finally. One arm slid across her chest to cover her exposed breasts, and the other went to her crotch. One of the tentacles blocked that one, which seemed to catch her attention as her head cocked again, and she let out a wail. "Ninggtess!"

She was shocked. He got that by her mannerisms, which told him that Margie was still in that body somewhere, at least for the moment. Then, further differentiating what had just happened from anything in the natural world, the tentacles drifted to the ground beneath her and lifted her into the air as they pushed against the floor. Gliding atop her new appendages, Margie didn't bother covering herself any longer.

Given her current state, modesty wasn't the most critical thing. Her head tilted to the side again, and she twisted her neck to stare through the opening above the dining room. In a couple of short tentacle hops, she flew up through the opening and disappeared out of sight into the city.

CHAPTER 5
HOME INVASION

THE ROOM SPUN around Thaddeus's head. He stared at the doorway sideways and watched four people in what looked like black riot gear push through the smoking remains of the door that had been fully intact only a second before. Where Thaddeus had been standing *two* seconds earlier. That had all changed in a single blinding flash. His eyes slowly pulled details out of the haze. The first to enter carried a weapon that looked like a rifle except that the barrel extended farther than the usual two feet. This person seemed taller than him by about six inches, though it was hard to discern with them sideways. Another trespasser seemed average height, though with a thicker body like the first person had been squashed down into body armor two sizes too small. The last two seemed about the same size from what he could tell from his vantage point on the floor. The room's spinning slowed enough for Thaddeus to discern that the first person had leveled their weapon toward Thaddeus's head.

"Where did she go?" said the woman. Her physique was impossible to tell from the uniform, but the voice was clearly feminine.

"Where did *who* go?" Thaddeus cringed as the words came out of his mouth. He had wanted them to be a challenge, so that whoever had destroyed his home got the message that they couldn't simply blow a hole in his front door. In truth, his voice carried a tinny edge to it that reminded him of a five-year-old complaining about having to wear pants—like a child had played hide-and-seek for too long and then who was left quivering in the shadows calling for help when all the other children had already gone home. The voice depicted exactly who Thaddeus was at that moment. And that was the problem. The person with the gun didn't seem to believe in Thaddeus's authority any more than he did.

"I said where is she? Stop stalling and tell me the truth."

"Katie, I think you were right," the shorter stocky one said with a male tenor.

Katie must have been the one with the weapon because she turned when her name was called.

"You're the one who wanted riot gear, Neko."

"I didn't say to blow up the door."

"Wh…who are you?"

"Sorry, Mr. Vlissides. Kathryn Villin, CDC. You can call me Katie. This is my team, the Biological Security Task Force. We're looking for," the woman looked down at her mobile phone and back up again, "Julep Hode. Does she live here?"

Probably made up the name Biological Security Task Force, Thaddeus thought then jerked his head up as one of the other alleged CDC team members spoke.

"Look," said a third, skinnier and just a hair taller than the stocky one called Neko. "It was precaution. What if there was a tentacled freak in this apartment? Then you'd be thanking me."

"It's been over a day, Neko. She took off like all the others," the woman who called herself Katie responded.

"I don't know where she is," Thaddeus said. He motioned

with the arm that didn't throb from the blast up toward the gaping hole as he worked his jaw. "And I don't know which her you're talking about either."

A thousand things went through his mind as he finished his sentence, once he'd worked his way past the most obvious question. Why there were four armed people in his living room? Clearly, they were looking for someone they thought was dangerous, otherwise why bother? And up until this morning, Thaddeus would have hardly considered either Julep or Margie dangerous, except possibly to him. Their relationship problems hardly warranted this level of intervention. And they had only been there for one of the women, who he belatedly considered was likely Margie, since she'd arrived and left moments before they got there.

Margie and his Julep, who he'd wronged so many times. Even if Julep did deserve the way he treated her sometimes— because she wasn't exactly innocent—she didn't deserve to turn into whatever it was Margie had become. Which, as he saw it, looked more and more likely to be what had happened. Thaddeus pushed himself to his knees and straightened his back as he tried to stand. Rickety feet supported him more than he thought they would.

And what was it that Margie turned into? His hands shook involuntarily, and he pulled them over his face to both steady them and hide from the world. Thaddeus's eyes slammed shut as he tried to block out the image that had already seared itself into his mind, ineffectually so. He still saw the gray-green scales and dripping flesh, the tentacles protruding from her belly, and the...he didn't want to think about it anymore. His jaw seized shut as the intruders knocked over a dresser by the door and then pushed past him farther into the house.

"G...get out!" he managed, through his splayed fingers. Thaddeus gulped air down and filled his lungs, then tried again. "Get out!"

"Sir, calm down," Katie told him.

"Calm down? Calm down? You come barging into my home and tearing apart...everything. What are you looking for?"

Thaddeus peeled his hands away from his eyes in time to see one of the people approaching, hidden behind what seemed to be a gas mask. This one walked with a careful pace, sidestepping the shattered figurine that used to be a fairy princess. A shattered dragon's head lay next to a broken fey wing. The person pulled off a helmet, revealing the shaved sides of a head topped with flowing orange locks, not naturally orange but a dye job so poorly done that even Thaddeus could see the different shades within. His eyes slid down to the face and fell upon flashing-hazel eyes and a smile that was just slight enough to convey that she didn't want to be there any more than he wanted them there. *Kind of a lot to fit into a smile,* he thought.

"Mr. Vlissides," Katie said, as one hand guided into a pouch hidden in the front of her suit. "We're the CDC Bioengineering Task Force. We've had reports of a strange creature in the vicinity."

"You broke into my home."

"We did. The government will reimburse you for the damage. Where is your wife now, sir?"

He looked into the woman's kind, expectant eyes. His mind spun back to Margie digging through the broken remains of the vial before she...before she...he shook his head.

"What is it, sir?"

"Doesn't matter. It's over there," Thaddeus said, pointing to the floor beneath the gaping hole. Storm clouds gathered in the sky above, threatening rain. That, of course, would simply be the perfect end to a day that had pushed him past his tolerance. The woman glanced where he pointed, then said something in a language that didn't *sound* like English, but his muddled mind could have been mixing things up. She pointed, and one of the other individuals in black skipped to and began to gather the pieces into what looked like a thin plastic bag.

"Why do you want that?" he asked.

"What did you see?" she asked right back, her smile unwavering as the others collected the remaining shards of glass. "I'll tell you if you tell me."

Didn't seem very professional, but he could play tit-for-tat games.

"You won't buy it. I don't buy it either. I've been under a lot of stress lately…with work," he said, not mentioning that sneaking around with Margie had become incredibly difficult since they'd moved into the new apartment just a few blocks away. Thaddeus had thought it would make things easier, but that close was just too tempting for Julep as she dropped in on Margie's home a couple of times while Thaddeus hid in a closet or out on the fire escape. That was why he was planning to let Margie go—*before* he'd found out about the baby.

An involuntary shrug. None of that mattered now if what he'd seen was real. Now all he wanted, surprising even himself, was for both of them to return safely. Margie. Julep. Even the baby. They could be pissed at him, he bargained. They could cut him out of their lives completely and raise the child as a team. He'd gladly trade his comfort for them—both of them. That wasn't a bargain Thaddeus had ever been used to making. He cleared his throat with a cough.

"She changed," he said, gambling on the truth. "She changed into something…a monster. Tentacles extending down to the ground from her belly. *Tentacles*. And it happened so fast. Midsentence. She was pissed, and we were fighting—"

"What about?"

"Doesn't matter, does it? She cleans when she's angry. Margie bent down, stood back up, and then she suddenly kept repeating herself and not making sense. A second—no, about thirty seconds—later, and she wasn't Margie anymore."

"Margie? I thought we were talking about Julep. What about Julep? And who's Margie?"

Thaddeus shrugged his shoulders. He must have looked pathetic, a grown man standing on shaky legs and staring distantly forward as he tried to kick-start his mind into working again.

"I...I don't know about Julep."

"She smashed the vial into the wall there. That didn't have anything to do with you?"

His mind went to the night before, back when he'd had what he thought was the worst day of his life. But right now, he would pay to have yesterday back.

————

The store clerk at Home Sweet Awakenings had promised, had *sworn*, that the pendant in which the now splattered fluid had lived would save his relationship. It had been the three drinks that coaxed Thaddeus into telling the clerk his life's story, though he may have embellished a few parts. Margie hadn't hit on him at his engagement party, for example. That had been the other way around. Thaddeus was bored after his fiancée overindulged in cocktails and without a warning left him to entertain the fifty or so guests by himself. He'd gotten some funny looks then, as though people had expected him to follow her lead and disappear, but the couple had only just arrived, and Thaddeus had spent over a thousand dollars on the party so he was going to indulge at least a little.

Besides, it wasn't what people probably thought, he rationalized. They probably assumed that Julep had run off to make herself sexy and awaited him in their hotel room. What had actually happened, and what Thaddeus had worked with more than one Julep's girlfriends to conceal from prying eyes, was that Julep had once again locked herself in the hotel bathroom while she puked her guts up. Praying to the porcelain goddess, as she liked to call it. And that was how Margie and he had found common ground. He'd needed someone to vent to, and Margie knew her sister's habits full and well. He hadn't even had to explain. Margie guessed within seconds of their talking.

He had blabbered on about Margie probably more than he should have given that *she* wasn't the one who was going to get the gift. The store clerk was French and in America on a visa, so he probably only understood every other word. But he'd latched onto the word *love*, which Thaddeus must have used at some point, though whether he was discussing Julep or Margie at the time was lost to his memory. Still, the store clerk told him about this vial. If he had anything of her DNA—even a wayward hair—and Thaddeus's DNA, then the single most unique thing that Home Sweet Awakenings offered was a love vial. It would add enhancers to their DNA so that they would amplify in different colored fluids and trap them in a crystal vial together, forever merging and changing and splitting apart so that the colors would always change. For an extra thousand, they could add a glowing agent.

Thaddeus was terrible at love, but he was extremely well-paid for his ability to keep his mouth shut about government secrets, so the money seemed like a good deal.

"This, oh, this," the man had said in his seductive French accent. "This will change your life and hers. She will love you forever for this and show it off to her friends."

Not a moron, Thaddeus knew that if the ten-thousand-dollar diamonds Julep wore hadn't gained her love forever, then the vial wouldn't do it either. But what it might do was patch over the fact that Julep had found an image of Margie in lingerie amidst the photos on his phone. It might make her more willing to accept the completely unbelievable story that

Margie had asked him to take that image so that she could surprise the new man in her life with a printout and that storing it on her own phone would allow her imaginary man to find it and might ruin the surprise.

Yes, it was weak. And yes, he knew exactly how bad the story was. But twenty-thousand dollars on a unique one-of-a-kind love trinket was exactly the sort of thing that could make Julep forget all about that image. Didn't work on all women, of course, but Julep and he were a lot alike. He could see that working.

He had a hair from the hairbrush she'd thrown at him earlier still clinging to his shirt. So the clerk—that's right, Armond, the clerk—earned a healthy commission. Twenty minutes and twenty-thousand dollars later, Thaddeus was in the possession of the most unique love trinket in the world that might save his marriage. That was before he figured out that Julep hadn't just broken into his phone just that one time, and that she'd learned something else about him and Margie. Twenty-thousand dollars would go a long way for patching mistakes, but there wasn't enough salve in the world to patch the wound of a sister carrying her husband's child.

A miscalculation on Thaddeus's part about how much Julep had known. That was how the vial went flying through the air, just barely missing his head, and smashing itself into the wall. That was how he'd spent the evening out drowning his sorrows and staggered home too drunk to see the huge gaping hole in the ceiling. He'd collapsed onto the couch, noticing the chill enough to groggily get up a moment later and up the thermostat on autopilot. Even then, he hadn't seen the hole that was *right fucking there over his head*. He'd curled up like a baby on the couch and drifted into a deep sleep, interrupted by bathroom trips.

And no, he didn't notice even when he staggered through the bedroom to the bathroom in the middle of the night that his partner wasn't actually in their bed. He'd been on the couch enough that most of his activity there was rote and didn't require even knowing which house he was in (though he'd gotten at least that part right). But come morning, it was him and a broken vial and a hole in his apartment.

———

"You really are a piece of work, aren't you?" Katie asked after the story, her smile still present, but flickering around the corners. "You really didn't notice?"

"That my wife had disappeared? No. Not until the morning. That's when I saw the hole, and that's when I called Margie."

"Your wife disappears, and you call her philandering sister instead of the police? When there's this huge hole here?"

"Are you a cop or something?"

"Not technically, no. But seriously. That's the best you could do?"

"Who do you call when it looks like World War Three happened in your apartment? What was I supposed to tell the cops anyway? The first thing they would do is probably lock me up for spousal abuse."

"Interesting that's where your mind went. Guilty conscience?"

"Well, not anymore, Ms. Bioengineering Task Force," he said and rubbed his hand down his face. "I just want her back. I want them both back. Lock me up if you have to. Just find her."

He hadn't realized tears were falling down his face until his hand came away wet.

"Call me Katie," the woman said. Her smile was completely gone. "Or Agent Villin if you want to be formal. Look, Thaddeus, we know this wasn't you. And you're right, calling the cops would have been a mistake. We're going to look for her, okay? But if we find her—and I'm not saying we will because what happened to her isn't done happening yet probably if it's only been a day—then she's not going to be herself if what you've said is true, Thaddeus. We don't know yet how to undo whatever this is. There's very little to go on."

"What happened to my wife, Katie?" Thaddeus said, the salesman in him knowing to use her first name if she'd let him and try to put a wedge between herself and her professionalism.

"All we know so far is that a handful of people who have bought from Home Sweet Awakenings are disappearing, and people have said that they've seen them turn into monsters. That, and we found something that looks like a snake-squid the size of a human in Arlington. That thing...that thing..." She shook her head, and he knew the feeling. "If it started out human, it isn't any more."

"And you think this is what's happening to my wife? She's turned into a snake-squid?"

"What do you think? You saw what happened to Margie. I didn't."

Checkmate on his denial. He had seen, and he still couldn't unsee it. The tentacled monster rising up above his head and deftly using her new appendages to work her way through the opening above. No, there was no unseeing that. But still, his heart clung to the hope that Margie might be able to change back somehow.

CHAPTER 6
BIOLOGICAL ENGINEERING TASK FORCE

AS SHE STEERED the unimaginative black SUV down Arlington Boulevard, Katie imagined her mother laughing and pointing at her with that near-toothless mouth and cracking knuckles.

"I was right all along," the woman would say, her dry, cracked lips pulled back into a ghastly grin. "I told you."

It was too early to call, though. Katie hadn't seen what Thaddeus claimed he had, and Thaddeus wouldn't be the first lover to use acts of the supernatural to dispose of a spouse. There'd been the incident in Texas where a woman had claimed aliens had abducted her husband. Katie and her team had eventually found the man's body wedged into the bottom of a well where the woman had put him after she'd sliced his neck with a butcher's cleaver for talking during *Jeopardy!*, and Katie imagined probably a lifetime of other slights.

"What was that?" she asked the shaken Neko. Neko shook his head and said nothing, holding his hand in the universal sign for stop.

Viv wasn't nearly as withholding.

"You saw the person-shaped hole in the roof, right? Did you see anything around to create that?"

"You believe that the man's wife changed into a squid creature, punched a hole in the ceiling, and escalated herself through?"

"His wife is gone. Her sister is gone. Both in his apartment," Katie said. "Something feels wrong about that."

"And the hole?" Viv replied.

"Anything can be staged. Just because we don't know how he did it yet doesn't make it real."

"I'm with Viv," Neko finally said. "Anything can be staged. But you saw the slime on the walls?"

"Just a broken vial," Katie replied. "Could have been anything. And what's more likely, a man going to extremes to cover up a double homicide or two women turning into monsters?"

Neko's eyes turned downward. Katie knew he had to acknowledge her point, even if he stopped short of saying so. Viv shifted her weight from one leg to the other and ran her delicate fingers through her ash-blond hair, pulling her shoulder-length locks from one side of her neck to the other. Her eyes seemed more sunken in than usual, as though she'd not slept the night before. Possibly true. Neko looked just as ragged, and his bald spot had more of a sheen than usual. Maybe they'd had a little too much fun the night before. Whatever it was, they were both letting their imaginations run rampant.

"I think he's lying," said Neko.

Katie turned back toward him and blinked once before remembering she was driving. Then, she turned forward and swerved into the left lane to avoid colliding with another black sport utility vehicle. She'd forgotten that in Northern Virginia they were as common as the poplar trees that lined the road. As they passed, she caught what had to be the most expressive glare hiding behind aviator glasses and a crew cut she'd ever seen. She glared right back.

"That hole, anything could have done that. There's no way his wife and girlfriend both turned into monsters. One… maybe. Two? Uh-uh."

"Before you say it's uh-uh," Neko said while he straightened his glasses, "maybe we should check the next stop and see if there's anything to make of it."

Katie rolled her eyes.

"It's a good thing we wore riot gear." She smirked. Viv said nothing in response, so Katie continued. "Anyway, that man wasn't even a little sick. There's no contagion here. It's just a man trying to get away with murder. I'm with you, Neko. Let the Arlington police handle it."

"It wouldn't be right if we didn't investigate the other two reports, Katie," Viv replied, somewhat subdued, from the back seat. Her easy smile had been replaced with a thin line below her nose.

Katie sighed at the idea of her planned evening, simple with a few drinks at the hotel bar and maybe a wine-induced bubble bath, being sidetracked. She checked her phone.

"There's plenty of time until happy hour," Neko said. Katie smiled at his overly acute observation and the odd turn of events that put her in the position of pushing for escape from work and the two of them trying to stay on the job.

"I guess," she said. "The next one is over two hours away though, down near Richmond. Bus accident and a handful of survivors. Last chance to blow it off and head back to the hotel."

"Not doing it," Neko said, his comb-over appearing especially thin as he shook his head. "I think something is happening, and I want to know what. Maybe I can get a disease named after me."

That broke Viv's stress out as she responded with a slight laugh.

"Fine," Katie said. "Here we go."

———

Katie leafed through the manila folder after parking, as the others exited the vehicle. Someone had called in to the Fredericksburg Police Department from their mobile complaining of two things: a bus had crashed on the highway and a creature had been seen ripping people apart. Of course, the police report that Katie had gotten was sparse and written in the sarcastic manner of someone who clearly didn't believe the caller. It had only been referred to Katie's desk by an administrator who Katie guessed probably trucked in conspiracy theories as much as Viv did.

The bus was on its side atop an overpass. Suspicious, sure, but it was a bus accident, so not so suspicious. Disbelieving or not, from the squad cars nearby, Fredericksburg's finest had beaten them to the scene and were busily cordoning off the area. Whether they would be cooperative or not remained to be seen. Often the police could be the most useful allies, but sometimes they could also get in stupid pissing matches, and Katie would have to inform them that she outranked them even if she was "just CDC."

She put the folder down and stepped onto the hot asphalt. The first thing she noticed made her stomach sink: a hole the size of a Toyota Prius had been ripped into the roof of the bus and from the looks of it, if the Prius had had claws and had been trying to get out as opposed to pushing its way in. She brought her hands up to her eyes and squeezed. If there was another snake-woman involved, she'd have to write a report that she already didn't believe, and then they'd have to spend a month chasing down clues to nothing. Or worse, they would find some truth in the rumors and then her mother's world view would have been exonerated. Katie exhaled.

"Neko, go find out what the police know. Viv, find any survivors and give them an interview. I'm going to find the scene investigator."

The man was easy to find and appeared used to the Virginia summer heat from the look of his sunglasses. He wore a Hawaiian shirt and blue jeans atop tan cowboy boots that didn't really work with the combination. She guessed he also had a motorcycle at home and a Hells Angels jacket in his closet.

"You in charge?" she asked.

He looked over at her and said nothing. He gave her a cursory nod as she crossed the caution tape. Closer to the bus, Neko had already begun chatting with one of the other policemen. Viv seemed to be lost as she wandered around the vehicle, occasionally poking her head up to a window to peer inside.

"Yep," he finally said. She couldn't tell where his eyes went behind his aviator glasses. She corrected her bulletproof vest and he smiled. "What's that for?"

Katie flipped out her badge and flashed it at him.

"CDC," she said.

"In Kevlar vests? Aren't you hot out here?"

Katie didn't ingratiate the man with a response. She was confident the beads of sweat pouring into her eyes were enough to prove how hot she was, and it wasn't as though she was about to take off her gear, however much doubt she had. Viv's visceral reaction of trembling eyes and uncommon quietness had staying power.

"Nope," she lied. "Not hot at all. What happened here?"

"According to the driver, something came out of the bathroom and started killin' folks. From his description, something like a walking squid or Doctor Octopus or something."

"Where is he now? Can I talk to him?"

"Nope."

Katie paused for a minute to let the man continue. He was obviously testing her patience and bearing. She cocked her hip to the side and stared into his glasses through her own, unblinking. He made it about thirty seconds before he made a chewing motion with his chin and cleared his throat.

"Died."

"I thought there were survivors."

"There were. Three of them we know about. Two more unaccounted for… a…let me see…" He fumbled with a clipboard she hadn't noticed he held and pulled it up to his face. "Passenger list. Let's see. There should be Aristide Decuir and Evian Baptiste on the bus. Also, there's also about half of a bridal party still missing—signed up as a group, so I don't have their names yet. Not sure if they're alive or dead, by the look of the inside of that bus."

She glanced across to Neko, who seemed to be having more luck with one of the beat officers than she was with the investigator, who seemed to want her to work for every word he uttered. Katie stared at him again, noticing the scar below his left eye and the comb-over that made Neko look like he had a full head of hair.

"What else can you tell me about the incident here?"

"Well, there's a big goddam hole in the top of the bus. Something went through it."

She stole another glance at Neko. He and the officer he was talking to were staring into what she assumed was a phone.

"Excuse me," she said, offering more politeness than she should for the uselessness of the man she'd been talking to. She crossed the pavement, feeling herself slowly baking in her riot gear, hotter now than before the man's comment. As she approached, Neko's eyes, already wide behind his Coke-bottle glasses, seemed wider as they bolted up to see her.

"Snake-woman," he confirmed. "Look at this."

He held up a tablet with a video app, paused on a full screenshot of what looked like something out of a horror movie. What she saw wasn't a snake-woman, but close enough, and it was a woman, or had been at one time. She had claws that descended from between the straps of a formal gown that had been shredded somehow. Neko pressed the screen, and the video rolled into motion. Ridges that extended from between her eyebrows down her nose culminated in a mouth full of jagged teeth from which a massive protruding tongue whipped around and sliced through two people during the short video. The woman had no stomach beneath her exposed leathery breasts. In its place was a continuously biting mouth that seemed to emit little worm things that slithered toward anyone before her. The video lasted five seconds, and three people died during that time. Katie clenched her teeth, and her stomach fell through the pavement. But still, a mutant killer woman didn't necessitate the CDC. Unless infection or transmission was involved, and rapid spreading at that, the woman's condition was just an anomaly and nothing for her to report.

Except then it wasn't. Katie had to admit to herself, now that she'd seen the video, that the hole in Thaddeus's ceiling could have been caused by the same thing. And by now, the story they'd heard on Arlington Boulevard was starting to seem more plausible. If the Biological Engineering Task Force wasn't the right group on the case, she didn't know who else to call in.

Viv tapped on Katie's elbow and blew any remaining doubts out of the water. She held a tablet with a fracture extending from the top to the bottom, crossing the smooth face and splitting the device almost in two. It was a hairline fracture, so the device still worked, and from the sounds of it, someone else had the presence of mind to record. What Katie saw on that screen was one of the worm creatures slipping into a boy's screaming mouth, and then seconds later, a tentacle shot from his stomach and penetrated through a passenger in front of him. Thirty seconds into the video, the boy had fully transformed into something that H.R. Giger might have created.

It wasn't pretending or special effects. This was real. She could already see her boss reading the report and asking for Katie's resignation.

"Get me a copy of all the videos," Katie heard herself say regretfully. "It looks like we have a case."

The sound of a truck pulling up onto the on-ramp startled Katie. She turned to see a silver F-150 speed along the road, almost colliding with the caution tape before quickly stopping.

"Great, it's Greg. He'll have a field day with this," she overheard a policeman nearby say.

"Who's Greg?" Katie asked, directing her question to the slim man who looked too skinny to have room for his internal organs. He glanced away from her at first, then back over.

"Local crackpot," he said. "Claims his wife turned into a lizard creature."

Another policeman, this one stockier with a thick neck, stopped examining a hunk of sheet metal, made his way over, and nodded to Katie.

"Don't place stock in that, whatever *this* looks like. She ran off on him. Been cheating on him for almost a year, and everyone admits it but him."

She'd seen the creature on multiple tablets by now. It certainly looked like it had been a woman. Basic anatomy told her the creature had been female. Not much of that dress had survived. Yet nobody had recorded a woman transforming. The footage was primarily the woman-creature attacking whoever was holding the device. It was as though the creature had known that she was being recorded and didn't want to be like a child lashing out on the playground after all the other children there taunted her.

"Bring him here," she said to the lanky one, who shook his head as though it was the biggest mistake she might make in her life.

"What about the other two?"

"Other two?"

"Do you recognize them, Bobby?" asked the portly cop.

"Nope. Not locals, Jim," the man replied. "But probably some strays he picked up at the bar. You know he's lost himself to the bottle since Miranda left."

"Get them all," Katie said, motioning with her head that he needed to hurry up. "I want statements. Bring them to me, and I'll get them myself."

The lanky man, Bobby, she gathered, sulked his way over to where Greg stood outside the taped off area. She watched them exchange words, and then Bobby lifted the caution tape to let them through. One looked military, like Katie's father was, with a high-and-tight haircut, with just the suggestion of hair on the sides of his head and slightly more across the top. He had a day and a half of rough beard that most military men kept from their faces. The woman with him had the telltale signs of being a military brat. Katie would recognize them anywhere because she was one. The woman seemed just as comfortable walking through an accident crime scene as a shopping mall. Except for the occasional glances over her left shoulder, the woman might have been shopping at Walmart.

The three stopped just short of where the bodies lay across the highway. Katie put herself between the three and the carnage and nodded to Bobby to dismiss him back to processing the scene, which he seemed only too relieved to do.

"Greg, right?" she asked once he'd come to a complete stop. His wide eyes were too busy soaking up the wreckage to acknowledge her. Katie cleared her throat and tried again.

"Greg, right?"

"Uh, yeah. Yeah, that's me. And who are you, ma'am?"

"Katie Villin, Center for Disease Control and Prevention." She flashed her badge out of habit and tucked it away again. "You have information for us?"

"Not me, ma'am. These two," he said, motioning to the Marine and the military brat. "These two were on that bus."

He said the words like he couldn't believe them, and she could see why. The sideways bus with a hole through the roof didn't exactly project the possibility of survivors existing. Other than a couple of scrapes, these two seemed pretty much unharmed.

"And who are you?" she asked, directing her question to the woman.

"Eviana Baptiste," she said, "and this is Aristide."

The woman stopped without giving his last name. The searching look in her eyes told Katie that she didn't know what it was. So these two had only just met. Maybe fellow travelers? Katie liked the odds that they had been on that bus. She turned to the scene investigator, who still looked like he harbored some resentment toward her for running her investigation right over the top of his. She flashed him a winning smile.

"Anywhere we can talk with these folks that's a little more private?"

"They can follow me," Greg said.

CHAPTER 7
GET IT TOGETHER, MARINE

THE VEHICLE WASN'T that impressive from the inside. There was enough seating for six adults though, so it was large at least, though the seat cushions were some sort of fabric instead of the leather Aristide hadn't known he was expecting to see until he was disappointed by it not being there.

Aristide and Evian rode in the far back two bucket seats. Immediately in front of them and casting wary glances at them for the majority of the short ride was a woman with a broad nose, sunken eyes, and stringy brownish-blond hair. A pair of pink-framed glasses rested atop her head and a charm necklace was just visible against the ivory indentation that peeked out over her black Kevlar vest. Her matching helmet, which she used as a fiddling drum for restless fingers, sat in the seat beside her.

A man with a bad comb-over drove. He kept obsessively running one hand over the top of his head in what looked like a vain attempt to keep the strands down and maintain the illusion of hair atop his head. This man also had sunken eyes, partially concealed behind wide, circular lenses. Like Aristide, he also had a thin scruff over his chin as if he hadn't shaved in at least a day and a half. Aristide didn't know his name, though he recalled being introduced. Just with so much happening, there was far too much new information to process than he was capable.

In front of Evian, a man big enough to be two men kind of squashed together sat. This man moved his mouth like he was chewing something but didn't seem to have a lot to say. Beads of sweat glimmered off of the man's bald head.

Aristide glanced over at Evian, whose chipper demeanor had half returned, and who ingratiated him with a slight smile. At least one of them wasn't freaking out inside. It was some solace to him that nobody seemed to see past his military bearing to tease out the fact that he was, in fact, terrified. His eyes relentlessly scanned each window in turn, looking for that creature—that *woman*.

Get it together, Marine.

"We don't know anything," Aristide muttered to Evian, keeping his voice low so that hopefully even the woman immediately in front of them couldn't hear.

"We don't know what we know," Evian said. "Combined with the evidence that they've got already, something we saw could be important."

"Important enough to miss your family in Louisiana?"

She nodded. "My family will understand. And I might have lied when I said they were expecting me anyway."

His eyebrow arched up. "You lied?"

"That was before I knew you, Aristide. You could have been a serial killer. I wasn't about to tell you that I, a single woman traveling solo, had no real destination and nobody was expecting me. Doesn't seem bright, does it?"

"But you spent half the ride with your head in my lap."

She shrugged. "I guess I decided you're okay after all. We didn't talk much more about destinations on the bus, remember?"

He thought back and realized that she was right. The "where are you heading" part of the conversation had all taken place in the hard plastic seats of the Triangle bus station. They'd moved on to talking about the family on the bus. Aristide nodded.

"Yeah, that's right," he said. His eyes caught something moving in the trees, and he fixed his gaze on a clump of juniper trees that seemed out of place against a backdrop of oaks. The tops of one of the trees shook. He felt his eyes go wide. Evian seemed to notice and turned her gaze in the same direction.

"What are you looking for?"

"Nothing."

"You're spending a lot of time looking for nothing."

The tree shook again, and her eyes went wide too.

"Do you think that's her?"

"Probably just a hawk or a squirrel or something," the woman in front of them said.

"Are you from here, Vivian?"

Vivian. That was it. Or her team members sometimes called her Viv.

"We're here," the driver said, as he pulled into the parking lot of what looked to Aristide to be a trailer barely larger than the bus had been. Aristide shook his head.

"Where is here?" Viv asked, clearly disappointed.

"Privacy," Katie said from her position in the front seat. "Privacy and a chance to let them process their crime scene without feeling like we're taking over their investigation. It'll go better for us that way."

"Besides we've seen all I want to see," Viv muttered, and the man in front seemed to nod his head in agreement. "How many monsters do we need to see in one day?"

"Well, after this one there's the one in Harrisonburg," Katie said. "Unless we believe that Greg guy about his wife and want to spend tonight looking around Fredericksburg for her."

"The sooner we get out of this creepy town the better," the man driver said, popping his door open to disembark. "The police here are definitely offended by our presence."

"Probably," Katie said, nodding.

"I bet if we were the FBI, they'd be a little more willing to work with us," said Viv as she slid out the side door.

Aristide recalled that he hadn't even asked about what federal agency they worked for. Katie had flashed a badge, and he went along with it. Dumb. He opened the back door and disembarked with Evian behind him.

"Who are you with?"

"Center for Disease Control," Katie said without pause, as though she'd answered the same question a hundred times before. Aristide guessed she probably had. "You're military, right?"

"United States Marine Corps," he told her.

"MOS?" she asked, also with such a casual nature that he knew she had some military affiliation.

"Forty-sixty-six, network engineer," he replied.

"My dad was an oh-two eleven," she said. "Intelligence enlisted." She walked as she talked, cutting across a parking lot fringed with dying grass and up the rickety steps. Katie fished some keys from her pocket and tried three before the fourth opened the door.

"Did you move around a lot?" the question came from Evian. It was directed at Katie and seemed to elicit a smile from her.

"All the time," she replied, glancing over her shoulder as the door swung inward.

The smell of the riverfront and decomposing fish carcasses hit Aristide like a brick wall, knocking him backward from the stairs where he'd begun to follow the woman up. She seemed to notice, and her face shot back around toward the interior. Katie uttered a massive scream before her body sank back, knocking Aristide over and clearing Evian's head in its flight. She landed on the glass in front of the SUV, shattering the window.

None of them had guns.

Aristide had noticed that right away, and now it seemed like a very shortsighted thing to do for any government agency. Especially once he'd recovered himself enough to glimpse at what followed the woman through the opening.

Shreds of fine fabric hung in clumps onto the sides of what Aristide could only describe as a lizard-woman. Her face still seemed vaguely human even if it extended out like a lizard and her eyes blinked sideways. A mouth opened and closed, flicking out a forked tongue in between. Two massive arms ended in claws which at first was what Aristide thought she'd used against Katie, but that was before he saw the glob of spit sail over his head. He followed it with his eyes in time to see it collide with Katie's face, covering her as she struggled, still clearly disoriented, to wipe the stuff away. For a frantic second, she cleared enough so that Aristide could see her eyes, just in time to see those eyes roll back into her head as she began a full-body shake.

Evian cowered behind him as he pulled himself to a crouching position. The man and Viv dove behind the vehicle, leaving Aristide and Evian to face the creature together. Aristide raised his hands up, expecting the claws to rip through his forearms at any second, when the sound of a gunshot rang out behind him.

"Git down, Miranda," a man's gruff voice came from behind.

"Greg!"

"Now who's being crazy," Greg said. Miranda, if that was who the creature was, didn't seem to know him or slow down.

She swiped one massive claw, and Aristide's arm was on fire, burning with four long gashes. He paused for a split-second, having been unaware that the lizard-woman's swipe had connected until that moment. Another shot, and Miranda went down. Her body convulsed on the floor for about half a minute before coming to a slow stop. Aristide lifted his gaze to Greg in time to see the man wipe his hand across his glassy eyes.

"That's her?" Aristide said, as softly as he could, once he finally summoned the courage to stand. He examined his arm as he talked.

"Yep," he said. "Still has that necklace chain on. Did you see that? Like it wasn't enough to humiliate me by galivanting all over town, but even when she transformed into whatever that was, all she kept was that thing."

Aristide then remembered Katie and turned quickly to face her.

"Grab her, Neko," Viv said. "On three, we'll lift her."

They'd gotten to her first. The man, Neko, hoisted her by her shoulders, and Vivian had gathered up her legs, one under each arm.

"There's a couch inside," Greg said, as though the doorway wasn't mostly blocked up by the remains of his dead wife's lizard body. "Give me a hand."

Aristide wasn't a scientist, but he wasn't dumb either. The lizard-woman was easily two hundred pounds, and from the pictures they passed on the way across the cramped living room to the loveseat, Greg's wife wouldn't have been close to that soaking wet. He grunted as he lifted her up onto the couch from her position, hanging down from where his hands grabbed her under the knees. Aristide nearly toppled over as a thick, scaly leg succumbed to the effects of gravity and swung down to swipe at his calf, barely missing with those razor-sharp claws. His arm stung as he bundled her back onto the couch.

Greg was already on his way to the fridge. He brought out two bottles of Shiner Bock beer and handed one over to Aristide before taking the only other seat in the room, a recliner large enough for three. Aristide set his beer down on a counter while Greg settled himself down into a cushion, cast a glance at his wife's body, and flipped on the television.

"You're not doing anything about that?"

"What's to do? The cheatin' bitch got what she deserved."

"But there's a dead woman on your couch."

"Yeah? Well, that's what you all are here for, right? Why don't you investigate her? I'm going to watch my golf."

The next through the door were Neko and Vivian, carrying their wounded leader (at least, Aristide guessed that she was, given the way they all supplicated up to her). Greg's eyebrow went up, and he stood, offering up the recliner to Katie's unconscious body, grumbling as he walked away from it. Aristide's stinging arm pulled his eyes downward. On the way, he thought he saw Katie move, but when he snapped his eyes back to her, the movement ceased. He felt a tug on his uninjured arm.

"Did you see that?" Evian asked. Aristide turned sharply, having forgotten that she was there.

"What?"

"That," she said and pointed to Katie's arm. Just beneath the surface, a bump rose and then fell away. Aristide wiped his eyes. He must have been seeing things. Just as he was about to turn away, it happened again.

"What is that?" he asked. Evian shrugged her shoulders. She wiped a stray hair from her face at the same time that Aristide rubbed his eyes. "Maybe we're just tired."

He watched her arm closely for half a second more. Nothing happened.

"Nothing," he said. "I think we must be imagining things. Can you blame us?"

Aristide turned to Greg. "Greg, is there a bathroom?"

Greg nodded his head toward a kitchen the size of a closet.

"Through there, the hallway on the right. This is the duty trailer. Past that is the bedroom. Don't touch any of the guns or Jim'll have words with you."

Aristide stepped in the direction that Greg pointed, only to be stopped by a touch on his arm.

"I'm coming," Evian whispered.

"I'm just getting a bandage or something. I can handle it," Aristide said as blood trickled down his arm from four shallow slashes on his bicep.

"Not a chance. I'm not staying out here with that hillbilly and the Power Rangers. Not to mention whatever that thing is on the couch and whatever's happening on the recliner? You're nuts if you think I'm staying out here with them."

"That's Katie. We're just both tired," he said.

"Then, it'll still be Katie after a quick trip to the bathroom, won't it? Besides, I know how to use a gun, and if there are some back there, I want one."

Aristide glanced at Greg to see if he was paying attention to their conversation. He'd zoned out again, watching a barely visible ball move through the air on the television screen with the sound turned down. In the corner of his eye, Aristide caught more movement against Katie's arm as Vivian fussed with the downed woman's face, wiping yellow goo from the sleeping woman's eyes. Aristide shook himself off and continued his walk with Evian so close behind that he felt her hot breath on his neck. A second later, her hand clawed its way into his.

At first, he was shocked at her touch, or anyone's, after what they'd seen. His arms still shook with the vibrant energy of anxious fight-or-flight. It didn't seem like the time or place for hand-holding, but he found himself comforted by the physical contact. And having her with him came in immensely handy seconds later when it came time to pour almost an entire bottle of hydrogen peroxide into the gashes on his arm. He felt his eyes water at the pain and bit his lip and squinted to keep from crying out. He was a Marine, and Marines don't feel.

"Fuck!" he said, as the fluid dripped down onto the sink, pink with his spent blood. "Goddamn it. That fucking hurts."

Evian laughed at him as he knew she would.

"Some Marine," she said. As he recovered his composure, she reached over and pushed the white plastic knob down on the door to lock it. He lifted an eyebrow at her. "Just in case."

Aristide nodded, then his imagination freed with the pain. He could easily imagine the woman getting back up from the couch, or worse, her arms or legs detaching and forming two entirely new creatures.

"What the hell is going on out there, Evian?" he said in a deadly serious tone. "And on the bus. How does someone turn into those things?"

"I hear they get scratched by one," she said with a side smile.

"I'm serious. That doesn't just happen. People don't randomly grow claws, do they?"

"All the time," she replied.

"You can't be serious."

"A hundred percent. People definitely mutate all the time. What do you think cancer is but a somewhat stable mutation? Most mutations fade away and turn up useless DNA, though. Trillions of times a day. Usually, mutations don't work together like what we saw, though."

He stared at her blankly. Her cheeks grew red, and she stammered, "I…I'm studying to be a nurse, remember? How do you survive with your short-term memory?"

"But that's cancer, and I don't know about you, but I haven't grown a lizard arm."

"Yet," she corrected, still smiling.

"Yet," he replied in a low grumble.

She retrieved a square gauze four inches by four inches from below the sink. She pressed it on his cut, causing another flare-up of scorching pain before it faded. Then she expertly wrapped medical tape around it until it was secure and didn't move. He flexed his arm.

"Good work," he admired. "Feels better already."

"Excellent," she said. "That means you can help me carry weapons. Come on."

"Uh…one second," Aristide said, spotting a closet half-hidden behind the edge of a dresser. He walked toward it, slung the door open, and blew out a sigh of relief.

"A little privacy?" he said. Evian raised a single eyebrow at him. He shrugged and motioned for her to turn toward the door, which she did. A few seconds later, he'd donned a pair of slate-gray pants and discarded his urine-caked jeans in the corner of the closet.

Aristide turned to see Evian approaching the gun rack. He could tell by how she gravitated toward the handguns that she knew her way around a weapon. The larger magazines meant more ammo usually, and handguns were way more effective at close range than trying to aim a bulky rifle. But there was still a need for the rifles in the large wooden gun rack. Aristide broke the lock with two solid kicks while Evian freed the handguns from pegs on the wall. She pulled down a Glock 19 and checked the magazine, then flashed the top of it toward him. It was full of rounds that looked like hollow points from where he stood. In total military mode, Aristide freed an AR-15 just in case they needed a long-range option. He also grabbed two pistols. He contemplated a third when a scream jolted him back from mental calculations and into reality. Instinctually, he checked the magazines on the two handguns and threw the AR-15 face-down strapped over his shoulder. Evian eyed the door. Another scream, this one with the distinct tenor of a man undergirding it.

Aristide let out a deep sigh and traded glances with Evian. He turned his head just once to look at the lonely window on the far end of the trailer. It seemed large enough to jump through if they wanted to try it. He caught Evian's eyes, and the tension in her face gave away her fear at last. She stepped toward the back of the room when another scream pierced the air, followed by something massive colliding with a wall. Then she shook her head, turned, and squared her shoulders on the door. Evian nodded twice, sighted in.

"We have to," she muttered.

"Yeah," Aristide agreed, sparing a longing glance for a young walnut tree beyond the window, leaves swaying in a gentle breeze. "I guess you're right."

The door opened inward, so Aristide trained his weapon on the opening while Evian yanked the door hard enough to crash into the wall. He pushed through the opening, holding one of the pistols out in front of him, his thumb switching off the safety simultaneously. The hallway was empty. The sound of chewing, like a dog working on a pig's foot, but louder, echoed through the enclosed space. Somewhere toward the far side of the trailer, Aristide heard the crash of something significant in the brush. Whispered voices followed around outside the trailer. A woman's voice and a man's voice that he could make out well enough to tell that it wasn't Greg. Neko and Viv.

"Shit," he said as he turned back into the kitchen. Aristide let out a deep breath. The kitchen was empty and spotless, like it had never been used. It was in the same condition they'd left it. He heard Evian shuffle behind him, close enough to feel her body heat.

"What do you see?"

He turned his head. "Noth—"

Suddenly Aristide was airborne. The kitchen flashed

beneath him as he was lifted toward the ceiling. At first, he couldn't tell where the thing had grabbed him or what it was that had done so. He lifted his weapon on instinct toward the center of the arc and fired. It all happened so fast that Aristide couldn't tell what he'd hit, but whatever it was stopped pulling in midair, and he fell from nearly eight feet high onto the paisley orange linoleum floor. Another gunshot rang out as he bounced and then slid. Whatever it was hadn't let go of him yet, and dragged him still toward something. He lifted his groggy head to see a giant scaled spider leg, as he looked on farther. Running his hand down his stomach, he caught hold of a sticky wire wrapped around his torso. It didn't seem to be tightening but was doing an excellent job of yanking him across the floor.

Aristide followed the cord with his eyes. His heart froze.

Katie's face stared blankly at him, only her torso ended at a massive scaly bubble that resembled a spider's abdomen. The cord ended at the very tip of the hard-encased underside.

Her eyes captured him. Just like Greg had said, he could see her in those eyes. Then it became clear why the gunshots didn't stop her. Her Kevlar vest remained intact over her torso with two indentations where bullets had connected. Even hollow points couldn't get through Kevlar. He relaxed on the floor and focused on raising his weapon to eye level. Katie's brown, hopeful eyes looked confused and disoriented. The tugging stopped for half a second as she opened and closed her mouth, trying to say something he couldn't discern. Her vest ruptured toward the base, as scales formed on her skin while he watched, creeping up from where her waist would be and splitting the thing apart.

Another gunshot. This one seemed to hit her in the leg, but from the sound of the ricochet made no impact. That was when he connected the dots.

It wasn't just the Kevlar. Her scales were as hard as

armor…and Katie wasn't through changing yet. The Kevlar vest ripped again, splitting and falling away, taking the rest of her shirt.

Something in Katie was still human, he thought, as her arm swung up to cover her nakedness. Aristide sighted in and pulled the trigger.

The tugging stopped. Aristide placed the hot muzzle of the weapon against the cord, where it hissed and cracked and emanated the odor of burning plastic. He pulled back on the trigger, and the blast ripped a hole, freeing him. Footsteps pounded up behind him.

"Is she—"

Aristide looked at Katie's face, still mouthing words he'd never know. Her eyes faded slowly into darkness.

"I think so. Look," he said, pointing to the boundary between scale and woman flesh. Even though Katie had stopped moving, the gray scales crept up her side for thirty more seconds, overtaking the base of her sternum and then slowing to a stop at the bullet wound in her clavicle. The body shook once, causing him to jump backward.

"Is she really…dead?" Evian asked, her green eyes glassed over. Aristide rubbed his eyebrows, then blinked a few times and stared at the body before them. No movement. Not even the slow rise of breathing, common to all animals, moved her body.

"I think so," he muttered then ran a hand through his hair. He glanced at the other body splayed on the floor in the entryway. "Both of them, probably."

"What's going on, Aristide?" Evian asked. He shook his head. His military mind saw only threats here.

"Looks to me like that one," he said, pointing to Greg's wife, "spit venom at Katie, and turned her into a spider-woman."

"Poor woman," Evian said, getting far too close to Katie's

body and running a hand through the woman's tangled hair. "She never asked for this."

"I'll bet she didn't either," Aristide replied, pointing to the other body. "And why is it only women changing?"

Evian looked at him then. Rather, he saw her eyes drift toward his bandaged wound, which had stopped aching now that attention was drawn to it. There was nothing unusual about his arm that Aristide could tell, considering a monster had taken a swipe at him. The bandage was clean, showing no blood, which was likely a testament to Evian's nursing skills. He flexed once. No pain at all. That seemed a little off. But they had other things to worry about than the fact that his wounded arm didn't hurt.

"Evian, I don't want to stay here," he said in as serious a voice as he could muster. "How do we even tell if these things are dead? Maybe they're just hibernating or changing. How many others are out there? We need to get away from here. Whatever is happening, it's happening here in Fredericksburg."

"And you want to try for Texas?"

He nodded.

"There are more guns than people in Texas. If we get that far, we'll have a chance on my dad's farm. I've got three months of basic training pay to work through. We can afford anything we need on the trip."

"And you want me to come with you?"

"Only as far as Shreveport, Evian, unless you want to go all the way. We need to get out of here. Now. Let the feds handle whatever this thing is."

Except he was the feds now, and it was only a matter of time before his phone rang—wherever it was—with orders to hightail it back to Quantico if this thing was as bad as he thought.

Evian's fingers slipped from Katie's head over her dazed

and open eyes, bringing her eyelids down. That made the woman look like she was sleeping, though it didn't help the scales that seemed—if he wasn't mistaken—to have crept even farther up her chest. Aristide grabbed Evian's shoulder and pulled her back.

"The truck's still outside," he said after she turned to face him. "We just get in it and drive. Greg's not going to miss it."

With those words, they both turned to where Greg's mangled body lay on the floor. Pieces were missing: a chunk of flesh near his shoulder and another near his upper arm. Aristide couldn't figure out exactly what had happened in that room after they left, but something had taken bites out of Greg, and he didn't see blood on the mouths of either woman.

"Let's get out of here," he muttered, tugging Evian toward the door. Absently, he checked his rifle's magazine. Ten shots left in there. He hoped to God they couldn't burn through ten bullets between the front door and the truck.

————

Aristide used zero bullets to get to the truck Greg had driven in. He slid into the seat and breathed a sigh of relief to see the keys dangling from the ignition. In all the excitement of getting there, Greg had left the keys in his beat-up F-150, probably because it was more than twenty years old and nobody would bother to steal it. Not the best choice, but he guessed the sleek black SUV that Katie, Neko, and Viv had come in had left with three of the four of them. Hence, the truck was all that was left. Evian slid onto the bench seat next to him without any complaint. On the second try, the engine sprang to life, and a handful of minutes later, they were back on I-95 heading toward Richmond.

They rode along in silence. An occasional bump in the blacktop made Evian reach for what Aristide always called the "oh, shit" handle, but otherwise, she stared ahead with wide, scared eyes. At least, she had that look every time he glanced at her.

"It'll be okay, Evian," he chanced, staring at her slightly longer than a second on the open road. She shrugged.

"No, it won't," she replied. "Why would you say that?"

"We're leaving, aren't we?"

"And all those people died. An entire bus full of people, and then Greg and Katie. And what the hell happened to Katie anyway?"

"Whatever Greg's wife spat onto her must have made her change into whatever that thing was."

"She wasn't finished changing, Aristide. Did you see the scales creeping up her neck? Even after she was dead?"

He nodded. However, Evian had been containing her fear, and it wasn't working anymore. Her eyes were wide and darting. She bit at her lower lip as though trying to gnaw her way out of a cage.

"Yeah, but we're not dead," he said. "Sometimes that's the best we got."

"I don't know how you can act like everything's fine. What happens when we get to Louisiana and everyone there looks like the Creature from the Black Lagoon?"

"You were fine a minute ago."

"'That was before...'"

She didn't finish the sentence. From what Aristide thought, nothing had really changed. But something had, hadn't it? For one, they'd just stolen a dead guy's truck and were literally fleeing for their lives. And Aristide himself had divulged that he thought things were going to get a lot worse before they got better. Maybe that was a bit more than he should have said.

Aristide glanced over his shoulder to where he'd put the AR-15 on Greg's gun rack.

"The creature died in a hail of bullets if I recall," he said. "We'll be fine."

"My family," Evian said.

"The ones who aren't expecting you?"

Evian's face took on a hard scowl. "Yeah, them. They need to know what's going on here."

He turned his attention back to the road. Aristide licked his lips and focused on the dotted line as it drifted past the truck on his side. He leaned back and adjusted his grip on the wheel.

"I was just thinking," she said. "Louisiana's not that far. Neither is Texas. Do the math. If these things can create more, every second that red-dress creature is out there, there could be another one being made."

Aristide shifted uncomfortably in his seat.

Evian continued, "Imagine if just two. If she creates just two more—and who's to say she didn't already on the bus? But if she does, those two create more, and so on."

"Then, it still won't outrun us on the open highway," he replied. "So don't worry."

"You think it started in Triangle," she corrected him.

Aristide gritted his teeth and let out a heavy breath. "And it wasn't?"

"How could it have been? That one in Fredericksburg— where did that come from? Greg's wife?"

"She could have been turned by Red Dress," he said. "Wouldn't have taken long."

"He said she turned a week ago. Red Dress was only turned earlier today. God, was it today?"

Aristide looked out the window. The sun rested on the horizon, fat and orange like it had all the time in the world to sink below. The highway drifted past, and the trees became less and less frequent until there were none at all, and the highway was surrounded by grassland. The sun's orange glow worked through the tall grass, waving in gold as the wind raked across the shafts. The sight reminded Aristide of what he would find at the end of his drive. Natural bluegrass and spear grass were nearly chest-high, so there was no telling what kind of critters might be hiding among the leaves. The tiny town of Caldwell, where he grew up, had no hayfields. It had yaupon trees and oak trees and bull nettle and spear grass. And snakes. And trapdoor spiders and scorpions the size of his thumb.

All tame compared to what they'd just witnessed.

She leaned her head away from the window and against his shoulder. "Want me to drive for a while?"

As she asked the question, she'd already begun to close her eyes. Aristide examined her from his peripheral vision as she nestled in. He lifted his arm around her and pulled her into his shoulder. Having her there seemed to help him think.

"No need," he said while she lowered her head against him. "Maybe in a few hours."

"Okay."

The rickety truck bounced down the interstate, its head-lights illuminating an otherwise black, moonless night fifteen feet at a time.

CHAPTER 8
JULEP ALL THE TIME

THE RAIN FELL IN SHEETS, enlarging the puddle under the gash in the roof and smacking Thaddeus in the face to wake him from where he'd fallen asleep. He shivered awake in the same clothes he'd worn all the day prior and the day before that. As his eyes creaked open, there was something different this time. He saw the opening from a new perspective from his back staring up through it. Somewhere above, the moonlight caught on something shiny stuck into one of the exposed and saturated rafters. From a distance, it had a red opalescent sheen to it. Thaddeus scrambled to his feet and spared a glance for the kitchen table where the placemat with dancing princesses had long since blown to the floor. He stood and stretched up toward the gap, but his fingers fell short even when he jumped. Thaddeus grabbed one of the kitchen chairs. Tall enough now, he reached up and worked at the object that turned out to be slender, like a small pen. When he tore it loose, it fell into the palm of his hand in a puddle of pink water as the rain spattered against his palm.

It might have been a tooth, but it was too slim and too long.

Thaddeus could tell that it might have been white. The red, he was pretty sure despite the pain in his heart, was from blood —*her* blood perhaps, the result of whatever had happened to Julep. Then he realized the object was symmetrical and had a hole from one side to another. The fluid leaked from inside and even in the water that had collected in his hand, made his palm feel slick. A second later, he felt a stinging sensation in his palm and dropped the object, which corrected itself as it fell, pointing the one side directly toward the floor which thudded into it and the tube stayed on end, quivering.

"What?" he said, as he wiped his hand on his pants. He knelt and flicked the tube, and it quivered more. In that second, it occurred to him that it was a weighted projectile, a bullet or a dart. The red fluid had to be whatever the dart's payload was as opposed to blood. As this concept sunk in, movement flicked in his periphery above his head. He lifted his head in time to see something large descending. At first, he thought it might be Julep. Her eyes were solid white though, as though her irises had been erased. Instead of hair, feathers extended from the front of bridge of her nose back over her head like a bad Halloween costume. Wings extended up from her back, slowing her descent. *Wings?*

"Julep?"

Her mouth opened, and he stared in disbelief, trying to glean whatever she might be saying from the movement of her lips. He recognized what remained of her pants as Julep's skinny jeans that she'd worn the same day she disappeared. But her face had elongated somehow as well, and those *eyes*...

"It's me, Julep. Do you know me? Can you see me? The CDC were here. You need to talk to them. They can fix you."

Something whizzed past his head. He turned in time to see another tube similar to the one on the floor embed itself in the tabletop. Instinctively, he ducked beneath the table's hardwood surface. Julep alighted on the ground, and that was when he noticed her feet for the first time. Giant talons punched easy holes into the oak flooring. She didn't seem interested in him any longer now that he was tucked under the table and out of sight. Her movements jerked as she clipped across to the couch.

"Hrnph," she said in a voice that was so like Julep he almost came out of hiding. She trailed a puddle toward the living room area, ripping gouges in the floor as she went.

Her hand slipped over the back of the couch. When he saw it, he bit his lip hard. He looked at her other arm, and sure enough, saw the same thing. Her hands hadn't changed, nor her arms or most of her torso. From the waist to her chin and arms the woman was Julep, down to the scar above her left elbow. If he focused his eyes and mind on those hands, and how she so delicately touched every object as she moved on clunky giant hawk feet, he knew it had to be her. His courage grew with this new certainty, and he emerged from beneath the table, slipping as he stepped across the princess mat yet gaining his feet in spite of it. The sound of his stumbling must have caught her attention. A green and gold feathered tail flipped around as she spun. Her empty eyes seemed to see right through him. Her mouth opened again, and he held up his hands before his face.

"Julep, don't. It's me, Thad. You know me."

She cocked her head to the side, raising her eyebrows in the process. Good. She was paying attention. He lowered his hand and put on his best smile.

"I'm glad you're back, baby. I missed you."

Julep closed her mouth and reached out toward him the way she'd reached for him one night not so long ago, before the suspicion of his cheating had crippled their relationship. Her upturned ring finger on her left hand still held the engagement ring he'd given her—twenty thousand dollars' worth of ring. He reflexively reached his hand forward to touch his fingertips to hers.

"Yaaaa," she said as she flitted toward him and cocked her head the other direction. The Mardi Gras mask of her face twisted to the opposite side, and she blinked twice rapidly. Her hand touched his. There was no mistaking the touch. He felt a lump swell into his throat.

"I'm so sorry, Julep," he said, stroking her outstretched hand with the very tips of his fingers. She lurched back, jumped up into the air, and came down with her talons sunk deeply into the couch they'd bought that first week, after they'd decided that moving in together was the right thing to take their relationship to the next level. Well, *she'd* decided, just like she'd decided everything else with a huff and a fight, including the ring. He clenched his teeth and pushed the thought away. Right now, he just wanted her back. They could work through whatever it was that poisoned their relationship. They could work it through and make her believe that her sister was...well, was a liar, right? She'd buy that. And it wasn't as though Margie was going to fight with him about it.

Just get her to the CDC. They'll fix her, he thought.

He didn't notice her mouth opening until it was too late.

Just beyond where her teeth should have been extended, a thin sleeve twisted like a turret snail shell two inches long. With a birdlike whistle, the projectile covered the space between them in less than a second while he tried to withdraw his hand from hers. She closed her fist around his wrist, making escape impossible. With unimaginable strength, she held him locked into place, and he felt the projectile sink into the soft flesh of his neck.

Hot plasma flooded his body. With his free hand, Thaddeus pulled the projectile from his flesh, watching in dismay as a spurt of blood followed, then another, then another, keeping time with his heart. His vision grew cloudy as he struggled to dislodge his wrist. She didn't seem to notice his efforts as her head tilted rapidly from one side to the other, and a slow blink brought a round eyelid down over her eye and then back up again. He tried to speak, but his mouth wasn't his any longer, and he wasn't even certain it was a mouth. The cold dampness of his jeans reduced to tingling as they seemed to shrink around his legs, cutting off circulation and bringing him crashing down save the excruciating pain of his wrist twisting backward under his own body weight.

"You know what you did," her voice said, materializing in his head like a surfacing memory.

"Julep? What are you doing to me?"

"What have you done to yourself?"

A ripping sound echoed around the apartment as his legs freed themselves from the constricting jeans. The sound was so terrible that it forced his head down despite his twisted wrist, and he winced at the movement. Julep released him at the same time as she cocked her head back. A single clawed foot shot up from her perch on the back of the couch and collided with his chest, pushing him backward in its pressure and pinning him to the ground.

The spray of blood slowed with the failing of his vision. The fire that had flowed in his veins concentrated in his chest and gave one last incendiary burn before flaring out with his consciousness.

———

"Don't speak."

Thaddeus moved his mouth or what he thought his mouth should be. Instead of the sounds of words, he heard a flapping, sputtering sound and felt something heavy move on his upper chest. Daring to crack his eyes open, Thaddeus saw one big eye winking at him. His head rested on something soft and pillow-like. It took him a second to realize that his head lay on the multicolored feathered leg of his lover. Or former lover. Startled, he yanked himself forward into a sitting position with his hands back behind him for support and turned his head to see her more clearly. Several heavy somethings slithered over his chest.

"*What happened?*" he pondered.

"*You cheated on me,*" came her unexpected response.

He tried to shake his head, but her expressionless face stopped him. It hadn't been a question, he realized, so there was no point in denying it.

"Mrphhlske," he said.

Thaddeus shifted his weight to his right arm—the arm leaning away from Julep—and chased one of the slithering things on his chest with it. He closed his hand around a snake-like thing too close to his neck for him to fully see, then yanked on it in an effort to fling it across the room. His cheek muscles clenched in protest and an excruciating pain flared along the left side of his face.

"*You are like me now.*"

He shivered at the words and did his best to find his feet.

There were no feet. Or, there was one foot on a single leg. Only it wasn't a leg, but a long serpentine tail, the thickness of his body that extended down into a spiky coil. His belly had disappeared, replaced with a flat washboard stomach that ended at his waist where his nakedness was on full display. He cupped his hand over himself. Beneath that was only the single trunk where his legs had once been with bifurcated scales on what would have been the fronts of his thighs. Studded spikes extended along the backs of his arms that he had crossed in front his body.

"*What have you done to me?*"

"Me? I tried to kill you."

He lurched again. When he did his snake-bottom half didn't move, and he merely succeeded in planting his face into the floor hard.

"Couldn't," her voice said in his mind.

"Thank you," he thought back.

She still loved him. Perhaps even in these forms, they could find something together. He righted himself the best he could. He tried to speak again and reaffirmed that he couldn't. Every time he tried, he felt the slithering across his chest. Thaddeus pulled his snake tail under him to hoist himself up by folding it like two legs together. He wasn't stable, but he was high enough to see his face in the mirror-like surface of the apartment window. Four bulbous tentacles almost two feet long apiece extended down from where his mouth and cheeks should have been over his chest.

"Your outside looks how it should now."

"You did this to me."

"I tried to kill you," she responded, and he took her meaning. Her giant bird eyes seemed focused on his chest. When he looked down, he saw five scratches in a wide circle on his chest where her claws had tried to penetrate. *"I couldn't."*

It wasn't because she didn't want to. He ran a finger over his skin. It had thickened like an armor, and the spikes made him an intimidating sight. Thaddeus pounded a hand into his chest as hard as he could. Only the mildest sensation of pressure made it through his thick protective layer to his nerves. She couldn't kill him because he'd turned into a monster and not for any other reason.

And she might try again.

He moved his snake tail back and forth, trying to figure out how the multitude of muscles could work together. Julep opened her mouth again to expose not only the tubelike tongue that had forced his transformation, but also two rows of razor-sharp teeth. She gnashed them together once and then started in on him, her teeth clanking together making unnatural chattering sounds as she lowered her head toward his neck.

Somehow his tail wrapped itself around her legs. As she approached it pulled in the opposite direction, tugging her so that her teeth stopped just short of his flesh.

"I will have you," she warned. *"You can't be entirely protected. There are soft spots, aren't there?"*

Seemingly unable to focus her eyes more than a few degrees from where she looked, Julep jerked her head downward where one hand remained concealing his privates. *"Perhaps I should start there?"*

He hadn't accounted for her clawed feet. One shot forward and closed around his wrist, pulling it away from his waist. When he pulled back from instinct, her entire body moved with his flexed arm muscles. In a quick, desperate response, he continued, and the momentum flung her toward the window. As quickly as he had, she spread her wings and slowed her movement. She landed atop the kitchen table and crouched down beneath the hanging lights and their crystalline shades.

"I will kill you," she assured him.

"Look at yourself. Look at me. Isn't it…"

He lost the words. There was something he wanted to say, something kind and offsetting that would calm her. It was something about letting bygones be bygones, but not nearly so droll. Thaddeus's brain wouldn't produce the words he needed to say. All he could think about was the fact that she intended to kill him. Dead. And she could do it if she tried long enough. How long would his armored body hold against her razor-sharp talons anyway?

"You'll kill me," he said, only not using words. None of their conversation, he realized, had been words. They'd been thoughts, whispers, and suggestions in his mind. All the same,

he knew that her words were from her, and his words, as clunky and useless as they were, had come from his own mind.

The words echoed hollow. Behind it were images of their meeting at the Signature Theatre when she'd abandoned her friends and he his to go to an afterparty at a jazz nightclub just down the street from the Busboys and Poets Café. Only neither of them had enjoyed the jazz nearly as much as the two bottles of wine and spending the evening in his nearby apartment. They'd never separated after that and yet...

Reality descended over his imaginings like a dominatrix without a safe word. Julep sprang across the room, talons first, with her hair splayed out behind her. For a moment, all Thaddeus saw was her face and torso, and it reminded him of that night again. She'd been shy to reveal herself to him. All the lights had to be shut off completely except a candle that smelled of sandalwood that he used mainly to cover up the smell of pot.

Her claws connected as he was drawn into his mind again and he shook himself back. Thaddeus didn't have the luxury to ruminate. He felt something that time, with both clawed feet scratching at his chest. Thin rivulets of blood sprang from two small gashes, and she hadn't backed off again. Her strong arms had latched onto his shoulders and her projectile tongue was aimed directly at his eye before he realized it. With one arm, and amazed by his own strength, he hurled her across the room again. This time, she flew over the couch backward and crashed into the television above the mantle.

"You'll kill me?"

When the words came back, they were wrapped in sadness and anger all at once. He sprang at her, using his snake tail like a coiled spring and with outstretched arms pinned her down. Thaddeus rolled and lifted her up, mustering as much concentration as he could to get his tail to behave and wrap up her legs. Then, the tentacles that extended from his face all rose at once and without his control or will stabbed into her delicate, porcelain-like cheeks. Her large iris-less eyes stared out of their sockets and her feathered head bobbed at him, fangs bared.

Everything happened at once. He felt strength flowing from those tentacles into his veins starting at his neck and working down into his body. Thaddeus felt suddenly as though he could throw an Abrams tank, and deep inside he knew that he could. But as he looked on, reveling in the strength, he saw the light flicker behind her eyes. Julep's entire body shook in his grip and then went slack, but the juice went right on flowing.

Thaddeus tried to recall the conduits that had attached themselves to her before it was too late. He willed them to retract while the ecstatic bliss of siphoning her life force fought against him. With one horrendous shove, he pushed her away and fell to the ground, coiled up around her laying breathless in front of the couch across a shattered coffee table. The bliss had been replaced by salted wounds. Motionless, he lay there, having learned his lesson: once the tentacles latch on, don't ever let go again. Something else stirred within him. That emotion, that bliss, that *strength*. He wanted more. He turned an eye toward Julep, whose wounds had already begun to heal.

"You'll kill me?" he thought the words, and now all he felt was rage at her and at himself. Thaddeus knew that she'd been serious. She had a right to, he knew that as well. Somewhere out in the city Julep's sister hid, pregnant with his child—something he would undo if only he could. Not an hour earlier, he remembered telling himself that all he wanted was for Julep to be alive. Now, all he could think of, all he could wish for, was that he had the strength to kill her.

Thaddeus couldn't do that. He hadn't, had he? He'd only disabled her for now, and she would get strong again. And he could have his bliss again. Everything other thought flew from his mind as he felt the craving take over. She would be fine.

Look at her. Healing up already. He could keep her, hoard her, just for himself. Then he could have his bliss whenever he wanted, and eventually, someday, she would have to forgive him.

If she ever wanted to be free again.

CHAPTER 9
FEAST OF RATS

WORKING MARGIE'S NEWFOUND EXTENSIONS, those tentacles that extended from her belly and lifted her effortlessly into the air, had become as second nature. The shock of what had happened to her had paralyzed her mind for almost an entire day. Like a creature, she'd slinked away into the sewers and abandoned subway tunnels beneath Washington, D. C. in an effort to keep her modesty. An orange emergency light illuminated the ground beneath her, revealing a puddle and a second later, her reflection in it. She clenched her teeth at what she saw.

Constant secretions kept her hair falling into her face, thick and heavy. She couldn't even see her eyes through it, nor did she want to as she could only imagine what had changed there. Her skin, long since broken free of the remains of her clothing as she'd worked out how to move silently in the darkness, revealed a teal hue if she accounted for the infrequent emergency lighting's orange tint. Her arms were unchanged, and her feet had evolved into claw-studded flippers, which was why she used the tentacles to move instead. Those feet were too wide and unruly for walking. Sparse smaller tentacles hung like fibers from her arms, back, and thighs, giving her the look of a living fisherman's net. Those weren't so bad though, as beneath, her arms and legs still kept their smoothness. She wrapped her arms over where the four tentacles extended from her belly. Without those, she could almost look normal. Surgery to remove the excess and useless ones that decorated her skin, and she could have a normal life again. Almost.

"Mrelshhfd," she muttered.

Except she couldn't talk.

Curiosity forced her hand. Every time she tried to speak, what fell from her mouth were jumbled and useless syllables that made no sense when strung together. She didn't even feel her mouth moving when she did, as though she were forcing the sounds out through her nose. With shaking hands, she began at her chin and parted the dank, stringy hair. In that reflective surface, she didn't believe what she saw at first. Her hands kept going, despite her shock, pulling the hair the rest of the way up until it revealed eyes that seemed to protrude from her sockets in little flat bubbles.

She had no mouth.

It wasn't as though there was nothing there. Gill-like slits lined her cheeks, and they opened and closed as she tried unsuccessfully to sleep.

"Vasdfjlieiiis!" she screamed through those slits and watched in the reflection as they made the sound, flapping. Margie dropped her shaking hands and fled down the tunnel, toward the darkness. There could be no normal life any longer. Not for her, and deep down inside, she blamed one man, Thaddeus Vlissides. As she floated across the sewer drain, she remembered something—something she'd forgotten. Her child. How could someone forget something so serious? But her mind hadn't truly been hers for a while. Fear and anger and hostility had taken it over, hadn't they? She didn't have a child, did she? Not anymore. Tentacles extended from her abdomen where a child should have been.

A shimmery, fearsome thought coursed through her. What if those tentacles were her child? That would explain the gaping opening from which they extended. But she couldn't believe that. She couldn't believe that her entire body had absorbed her child and turned it into an appendage, little more than an arm or leg. In a quick answer to her question, she felt a movement deep inside, behind the tentacles, behind the putrefying stench of her overactive glands gushing out fluids to oil her skin. She couldn't smile, but she felt in her cheeks that her skin folds flapped in mild celebration. No, she hadn't lost the child. Somewhere in there, she knew he hid tucked away, safe from the world. One shuddering thought stopped her flaps cold. What would he look like when he was ready to join the world?

Movement.

Every movement around her seemed vivid like little explosions. She turned her head toward what turned out to be a sewer rat running along the ground. Behind it was another. A vague and fading memory of dinner, brunch, with glasses of champagne and eggs Benedict surfaced as she examined the creatures. Floating along on her tentacles, she tried to remember, tendrils of her mind grasping toward her dwindling humanity.

———

"And here I am, a third wheel. Seriously, Julep, there couldn't be a worse way to meet your new boyfriend. A little warning might have been nice."

"Would you have come, Margie?"

She gulped and swallowed. Probably not, but she nodded her head anyway.

"Right. Sure," Julep replied.

Thick buttery syrup dripped down the sides of a stack of waffles. Margie could smell the tantalizing cream layered over the top and the freshly cut strawberries. The sunlight kissed everything, adding a layer of brightness over the scene that made it seem magical and fairy-tale like.

"So who is this?" Margie asked, turning her attention to the man beside Julep. He had thick black hair combed back with every strand in exactly the right place. A five o'clock shadow, which she would eventually learn to be perpetual, covered his lower face, accentuating his strong jawline. She felt the flutters of embarrassment bouncing around in her chest. She felt as though she *knew* this man and had known him forever.

"Thaddeus," the man said, extending a thick, calloused hand in her direction. A working man's hand, like their father before he passed. "Vlissides."

She took his hand, and it was just that little stroke of his touch between her forefinger and thumb that sent sparks up her arm. Margie glanced down at her pancakes in a vain effort to turn attention away from her physical reaction.

Julep saw.

Margie knew it as soon as she glanced back up and any trace of a smile that had been on Julep's unguarded face had disappeared in that few seconds. She hadn't even done anything yet, and already, Julep's jealous nature had cast Margie into Thaddeus's bed. Although, for all the times that Julep had stolen Margie's prospective lovers, perhaps a little insecurity was warranted. Margie relished the idea as she recovered and flashed a quick smile toward Thaddeus.

"She didn't tell me her sister was almost as beautiful as she is," Thaddeus said. Julep's face twisted back up into her reserved smile. Margie would recognize it anywhere. Julep turned her gaze to Thaddeus.

"Thaddeus, you're too much," she said, then turned to

Margie and added a handful of teeth to her smile turning it into something like a sideways grin. "He said the exact same thing to Mother."

Margie's stomach had fallen, and she pulled her hand back. Of course, she wasn't a threat to Julep. And this brunch that was supposed to be sisters catching back up was just to parade her new boyfriend in front of Margie and let her know what she could never have.

"I...I have to go," Margie stuttered out, standing and pushing away from the table.

"I only just met you," Thaddeus said. "It's important to me to fit into your family. Can you stay for a while at least and we can get to know each other? I asked Julep to invite you."

"You did?"

"After all of her stories, I had to meet the source. Julep speaks so highly of you."

"She does?"

Margie looked over to her sister, whose features had softened into a warm grin complemented with wide eyes. Likely a trap. Margie, as usual, had no clue what was going on in Julep's mind, but she was reasonably sure that nothing about the moment included concern for Margie. She realized she shook her head as she thought it through and forced herself to stop.

"Yeah. The way that you shielded her from that dog attack. You put yourself between her and—what was it, a Rottweiler? Bulldog?"

"Poodle," Margie said. "It was a full-sized poodle, and for some reason it decided to attack us."

"That scar," he said, extending his rough hand out again and pushing aside the hair she'd so carefully draped over her shoulder. "There. That one. A badge of courage. I don't know how to thank you for keeping my Julep alive long enough for me to meet her."

His thumb brushed against the scar and again, Margie felt the betrayal of sparks sliding up her neck and down her spinal cord. She felt her cheeks heat up, and an eye toward Julep brought it all home.

Julep knew what Thaddeus was like. Naturally she did, and she knew that he was exactly Margie's type more than her own. The point, Margie realized, was to flout him, hold him over her, and weaken Margie with his presence. *Look at what I can have, and you can never have.* Margie's hand went up and pulled Thaddeus's down and straightened her hair.

"Please don't do that," she muttered.

"I was only—"

"But it's my body. Don't touch me, please."

"I'm sorry. I didn't know you were so sensitive about it."

"It's my body," she repeated. "Sensitive or not, doesn't matter. My body, not yours."

Not yet anyway.

With that, Margie dug into her pancakes with such gusto that she was certain she'd offended nearly everyone within vision range. But she kept eating, biting through the thick pancake slices and crunching through the fork as it broke into little fragments.

———

Margie came back to the present as she crunched through a fork in her mind. That part had never happened, but her jaw worked up and down on something. What jaw though? Her hand moved itself up to her head and worked itself around her face. No jaw, no opening for a mouth. All she had there were the strange slits, and nothing else. But she had the sensation of chewing. Something broke, crunched, snapped, and rent in her body somewhere. Margie followed the sensation down from her mouth through her neck and to the origin: her stomach appendages. Fear gripped her as she looked slowly downward.

On the end of one of her four tentacles hung the dripping remains of a sewer rat in a round, tooth-filled opening. It crunched squeezed and undulated as it distorted the screaming rodent into a shape that could slide into the four-inch opening and past the inverted teeth. The worst part about it was that she lusted after the flesh. The flavor coursed up her tentacle and into her brain, gamey and saturated with salty blood. Margie felt a tear slide from her left eye as she unrelentingly crunched down on the creature and watched it disappear into the end of her tentacle. She felt it slide ever upward and watched the bulge of it disappear into her belly.

More movement.

To her right was another rat. And another. And another. And she was powerless. Her appendages, now on their own and with her unable and becoming more unwilling to stop them, floated her toward the mischief of rats and flashed out like lightning and grabbed the rodents, crunching down on them two at a time, leaving at all times two tentacles free keeping her aloft.

Margie shed one tear, grieving for her humanity, before she gave herself over to the gratifying crunch and the echoes of rat screams bouncing through the dark emptiness of the sewer. Bliss filled her body as a rat after rat funneled up into her belly, the salt in their blood filling her veins. Then, finally sated, she lowered herself to the ground and curled up, wrapping her tentacles around her in a protective cocoon, and she rested.

Margie had run out of rats at the same time that she discovered another appendage hidden beside her tailbone. A small stub that looked like a deflated balloon suddenly expanded and ejected a fine line of white mucus that splattered onto the watery rocks below. She spat in disgust and held her hands before her eyes. Claws, barely human-like anymore, waved before her.

Hideous. She'd never convince Thaddeus to leave her sister looking like that.

But she was so strong.

Hovering almost ten feet above the floor of the massive tunnel took no energy. Movement along the tentacles now seemed second nature, like she'd been born with them. To test, she sped along ten feet forward and then back again. Perhaps she was thinking about the situation wrong. She didn't have to convince Thaddeus of anything. This time, this one time in all of her history with men, *she* was the stronger one. He could try to leave if he wanted to, *try* being the operative term. She would have him, and once he realized how much she loved him, he would be hers.

With a grunt, she swung herself forward down the tunnel, holding, one thrashing tentacle after another into the darkness.

CHAPTER 10
GENIE

TAMITHA VEGA FOUND that the tubules, about sixteen from the last twenty times she counted, made it almost impossible to relax. Relaxation wasn't what she hoped to accomplish quite as much as a way out of the auto pit she'd fled into for safety. No phone, and she was just short enough that attempting to climb out of the pit was impossible. 'She'd also tried that at least twenty times. Her sole consolation was that the itching had, in fact, stopped, which implied to her that whatever transformation was happening on her back had stopped, finally. Now all she felt was the raw sensation of air over an open wound across her sixteen new appendages, which wasn't much of an improvement but she could appreciate the change still.

The werewolf-man had gone. He hadn't come back. 'She'd spent most of a day in the pit. The lights above the pit had slowly dimmed, and now she lay uncomfortably on her side watching the last of the light drip away. The darkness was too dark, somehow, when it finally arrived. She couldn't see anything at all in the pitch black. Occasionally, paranoia (or good sense) caused her to fire a flurry of darts out into the black. So far, she'd hit nothing.

She sulked in the darkness while new pain grew in her abdomen. She stood and paced back and forth while trying to decide if her rapidly filling bladder would become more of a problem. Her bladder responded with a twinge of pain, letting her know that yes, in fact, that was going to be a problem. She sequestered herself into what she considered the most unlikely corner for someone to see her if they happened upon the auto pit, pulled up her dress above her knees and squatted. While she relieved herself, she recounted the story from her childhood, using it to distract from the fact that yes, she was peeing in the bottom of an auto pit.

In the story, a genie had been tricked into a lamp. After the first thousand years, the genie had sworn to himself that whoever rescued him would gain untold riches. After another thousand years, the genie swore to himself that whoever rescued him would gain unlimited power. When that second thousand passed, the genie grew jaded and angry. He said that he would kill whoever happened to find him and free him. Then, an unfortunate fisherman discovered the lamp and released the genie, who, despite feeling despondent about it, told the fisherman his story. The fisherman learned almost too late that the genie intended to kill him.

Tam shook herself off as she stood. She clenched her teeth as she pulled her dress down past her knees. One humiliation accomplished, and zero dead werewolves. She could remedy that though, as soon as she escaped. Once she set her sights on a man, that man ended up dead. There were no exceptions to this rule. Not Eddie, her third, even though he'd temporarily made it back to his family. That had almost given her pause. She typically didn't truck with married men, but Eddie had lied to her about that in his online profile. But she'd followed him to his house, tracked him for a week before catching him leaving his work one day. He'd, of course, called her a "crazy bitch" and tried to run until she ran him over with her car. Well, not her car, but his car, which he'd been stupid enough to leave unlocked.

She'd felt bad about that. Not killing him, necessarily, but more because she deprived the family of him, and now some little girl faced her same fate. The blackness wasn't empty, and in it she saw her own childhood. A child, abandoned by her father and alone with her mother and an endless parade of would-be stepfathers, many of whom were lecherous and untrustworthy.

That had started her habit. For a few months, the older man who looked like Santa Claus had treated her like he was Santa and owed her several backdated presents for all the Christmases she'd missed due to her mother breaking up with someone or starting a new relationship. He'd reminded her of Santa even to the point that he invited her to sit on his lap. That was when she decided that his wandering hands weren't worthy of her mother, and she would fix the problem.

Of course, her mother hadn't believed her. So she'd encouraged a second round with the man and drove a steak knife into his heart. Then, she and her mother moved.

She felt nothing about that either, except that she'd solved the problem. He didn't die. Her mother had gotten to him in time and taken him to the hospital. But he did stop coming around, and soon, just around Christmas time in fact, her mother had gone into her breakup spiral and beat her regularly through the holiday season.

But Tam had done the right thing. And she always did the right thing. Men couldn't be trusted, and if she was the only one who understood that fact, then she was the only one. One man, then another, then another. Before she knew it, she was, quite ironically, up to sixteen. The werewolf would have made seventeen, but she wasn't really sure how to handle that one.

She wasn't a tracker, and her best guess had to be that Jason had fled and wouldn't be coming back. He might not even be changing back into a human now that she considered it. There wasn't exactly a full moon or anything. As her mind struggled to shove her memories of the man into the werewolf myth, she realized that he couldn't have been. And, if he had been, lore directed that she should also be a werewolf, instead of whatever she'd become. It was a puzzle, and one that she lost interest in almost as quickly as she wandered into it. The simpler fact was that the tubules on her back and their projectiles only made her mission easier. How many men could she kill with these things on her back, she wondered.

CHAPTER 11
CHEATER. CHEATER. CHEATER.

JULEP HODE AWOKE with a pounding headache. Her eyes shot open, and the bright and unforgiving light blasted her in her left eye. She quickly cocked her head toward it to move the glare directly in front of her face, sharing the burden between two eyes instead of abusing one. Her memory of the room contrasted with what she saw. Before her, resting atop coiled snake appendages, lingered her former lover, if he ever was hers. She clenched her teeth to see him, and her fingers tensed themselves into claws with her nails ready to dig into his flesh. A bright orange-green color tinted Thaddeus's skin, accenting the spikes that had sprouted across his shoulders.

Had she known that would happen when she spit her projectile at him, she wouldn't have done it. His strength had become formidable, and even her talons could only barely pierce his hide. She would have left him his dull humanoid self just so she could rip him apart.

Cheater.

Cheater.

Cheater.

She flexed her left talon-leg in an effort to pull it up and try for his eyes. She already imagined the joy of feasting on one of those blue-green orbs. Julep was so very hungry too. As soon as her leg flexed, she screamed as the pain set in. She'd put too much into the attack and hadn't realized that she was strapped to a chair. Her leg stopped mid-swing, but the strength didn't stop pulling and her muscle cramped up, leaving her in excruciating pain.

"I saw that," Thaddeus warned her. *"Don't do that again."*

"I will kill you."

"So you say," he replied. Was that a smile on his face? *"You would have to escape first, and since you can't really talk, not much you can do, is there?"*

She wrenched with her other talon to try to reach his face, but this fell short as well. Julep bared her fangs at him and tried to bring her human-claws forward to do the job, but they were as secured as her talon-legs. Julep couldn't even get them from around behind her back to her front where they might be at least moderately useful to keep him off of her. His four mouth-tentacles hovered in the air between them.

"What did you do to me?"

"Nothing. You're fine. And oh, so delicious," he muttered, not looking into her eyes.

One of the tentacles came an inch from her eye, and she made out the leech-like mouth on the end. A flash and she remembered those plunging into her face and neck. She couldn't let that happen again.

"Leave me alone."

"After you tried to kill me?"

"You deserve to die."

That was the truth, wasn't it? Cheating was worth killing over, and he'd definitely been cheating. She'd seen him. He didn't know how empty his stupid fucking gestures were because *he* didn't know that Julep wasn't a dumb blonde. Julep had guessed her sister's email password three months ago, and from there, it had been cake to hack into her security system, which for paranoid Margie Hode, had included a healthy number of security cameras inside and outside her apartment. All Julep had to do was set the trap and then wait. Then when he cheated, she'd take him for all he was worth.

At least, that had been the plan. Margie was a weak woman and would take any opportunity to get back at an older sister who had been the star of the show for the entire thirty years of their lives together. But she had to play her part right. The wronged woman, pushed to the edge by her ever-cheating husband. And at the end of it, she couldn't talk to Margie again. That would be a blessing. The plan was built on the stack of reality. It was a good plan, except for one thing. She'd transformed into a harpy bird-woman.

That wasn't part of the plan. She cocked her head again to the other side and ground her teeth. She couldn't help doing it. The bird-like response was automatic as every noise could potentially be a threat and her body seemed hard-wired to respond. She could turn her head nearly completely around, but her hands and feet weren't moving anywhere.

"Are you going to kill me?"

"Why would I do that?"

Three of his mouth-tentacles swayed toward her like enchanted snakes, sending a chill up her spine. She couldn't get through his armor, but he didn't have that problem. Her body was light enough to fly, and that meant weaker in many ways. She didn't know it for certain, but she could imagine it wouldn't take much for his tail to crush her completely to death. It wouldn't take much at all.

"Hold still, and this won't hurt," Thaddeus said, his face-tentacles poised, two on the right side of her face and two on the left, all aimed at her.

"No!"

"I loved you," he said as the first tentacle dug into her right

temple just beneath her feather-line where her head of feathers stopped to reveal the skin of her face. *"So much."*

The other three planted themselves in order: one where her chin joined beneath what used to be an ear but was now a hollow indention, another on her opposite temple, and one more on the ear at the opposite side of her head.

Caught off guard the last time, she only recalled the pain as one giant ball of hurt. This time, the pain seared and burned, like a man o' war jellyfish she'd stepped on as a child that had nearly hospitalized her. Her insides turned to fire as the tentacles pulsated against her, pulling something from her body and into his. Blood? She didn't know, but she felt the weakness again, starting at the top of her head and falling down her body toward her talons. She stopped struggling, and the pain subsided so that she sat there with her head supported by his tentacled face, gazing blankly into it. It occurred to her before she passed out that he wasn't just taking from her; he was also giving her something. Her senses dulled, and she found herself losing interest after that final thought as darkness took her.

———

The next time she awoke, she thought she heard someone crying. Thaddeus's huge, multicolored body heaved and undulated against the far wall of their bedroom. Flashes of images came back to her: of him carrying her to her bed after a performance of *Wicked* at the Kennedy Center. She'd worn an opal gown that evening, and it dripped from her like lake water as he'd carried her across the room. She'd laughed then, when she'd had the ability to laugh. Her movements had been languid and assured, not like the jerky way she turned to see him now, out of first one eye and then the other.

"You drove me to it," he said. Typical Thaddeus, not taking responsibility for anything he ever did.

"I don't control you," she responded, cocking her head to one side then another. She wiggled a taloned leg only to find herself restrained. Looking down, she saw that he'd used electrical wires and duct tape to affix her to the desk chair. She tried expanding her wings, but something had trapped them. Even her useless human-arms had been pinned behind her.

It had been a lot to secure, though. As she wiggled her wrists, she found that they did move, and anything that could move would eventually break. She stretched them against their bonds, watching as he turned his tentacled face back toward her.

"You deserve—"

"To die," he finished in almost a mental sigh. *"Is there anything I can do to fix this?"*

He'd oscillated again, like an addict. One moment sucking her life force away and the next asking for her forgiveness. Forgiveness for turning her into a monster. She knew he'd done it somehow, but how was the question. What a convenient way to get rid of her. She couldn't even speak to defend herself, however human her face looked.

"Start by untying me," she said. *"We'll see what happens next."*

She bared her fangs at him. That part was instinct. Her new body kept no secrets, however useful that might be to get herself free. It was as though her body was hardwired to her emotions now.

"When you want to kill me? I'm not stupid."

"Of course, you are. You thought you would get away with it, didn't you? But now you're in the same situation as me. You're a monster too, Thaddeus. There's no normal for you, stolen just like you stole it from me."

His head quivered as he fixed his gaze on her. His feeding tentacles, she'd decided, pointed toward her with their sharp concentric teeth biting the air. Whatever else he was thinking, part of him was craving another sample...and this next time he might not stop until she was dead. She moved her mouth, feeling around with her tongue on the inside of her teeth. Something felt different since the last time he'd attacked her. She moved her mouth and forced air out of her lungs.

"Yooo daaah," she heard herself form words. Not good words, not well defined, but more words than she'd spoken in three days. Thaddeus's eyes widened at the sounds, and she stared at him as she thought of what other words she might be able to say.

"Maaarrggggg," she started.

Thaddeus responded by looking away from her, though his feeding tentacles didn't change direction as quickly as his head did. They poked around the sides of his head at her to remind her they hadn't forgotten the taste of her blood.

"Maarrggiieeee," she managed, forcing the end of her sister's name through her mouth. As she finished, she closed her mouth too quickly and clipped the edge of her stubbly tongue.

"I didn't mean it, Julep. It only happened once."

Thaddeus didn't know how much Julep knew, she realized. He didn't know how many times she'd watched and seethed at the video monitor when she'd hacked in yet again to her sister's security system. He didn't know how she'd clenched her teeth to each moan, each stroke. She bared her fangs again as she decided whether or not to reveal just how truly caught he was. If it wasn't for those tentacles waving at her like cobras, she might have. But even if her body couldn't keep the secrets of her emotions, she could keep him guessing at the details.

"Swear to me," she told him. *"Swear to me that it was nothing. Swear to me that my sister meant nothing."*

It wouldn't matter, but maybe he would think it did. Whichever way it went, Julep's wrists worked furiously, twisting back and forth, and she almost thought she could feel the tape starting to tear. Then, she'd have to figure out how to free herself from the rest of her bindings. One thing at a time. For a brief second, she longed for her innocence back. She longed to be ignorant again of his transgressions, and deep within her, she wanted that child to not exist. Everything else could be denied. Her mother had lived in self-enforced ignorance of her father's dalliances and seemed happy most days. Julep's life could have been like that. Maybe not the best, but all men cheat. If not all men, at least all of the men with whom she'd ever been involved. It was a fleeting thought, and even as her mind went through it, she found herself snarling at him. She wasn't her mother.

"*I swear it,*" he said, far too casually. And the tentacles, those things hadn't given up their feast. "*I swear it. Never again.*"

He slid forward in a serpentine manner, somehow keeping his torso upright. He'd gained more control since before she'd lost consciousness. She'd been the same. She'd smashed her way up through the roof on impulse and almost fell to her death from there. She'd flopped like a chicken when she'd flitted down to the ground below. He would only get better from here, and his tough skin coupled with actual motor control could mean the end of any chance she had for freedom, let alone revenge.

The tape on her wrists snapped. She kept her hands behind her back, concealed from him, as he approached.

Then his hands were on her shoulders, and the look in Thaddeus's eyes was one of softness, concern. It was no doubt one of his practiced looks that went along with his narcissism. She pulled her head back away from the tentacles. Whatever he meant by his approach, his feeding tubes had other ideas. He either didn't realize it or didn't care, and neither offered her much comfort as his arms then slid around her, and he brought his face within breathing distance of hers. The tentacles writhed before her eyes, hovering before her, and she thought she saw a bead of sweat on his forehead. A second passed before he wiped the bead away with his hand. The softness faded with that movement.

Julep quickly forced her head forward into his, colliding her feathered forehead into his face and smashing two of his tentacles against his right cheek. Thaddeus let out a loud screech layered over a guttural yawp that seemed to rip from his chest. The force of the call rattled the pictures on the walls. The one of them sipping beer in an Athens bar shattered on the desktop, and Julep kicked backward.

As Thaddeus screamed again, the chair fell, and its top came apart from its base as it hit the floor. Julep tumbled out, leaving half of her web of wires and tape behind but still with her wings too tangled to fly. Those wings were powerful. If she could only get free, they would take her right up through the ceiling and into the night sky.

Her talons were loose. If she could get them in the right positions, she could shred the makeshift spider's web that kept her trapped. She bent down into as small a ball as she could and tried to lift one talon behind her back. Too fast. Julep ground her teeth together as pain racked up her spine. She tried again, this time more slowly, and kept one eternally moving eye on Thaddeus the best she could.

Blood, or she assumed it was blood, leaked out of one of his feeding tentacles onto the carpet. Somewhere deep inside, rage flashed that she would have to clean that mess. No, probably new carpets. And it was *her* apartment that he ruined. The ridiculousness of the thought made her cackle at herself, ejecting a noise that sounded more like a bird's chirp than a woman's laugh. The bindings on her wings snapped under the pressure of her claw, which twisted back around to help her stand. Thaddeus still hadn't recovered. He let out another ground-shaking yowl and swing at her with his tail.

A free bird was too fast for that. With one quick gust, she lifted up to the ceiling, carefully so as not to rip another hole in her home. Julep came down talons first, directly into his face, slashing at the feeding talons. Thaddeus's tail missed its mark as he swiveled to hide his weakness, but he left an opening. His sensitive areas below his belly, two protruding knobs that floated out and vaguely phallic in shape remained exposed. Julep's left talon changed course and sank into the thick meaty flesh, eliciting another house-shaking scream.

"*Stop!*" he projected at her. "*Stop, please!*"

"*But you're so delicious,*" she mocked and twisted her talon, digging deeper

"*Anything, Julep. Anything. I'll do it. Just stop. Please.*"

For the next few seconds, Julep kept her grip so tight that she could feel the steady rhythm of his heart—or whatever passed for a heart—up her leg. Then, she slackened her grip but didn't let go.

"*That masterful job you did with the tape and wires,*" she said and bobbed her head in the direction of the rat's nest they had become. "*Tie yourself up. When I'm convinced, I'll let go.*"

Thaddeus began the awkward process of wrapping the remnants of her bindings around his body. Using his powerful arms, he tied down his tail as well. Eventually, the only part of him still moving free were the arms he'd used to do the binding and the tentacles, from which Julep had noticed the "bleeding" had stopped. She relinquished her grip and moved quickly to secure his arms behind him. To do so, she was forced to lean in toward his torso, where Thaddeus's mouth appendages flailed before her. Careful to stay back from them, she grabbed his arms and wrapped spare wires around them, hoping that the wires were actually strong enough to hold him in place.

As she made her final tug to check the secureness of the restraints, Thaddeus jerked his body backward. Before she could react, one of the feeding tentacles stabbed into her neck and two into her chest. For a brave second, she struggled to pull away before she found herself slumping forward over his spiked shoulder. With the last of her energy, she arched herself backward and went slack, her body weight supported only by the tentacles digging into her flesh.

CHAPTER 12
MIGHT BE NOTHING

THE MILES FELL AWAY as Aristide drove and while Evian slept, first on Aristide's right shoulder and then eventually with her head resting on his right thigh. The hours brought the night with them, and soon Aristide found himself staring into the darkness, greeted only by the occasional road sign. Adrenaline still pounded through his body even three hours later. Evian shifted her weight as he went over a pothole. He glanced down to see her aqua eyes blink themselves open.

"Sorry I slept so long," she muttered, righting herself in her seat and looking out the window on the beat-up old truck.

"Nothing really to see on this stretch of road anyway."

"I mean, it's probably my turn to drive now, right?"

He forced a grin. "I guess it could be if you feel like you want to. If not, that's fine too. I've got some hours left in me."

She examined her surroundings. "Where are we?"

"Right now, we're on eighty-five about two-thirds of the way from Richmond to Durham. We can stop there and get some food, maybe switch it up, and you can drive for a while if you like."

"Sure, that sounds good," she said, her voice thinning to a

whisper. "Was it real, Aristide? Did we really see what I remember?"

Aristide set his lip into a straight line and nodded.

"Yes. I've been asking myself the same question for almost the past hour. It had to be real. This truck isn't mine, and I don't own an AR-15 or any hunting rifles," he said, motioning to the gun rack behind him. "I never met you before today."

"I was afraid of that," she said then stared out at the highway before them. "Did you say between Richmond and Durham?"

"I did. Also, I said we're on eighty-five."

"Where's the traffic?"

"Hasn't been any."

Aristide looked far down the road, as far as he could see. No lights. Not even on the far horizon where Durham should be waiting for them.

"And that's not strange?"

"I've never been through Durham before. Is it strange?"

"This close we should at least see the lights."

"Maybe it's nothing," Aristide said, though he didn't believe his own words. "Could just be a blackout or something. We passed through a storm about an hour ago."

"Sure," Evian agreed. "Nothing."

She stared out at the road ahead. Aristide stared too. There didn't seem to be anything else to say. The mile markers flashed green in the headlights one after another.

CHAPTER 13
LOYALTY HAS LIMITS

"WHAT THE FUCK WAS THAT?" Neko asked, his foot glued to the floor as the SUV tore down I-95, heading southbound, which Viv noted was *away* from where they should be going. The offices in Quantico were north of them—thirty miles north and that distance grew every second. She said nothing. The last image she'd seen hung in her conscious mind like an unwelcome invader. Her friend and boss Katie had morphed into some sort of half-spider creature before her eyes. Viv could see the scales spreading down her arms like shingles or highly-concentrated psoriasis. Suddenly, she wasn't Katie anymore. Then, the disoriented woman-thing flung herself around like rag doll, and Greg had to send two ineffective bullets her direction just to slow Katie down. And that was all before they'd realized that Greg's wife wasn't as dead as they'd thought. Then, all hell had broken loose, hence the "what the fuck" to which Neko referred.

"I don't know," she muttered, far too late to be answering the question, but she answered anyway.

"Katie *attacked* us. She turned into a spider-woman and attacked us. You saw it, right?"

"I don't know what I saw, Neko," she said.

The man's glasses were fogging up, and just about then she wished she'd driven instead of once again being relegated to passenger. He swerved around a pothole, clipping the end of it which caused the SUV to jump and land back on the blacktop.

"Slow down, Neko."

The radio blared static and then a voice.

"Kathryn, are you there? It's past check-in, Katie. What's your status? Is it a pandemic, or isn't it?"

Neko looked like he was going to grab for the radio, but Viv was a second faster. As her hand closed around the receiver, Viv felt his fingers connect with the back of hers, and the receiver slipped down and swung by their knees. Her eyes slid over to Neko beneath furrowed eyebrows. Neko's eyes were wide and bloodshot, and his bottom lip shone slick with saliva.

"Don't answer," he said. "They'll send us back into that mess."

"It's our job, Neko," she said. "And what about Katie. What if she's confused, lost, needs guidance? Imagine if that was you."

"If that was me, I wouldn't have tried to take a swipe at you."

Viv winced at that response, but he wasn't wrong. Her left arm still hurt where Katie's newly forming claws had connected. The radio blared out again.

"Katie? Neko? Vivian? We have reports of another one we need you to check out in your area. It could be nothing, though. You know how these things go, right? What about the bus thing? We still don't have your report and…oh shit, there's another one. Katie? You're the only field agents in the area, and we need you on this. Fredericksburg…no, Warrenton. Both. Another one in Spotsylvania. Pick up, Katie. We need you."

Viv glared at Neko, daring him with her eyes to try and

stop her again as she reached for the receiver dangling near the floor. The SUV immediately slowed and drifted to the side of the road. She ignored his actions and clicked down the button.

"Vivian here," she replied.

"Vivian, great," came the response. "Any word on the Fredericksburg situation?"

Vivian took pains to talk through the entire series of events in great detail, starting with them being redirected to Fredericksburg and ending with them in the car driving down I-95, in fear of their lives.

"I was afraid of that. We're getting reports all over now. North Carolina is completely dark. An entire state. How does an entire state go dark all at once?"

The driver's door swung open, and Neko stepped out into the night.

"Hold for a second," Vivian said and hung the receiver by the dash. "Neko, wait!"

"Nope," Neko said. "Not a chance. If you want to play lackey and go putting yourself in harm's way chasing down creatures, be my guest. I'm not going to be part of it."

Her heart dropped in her chest. "Neko, you didn't hear. NC is dark."

"What does that mean?"

"I think it means it's like a power outage, statewide. Not sure yet because I hung up to yell at you."

"I'm sorry, Viv. I work for the CDC, not the Space Force. It's not my job to chase around monsters unless they can only be seen under a microscope. Leave that business to the FBI."

He'd stopped moving away from her, but he hadn't come back.

"At least wait until I finish finding out what's going on," she said. "Then we can make a plan. *Together.*"

She listened as the silence dragged on and on in the darkness that enshrouded the vehicle. Vivian hadn't realized how late it had become in her daze since the incident. Neko had stopped moving, and her arm itched. Furiously. She reached her arm across and closed around where the scratch had happened, only to find that there wasn't a scratch anymore. And the skin felt...funny to her fingertips—slick like rubber moving her fingers in one direction and then prickly as she pulled them back. In a single frantic movement, she flicked on the light in the vehicle and lifted her wounded arm before her.

Vivian's arm was the smoky greenish-gray of the meat that her impoverished mother had sometimes come home with from the only market within walking distance. The wounds had closed up as well. Vivian bit her lip.

"Hello? Vivian? Are you still there?"

Vivian blinked away tears in her eyes and looked quickly to the mirror. No sign of anything on her face. No change at all there, only her arm. She quickly wiped the tears away and took a deep breath. She could hide it. From the looks of it, the change was happening slowly, and she could keep it hidden. But whatever plan they came up with, her and Neko, they would have to stay with the CDC. If anyone could figure out how to fix her, that was who would do it. She didn't even have the option that Neko was trying to force. She exhaled through her nose and reached for the receiver. Her eyes fell to the open door where Neko stood, his eyes even wider if it was possible.

"You," he said, shaking his head. "Not you."

Vivian could taste his fear. He wouldn't stay with her like this. She only nodded.

"Fucking decide," she told him. "Are you with me or not?"

His Adam's apple jumped as he swallowed. His lips moved, but the words that flowed were unintelligible gibberish.

"I—"

That was all she needed to know. She sighed loudly and reached for the receiver.

"Vivian here," she said. "I'm coming in. Two down in the field."

She spared a glance for Neko, who still hadn't gotten back into the vehicle. He shook his head, still muttering, and stepped backward instead.

"Nek—" she started, but it only made him back up more quickly. A second later, she watched Neko turn and bolt, away from the SUV, across three lanes that were strangely clear of traffic, and into the brush on the side of the highway.

"Roger, Vivian. Come in and give your report. I'm sorry about the casualties. If you send me an address, we'll send a crew to pick them up."

She gave him the address of the trailer, then crossed the aisle in the car to take the driver's seat. Vivian looked out the window after Neko, but he'd already disappeared. She absently scratched at her injured arm, which itched even more. She started the vehicle back up, looked in her rearview and forward, and spun the car in a large circle.

Neko was gone. Everything that she'd thought they had together—which wasn't that much, but still—gone in an instant. Her heart raced as she realized the full implications of what was happening to her. But then, she didn't know. All she had now was a patch of thick gray-black scales on her arm, different in color and texture than whatever had happened to Katie, and different still from Greg's wife's greenish-red armor. Even the creature on the bus had been different. And Margie had turned into something that didn't resemble either of the other two.

So what could Vivian expect? Her eyes dropped to the gray patch, and she sucked in her breath. Already, it was twice the size as it had been the last time she'd looked.

———

Vivian was fortunate when, an hour later, she pulled into the CDC offices in Quantico. The gray had already covered her entire arm and was working its way up her neck, but it hadn't marred her face yet. If she shifted her clothes right, she could hide most of it from view. That had been enough to get her admitted through the gates, but the transformation had quickened. Her fingers on her right hand had merged while she watched, trying to drive and too terrified to take the time to stop though she probably should have. Wires first, tan and gray, pushed out from her ring finger to her middle. She'd tried to pull them apart. The pain was unbearable.

The worst part of it was what was happening inside her body that she couldn't see. Her breathing had stopped for about half a second and then started again, changing from her shallow, fear-saturated breaths to raspy, thick, mucus-y slurps. That had made it awkward to talk to the guard.

The parking lot that she pulled into was reserved for the senior vice president. He wasn't using it, so she took it. She swung the door open as soon as she parked, leaving the car on but not in gear. As she stepped down onto her left leg, it crumbled beneath her weight. Vivian's legs kicked into the air as she fell over. Her black uniform pants slid down revealing slender bifurcated feet without toes that ended in points. Her ankles had shriveled into the thickness of a water hose, yet were stiff and the skin had already gone completely gray. Her heart pounded in her ears. She tried to lift herself, but her arms were undergoing a similar transformation. Something thin, like an electrical cable line but shorter, swung before her face.

"Vivian!"

She looked up at the man who she hadn't seen come out of the entry to the building.

"Paul," she said, her voice sounding barely more audible than a croak. "Help me."

The changes weren't done. As Paul came toward her, he

tried to lift her onto her weak legs. His wide eyes seemed to blur into luminescent orbs and even his heavy smoker's breath was intoxicating and smelled like clean cotton and chocolate. Something stirred in her at the smell, and she lifted her head toward him. He lurched backward.

"Vivian," he said and bolted inside, leaving her a mass on the pavement. The building faded from complex multicolored to shades of a color she'd never seen before—a cross between purple and blue. Vivian's eyes landed on the flowerpot near the front door. All flowers were the same color, only different shades, and the background all seemed to blur together. She brought her hands up to rub her eyes, but when she saw the blue-purple talons that her fingers had become, she stopped herself. Her back shuddered under her, and she squirmed one side to another as her supine position became intolerable. Jagged spikes punched through the sides of her legs and something was on her back—something she could only feel that crinkled like newspaper.

A second later, the door ejected three people in hazmat suits pushing a gurney. A second after that, she was on the gurney being spirited through the door. She didn't have to guess where they were taking her. Observation. Three floors above where she'd entered. And once there, they would discover what was wrong with her. They *had* to. And when they fixed her, the first thing she would do is find Neko and let him know exactly what she thought.

Only they weren't fixing her. Thirty seconds later, she couldn't breathe. Vivian could push air out of her mouth somehow, but when she tried to inhale large volumes, she had no relief. It was as though her lungs had simply stopped working. She clutched at her chest with her clawlike fingers, shredding her clothes trying to remove the constriction until she could feel her chest dampen with blood from her efforts. The blue-violet colors dimmed around her.

"Someone, restrain her," a strong voice said. She recognized it as Katie's boss. "I'm so sorry, Vivian. We were sure this was a series of prank calls, or we would have sent you in more prepared. The next team will have better weapons and training because of your sacrifice."

The woman talked, but Vivian couldn't hear. Her ears had stopped working, and she only had the vaguest resonances from somewhere. Her forward-head antennae had sprouted tiny hairlike arms and with these, she felt the trembling of the voice but couldn't make out the words.

"What the hell happened to her?" someone said in the background as her arm hair sensitivity grew stronger. That time it came in loud and clear.

Suddenly, she began breathing again, but it didn't *feel* right. For one thing, the air didn't come from her nose or mouth. Both had been reduced to ornamentation except for the small, shallow breaths she still made in her unceasing attempts at reinstating her habit. Instead, her entire body tingled as the air around her seemed to saturate her, flowing unstopping into her body. The purple-blue world reasserted itself. Vivian realized then that she couldn't move. Her arms and legs both had been strapped to the gurney. The only thing not strapped down was whatever was itching her back, and her body was prone against it.

Lights passed by on the ceiling.

"I'm fine," she tried to say, fearing that the worst had happened and like the others, she may have lost the ability to speak. She recalled the video of the creature on the bus, and the gibberish she had spat through the tattered remains of the red dress. That wouldn't be her. "Let me go."

She understood it then. The fear, the disorientation. The massacre on the bus might not have been intentional. She felt urges that she barely contained every time one of the workers neared her mount. Bloodlust. But she managed, only because she'd known what to expect. In another life, where she hadn't been surrounded by her coworkers, where she'd been alone on a bus and freaking out in a bathroom…she wouldn't have been as capable. Who knew what would have happened then?

"Seriously. Let me go," she said, getting accustomed to using her breath only for speaking.

"Not a chance," was the reply she was given.

To her dismay, she recognized a change in tiling in the ceiling. The low-hanging crumbly cheap tiling had been replaced with thick slabs of what might have been marble. Not for looks, she knew, but for security. She was heading into the isolation ward, where she'd be "protected" by means of locking her up. They would do experiments on her to reverse the reaction. She wiggled a clawed hand. Vivian wouldn't be locked up. Her claws had grown longer and very nearly reached her leg restraints, if only she could stretch far enough. She extended them as far as she could, but one of her "escorts" saw her and quickly slapped her hand back down.

"None of that," came an accompanying voice. "We don't know how contagious you are, Vivian. We need to put you in observation."

"I'm not contagious," she disputed, but nobody seemed willing to argue with her. Instead, they all just focused on the hallway before her. The cart clipped along over the floor tiles until she came to a wide glass-encased room.

Vivian fought. She pulled and tugged at her bonds and even took a swipe at one of her escorts with a finger blade. Nothing stopped them from pushing her through the door and slamming it behind her. Then, she was alone on one side of the glass, and they were all on the other. Vivian turned her head, though she knew what she would find. A single bed with paper-thin blankets, a toilet in one corner in case she still had something like a digestive system under what she increasingly recognized as an exoskeleton. The pressure of her body against her bonds had grown and the itching in her back was impossible to ignore. On impulse, Vivian flexed her back muscles to try to scratch it only to wince as her body lifted, and the restraints yanked against her wrists.

She heard a creaking noise, though. The gurney was designed to keep humans constrained, not whatever she'd become. She tried it one more time, and this time as she gritted her teeth against the pain, she felt her restraints give, popping one by one until she was free. Vivian rose into the air as the itching on her back lessened. Then, she flexed her back muscles again, aware of how cramped they'd become. As Vivian walked, her body seemed to sway side to side. A quick glance backward showed her the purple outline of an insect-like abdomen. If she'd still had much of a recognizable human digestive system left, she would have vomited bile at the sight.

Her coworkers and escorts no longer offered words of encouragement through the glass. She rose up onto her taloned feet to almost touching the ceiling. Something on her back made contact with the ceiling. Her antennae detected a crinkling sound of old newspaper, followed by a breeze. The saucer-wide eyes of her coworkers and associates stared unforgivingly. She felt downward pressure on her shoulders and upper back. Vivian slowly turned her head on her shoulder and saw the tops of paper-thin fairy wings peeking up over her shoulders. Deep inside, a little girl's excitement at having fairy wings bubbled up, lived a brief, stressful life, and then died as she saw her inhuman claw wandering into her peripheral vision.

CHAPTER 14
SPIDER WOMAN

SHIT.

That was what Katie felt like. Absolute shit.

Her memories were spotty at best. There was a struggle, she recalled. She couldn't see anything, but something tried to attack her so she retaliated. Then, a couple of quick firearm reports and darkness.

Then light.

She lifted herself to her feet slowly and worked her jaw. So far, so good. Katie lifted her hands to her face to wipe away the goop that she'd expected to find, but it was already gone. And, despite how disoriented she was, Katie's jaw felt intact. She ran her hand back through her hair and then rubbed her eyes. She strained to focus on the room around her and instantly everything became clear. Crystal clear. It was as though every single item in her line of vision had come into focus at one time, and she could see the details of the orange stove with the crack in the glass as well as the tiny fibers of the washcloth that lay atop the sink full of dirty dishes.

Katie closed her eyes and twisted her head, rubbing the back of her neck. The vertebrae in her neck popped and slipped, and the muscles gave up their tension. She felt pretty normal, actually—more normal than she'd felt in a long time. When Katie stretched her arms to work out the kinks in her shoulders, she realized something was amiss. Shuffling on her chest brought her eyes downward where the remnants of her Kevlar vest clung to her equally destroyed (and very professional at one time) dress shirt beneath. Under that, gray fabric. Or she thought it was. Strange because she hadn't put on anything under her clothes except a very sensible red bra that wouldn't show through the white cotton pressed shirt. She bit her lip softly and winced, then forced her mouth back open. A five-second examination with her fingers revealed that her incisors had somehow grown and seemed to be angled outward. Possibly she'd been injured and just hadn't realized how badly yet.

Katie closed her mouth and continued to examine her clothing. She picked away at the vest and then the shirt beneath to reveal what she'd originally thought to be fabric, only it wasn't fabric. When she ran her hand down the center of her sternum, she felt the pressure all the way down. She recalled running toward the door to the trailer—probably the one she was in from the look of the tiny kitchen. Then, she remembered being slimed, and then…fighting Neko and Viv. And the man with the gun…Greg. Why would she do that? She turned her head toward where she'd though the fight had happened. There on the couch, near the lizard-woman, lay Greg. He was unconscious or something, from the looks of him not moving.

"Greg?" she tried to say. It took her two tries to get the word out, and when she did finally get his name across her lips, the sound of her voice had a deep tenor to it, like it dripped with venom. Katie rubbed her neck again. It was time to test the rest of her and see how bad the damage was. Anything that could shred that vest had to have hurt, but as she examined her torso, there wasn't a drop of blood anywhere on her gray skin. Why was it gray? Gunmetal gray, like her toaster oven back at home. It wasn't a natural color, and it was too uniform for her to have been sprayed with paint. Unless the venom had discolored her skin. That was a possibility.

She popped her back quickly and stood.

She watched the floor get farther and farther away. When she was as high as her normal standing height, the floor kept receding. Even when her head bumped into the ceiling, she hadn't yet finished standing. The shredded clothes fell down to her midsection. The remnants of the shirt, bra, and vest hung around her waist like a skirt. But what was under the skirt wasn't the two legs that she'd been born with. Beneath the skirt and stretching out beneath her were eight spider legs. From her torso down, the gunmetal gray turned to black gradually, and the legs propped her up.

Katie's breathing raced as she looked down. Her human torso, gray but human, seamlessly transitioned into the abdomen of a spider. From between her spider legs, she saw the tail of the abdomen and a stretched cord connecting to her body. With a grunt, she tensed her belly muscles and more wire-like spray pushed out and spattered against the wall. It stuck to one of the cabinet doors. When she jumped back in surprise, the door yanked off of its hinges.

"Fuck," she said, and she remembered the images of the woman on the bus. Suddenly the "no, no, no" made sense as it rattled around in Katie's head as well. Her legs had been stolen from her. And in their place was a spider's body, blown up large enough to fit a human torso—her torso—atop.

That was why she'd been fighting. And that was why Neko and Viv had run away. They couldn't kill her, and they couldn't save her. What else could they do? All because of the lizard-woman on the couch. Katie's eyes floated over to where the woman lay, and her tongue touched against the tip of one of her incisors. She didn't remember ever being so hungry. Her stomach churned with its emptiness. Whatever the transformation had done, it had taken most of her energy and now she had to eat. She bowed over forward, clutching her stomach.

"Uhrnnn," she grunted as the pain grew. Something in her body tickled the back of her mind. It was something primitive, something the spider brought with it. With another glance at the couch, the thought embedded itself in her mind.

Waste not, want not.

Katie scurried, careful to duck under the lights, over to the couch. In less than thirty seconds, she'd wrapped the lizard-woman in a cocoon of webbing. Katie then tilted her head back, and her incisors extended from her mouth like fangs. She stabbed them into the sack, and her sinus cavities pulsed as they ejected something through her teeth into the web sack. After half a second, she felt the motion reverse and a delicious potpourri of flavors gushed into her mouth. Lemon, raspberry, with a nutty edge to it. Katie was glad she didn't have to see whatever it was that she swallowed by the mouthful. All she knew was that she loved it, needed it, more and more. Half an hour later, she finished her meal and delicately wiped the edges of her mouth with her fingers.

That was a little disgusting, she admitted to herself. But still, when she considered her desk job, turning into a spider-woman wasn't the worst thing that could have happened. And, all things being equal, she still had her mind mostly intact, which didn't seem to be the case with the woman on the bus. Unless...the thought came in an instant. Unless the woman on the bus could think. There had been that moment that Katie couldn't think properly. An argument could be made that eating a lizard-woman like a slushie wasn't clear thinking either, but she had a new body now, and it wanted what it wanted. But she'd been seriously disoriented, not even herself, for more than three hours. If she had been the woman, she probably would have lashed out too, frightened and alone.

Somewhere out there in the wilderness was a terrified young woman as unsure of what was happening to her as Katie, but with far less experience in dealing with unknown contagions—which had to be what this was. That woman was alone and had just killed all of her bridal party companions. That woman needed someone, someone who could understand what she went through. That woman needed Katie.

Katie turned to try to go through the door and found that her oversized abdomen wouldn't squeeze through. She turned sideways and was able to get her torso and two of her spider legs past the threshold.

Spider legs. Katie took a deep breath and stilled her mind. She couldn't help thinking of her mother and the conversation the woman would have had if she'd ever known about Katie's current situation.

"I told you," the woman would probably say, her unkempt yellow hair sticking up like dried straw. "I told you. It was the government. Just watch, any day now they'll roll out a vaccine for it. You'll see."

Katie was a professional…spider-woman. She knew that it was too soon to even begin to formulate an opinion about who might be responsible. The CDC had to get to the "what" first, and to do that, they would need samples. She sucked in her breath, as though that might diminish her gunmetal-plated abdomen enough to squeeze through. She pulled with her arms and legs, but the thing wouldn't budge. Katie only succeeded in wedging herself into the doorframe and found that she couldn't back out either.

Tiny hairs on her legs and abdomen and the backs of her arms pricked up. Katie's entire body vibrated with the sound of an approaching vehicle. An approaching vehicle would arrive to see a half-woman, half-spider trapped in the door of a trailer containing two dead bodies, one of which she'd eaten. It wasn't like she was using the body any longer, but likely there would be no conversation. If she'd seen herself, she would go immediate fight-or-flight. She was almost certain by the sound of the engine that the occupants carried weapons. The truck sounded like an old F-150 which seemed to be a popular truck in these parts, and she overheard several male voices weaving together in the background. In an open-carry state like Virginia, one or two were guaranteed to be packing.

She struggled more with the door and managed to get another shining black spider leg through. The trail from the highway to the door of the trailer wasn't long, and she could see the truck chugging along at the end of it. Frantic, she pulled harder and harder and stabbed her legs deep into the earth to anchor. Creaking as the truck spun closer, then even more creaking. She thought the doorframe might break, but it didn't. Instead, she only became more tired as she pulled, and as hungry as she'd ever been in her life.

An idea struck her. Using her legs to lift her body upward, she wedged the bottom of her abdomen between her legs and shot webbing out into a mass covering two oak trees off to the side of the driveway. Then, she grabbed the cord with her hands and used it to pull while she pushed with her back legs. The doorframe creaked and complained, and the trailer shook with her efforts. For several seconds, she thought she might drag the trailer across the gravel parking lot.

The truck approached. She could see clearly now. Three men in the front, and one already hung out the window with a rifle. She needed to move faster.

Just when the trailer rocked again, the doorframe broke open, and she spilled out. The exertion left her drained and heaving on the gravel. The truck rounded the edge of the lot and then came to a stop with the man leveling his rifle at her.

Instinct took over. She shot another round of webbing over the truck, and her legs carried her toward it as the man's face caught the first blast. She scurried around it as she had the lizard-woman, wrapping the entire truck before any of the men had an opportunity to get out. Sealed up tight, she could make out the men's muffled cries. She knew one of them had to have a knife, so now could be her opportunity to leave.

Katie didn't flee.

She stood erect to her full height, with two legs on top of the truck and the other six supporting her body. Then she examined her work. Air-tight. If they didn't cut through soon, all three of them would suffocate.

Katie raised one spiked foot and stabbed into the webbing around the cab, puncturing it through. When her leg emerged, blood dripped from the end, and Katie winced. She couldn't see through the webbing, and it wasn't her fault, but there it was. She'd injured someone she hadn't meant to. When a rifle muzzle worked its way into the hole she made, Katie skittered away at a comfortable speed that had to have been fifteen or maybe twenty miles per hour. Her legs carried her toward the forest on the other side of the highway as her only thought was to get away from the men with weapons. She stepped out into the congested traffic, hopping over cars and clambering on big rigs. Crunching metal and squealing breaks provided the soundtrack for her efforts. Save an MG colliding with one of her rear legs and crumpling like an eggshell, Katie made it to the woods with no other incident.

The forest of old-growth trees provided her cover. She slid easily between them. Katie climbed up into the thin canopy and looked in the direction of where she thought the bus had been. Even from miles away, Katie was able to make out the overpass if not the bus itself. With slow, deliberate steps, she lowered herself down to hide among the uppermost branches of the mixture of fir trees and oak and made her way toward the wreck. Red Dress woman wouldn't be there anymore, of course. But knowing how it felt to transform, to have one's life upended all at once, forced Katie to believe that she had to be *near* there at least. If she could bring herself and Red Dress woman to the CDC, there might have been some hope for reversing whatever the process was that she guessed wasn't done yet.

Katie was so hungry, though. First, she would need a snack. In the distance, she could see deer grazing, unintimidated by her...yet. If she approached them, she knew they would run off. So she set about making use of her new skills. It turned out to be easier than crochet to spin a good net. Then she clambered across the treetops to get on the far side of the deer. In a few moments, she'd scared the deer back into the trap she'd made. Dinner was served.

CHAPTER 15
MISPLACED HOPE

BLACK. The color of the night without road lamps and a barely visible moon that kept getting snuffed out behind the clouds. Every time a cloud passed over the barely visible moon, Aristide couldn't shake the thought of that old myth about the moon being the home of the dead, where souls ascended after death only to be reborn again. It was an easy thing to believe when the woman he was travelling with, who he'd met only hours earlier, stared out the passenger's window in a catatonic trance at oversized cat tails lining the edge of a deserted highway. The dead moon's glow made her pale and meek in its light, as though it had washed the life right out of her.

Had it not been for the headlights on the pickup, Aristide wouldn't have noticed the city of Charlotte when they arrived. The moon that shone moments before had disappeared behind the clouds. The gas light plinked on, shining as an offensively bright teapot indicating the tank was near empty. Five quick miles later without a gas station, and it began to flash.

The exits snuck up on him in the limited range of the headlamps so that the first two that indicated gas stations swept right by. After that, he slowed to a slow crawl and committed to the outside lane. At the very next exit, the truck pulled off, and he felt it rattling and wheezing as it struggled to find more gasoline to burn. He patted the dash gently, and Evian snapped to attention.

"What'd you do that for?"

"Offering a bit of hope," he told her. "This truck may not make it much farther without a gas station."

"You think there will be a *working* gas station with no power?"

"No. But maybe a car that we can siphon from."

Flashes from childhood. In Podunk nowhere, there wasn't much to do. He and his friends had passed time with practical jokes. Siphoning all the gasoline out of a friend's car while they were out on a hot date was a staple in their repertoire, so he was certain he could still do it. Some things just came back. Like riding a bicycle.

They pulled into a pitch-black gasoline station that, to his surprise and a little relief, hosted two abandoned looking clunkers. One was a Ford Pinto, which Aristide was certain weren't even made any longer. The other was an MG that looked like it lost a fight with a Mack truck.

"Come on," he said, unlatching and swinging the door wide.

"I'll stay here," she said.""" "Maybe there's something we can use in this truck."

Whether that was the real reason she wanted to stay behind or not, Aristide couldn't know.

"Suit yourself," he responded, shrugging his shoulders at her. It was a one-person job anyway, aside from finding the materials. A tube and a bucket should do it, though a funnel would certainly make it easier. As he scanned the perimeter looking for something that would work, his eyes fell on the garage attached to the convenience store. Of course, there would be stuff in there. And with no power, there would be no alarm. It only took him a second to make the decision, but when he looked into the truck and then past Evian out to the garage, she glared at him.

"That's someone's business," she said. "I know what you're thinking."

"Evian, think about it," he said. "There's got to be something really bad happening. Nobody in the shop, and it's damn near apocalypse bad out here with monsters running around. I don't want to be dinner, and if we wait here, that's exactly what will happen. Or worse."

Aristide didn't elaborate on what worse was, but whatever was in Evian's mind caused her glare to disappear and her to pull her arms a little tighter around her body. She nodded once, and he slammed the door and left before she could change her mind.

The smell of burned oil and spent gasoline clogged his senses the closer he got to the garage. Inside, he already knew he would find a fire-hazard pile of oily rags. Every garage he'd ever worked in had a pretty lax policy on cleanliness. As he approached the building, he thought he heard rustling beyond the corrugated garage door. Aristide inched forward to listen and held his breath so he could hear. Nothing. Nothing but the beating of his heart. He leaned over to pull the door up. Mid-bend, his arm itched, and he reached over to scratch it. He found that he couldn't stop. The more he scratched, the more it itched, until it felt like his arm was a ball of fire tucked into the sleeve of a jacket.

He forced himself to stop. There would be time for more scratching, he said to himself as he continued his bend and grabbed hold of the door. With one quick yank, the door slid up and collided with the roof and flew off of its hinges. It crashed to the ground atop what looked like a Lamborghini that would have been in pretty good shape, had he not just crushed it with the garage door. Aristide definitely didn't expect such a car in a place like this, any more than he'd expected to rip a steel garage door from its hinges. He flexed his arm for a second, allowed himself a handful of scratches, and then stepped inside.

"Hey," came a voice from the darkness. Aristide stopped and backed up slowly. "Down here. Thank God, you came."

He scanned the darkness but saw nothing. A rustle caught his attention and drew his head down a second later to see a pair of eyes peering up from a grease pit. Aristide shielded his eyes as the lights seemed to all come on at once. Another rustle. He peered down and saw dark eyes, almost black possibly navy blue, he would have guessed. Eyelashes were the next thing he noticed, thick and black and matching an oil smudge above a left eyebrow. He carefully examined the space around the person in the pit. No extra appendages or new additions. She looked normal enough.

"What are you doing down there?"

"Power went out, and I couldn't get the lift to work. Too high for me to climb out," she said. "Toss me a cable?"

He looked around the floor. There he saw what looked like jumper cables lying next to the Lamborghini. Aristide walked over and picked up both ends of the cables. One end he lowered into the pit and the other he held onto with his right arm, trying to ignore the itching sensation. She grabbed hold with both hands, and Aristide lifted her out of the grease pit.

"How'd you do that?"

"Lift you? You don't weight much," he replied.

"No. How'd you see the cables?"

He stared at her confused. "The lights came on," he said. "Do your eyes work?"

Directed by his own words, his gaze turned to her dark blue eyes. Deep, and navy, and endless pools. She didn't seem to notice him staring.

"What lights?"

His fucking arm.

Aristide couldn't ignore it any longer. He scratched hard at his arm with his fingernails, and his eyes shot open. Something broke free under his nails like plaque psoriasis, only the size of a quarter. He shook his sleeve, and a black flake fell out onto the ground.

"Are you still there? Uh…sir?" the woman asked. The fear in her voice flipped him back into Marine mode. Another one to save.

"Aristide," he said. "Aristide Decuir. Just follow my voice, and I'll get us out of here."

"Tamitha Vega," she said. "Friends call me Tam."

"Tam, is there a gas can in this garage?"

"Over there against the far wall," she said. Darkness or no, she pointed in the direction, and Aristide exhaled a sigh of relief as he walked over and grabbed a red can marked "GAS" on the side. Another breath as he realized that the can was already full.

"You really can see in this?"

He nodded. Then remembering that she couldn't see anything, he replied that he could.

"Crazy," she said.

"Not so crazy," he replied. "The lights came on."

"If you say so."

"I do. Follow me. I've got a truck. You'll have to squeeze in next to Evian."

He turned toward the door to leave and stopped short. The entire landscape outside had lit up to nearly daylight. He could clearly see the truck, down to the crack in the window just in front of where Evian sat. He could make out her anxious eyes, wide and green-blue, though they seemed to glow and emanate a silver tint. What he saw was impossible, and his mind too quickly jumped toward the implications. As he walked, Aristide rolled his sleeve up. Every once in a while, he called back with a quick "you still there?" Beneath the sleeve, he saw nothing of the cut. Instead, a dark black patch of what might have been skin, with circular coin-sized scales overlapping each other in the area.

"Shit," he said. His eyes furrowed on their own, and he felt them going damp with the realization that the infected area was no longer limited to where the claws had dug into him. It had spread around his elbow and fanned to the back of his arm. Whatever it was, it was spreading.

"Tam," he said as he pushed the door open. "Listen carefully. Can you see that truck, about fifty yards out there by the pump?"

She nodded.

"That's what this gas is for. Take this and tell Evian, the woman in the passenger's seat, that I'm not coming."

"Why aren't you coming?"

Aristide sucked in his breath, looked at his arm, and clenched his teeth.

"I'm not safe."

She nodded at him in the darkness.

"I'm not either," she said.

A second later, he felt a jolt in the side of his neck, and he stumbled forward, fighting to stay on his feet and cursing himself for believing that this woman was helpless. As he fell, he thought he could be forgiven for that. Everything on her front looked perfectly normal. The tubule that pulled itself from his neck as he fell had come from somewhere behind her.

"Thanks for the help," she said. "Evian and I will become great friends."

He stumbled forward and put his hand out as the ground

rushed up to meet him. Tam walked slowly and deliberately forward toward the vehicle, and all he could do was groan on the ground as she went. A second after he fell, he felt a surge of energy course through his veins. Whatever she had done seemed to flood from the point of stabbing and filled his body like a warm fire, or the heat after drinking a ghost-pepper spiked cocoa. He knew from the sensation and the relentless itching that covered his entire body that his reaction had sped up. The blackness on his arm, he could see through blurring eyes, had spread down to his fingers.

Tam was five feet away when Aristide's shirt ripped from his back as gigantic bat-like wings exploded from his shoulder blades. His pants split from the rapid growth, and every item of clothing save the shreds of his T-shirt fell away. A guttural howl echoed from his belly through his lips and out into the night sky.

Tam stopped. She turned, and he saw her do it. The blurring stopped and reversed, and suddenly everything was crystal clear, down to the widening eyes of Evian, who, as close as she was to Tam, had to have noticed the growths on the woman's back. Like a giant infant, Aristide stumbled on his feet. He flapped one wing, and the force of it knocked him on his side. Tam let out a laugh.

"So that's what you meant," she said. "Why didn't you say so? We can be great friends."

Both wings flapped and lifted him about a foot into the sky before dropping him unprepared on massive, untrained legs. Aristide stumbled again, falling to one knee.

"Let's go, Aristide," she said, and then the illusion of her human form fell away as she showed a network of tentacles about a centimeter in diameter, each floating up behind her. Her face was still too human, and the network of fibers seemed like they levitated up out of a backpack or something. Aristide let out a deep growl before he pulled both of his new wings down hard behind him. They lifted him as he'd hoped and hurled him forward toward the woman, but she sidestepped quickly and flung a handful of wire-like tentacles in his direction at the same time. They all fell away against the black scales that now covered his entire body, but they did alter his trajectory, and a second later he barreled into the side of the truck.

He hadn't heard the window shatter. But when he recovered from disorientation, he saw that Tam had gotten past him and pulled Evian from the car.

"I'm so hungry," Tam said. "One step closer, and I swear I'll do to her what I did to my boyfriend."

"Your boyfriend?" he managed to say, although it came out as a near-incomprehensible roar. Evian's eyes looked toward him, and she clung to Tam for protection. "Evian, it's me."

Another growl. He was losing his words. Somehow, he had to convince her to move away from Tam, so he could deal with the threat. Fortunately, Tam did it for her.

"She likes me, Aristid…whatever your name is. See this?"

That caught Evian's attention, and she immediately pulled away from Tam, but Tam was faster. As Evian tried to flee, at least ten of the needled-hoses plunged into her back. It happened so fast that Aristide wasn't sure it had happened at all. Only when Evian plunged to the ground was he convinced. With an angry shout, of words that didn't sound like words, Aristide flung himself into Tam and knocked her back fifty feet. The gasoline can parted from her and sprang into the air. Aristide caught it and sprinted to the truck. He could outrun Tam, but Evian couldn't. He scooped Evian up and put her in the passenger's seat. Then he tried to get into the driver's side but realized he couldn't even fit through the door. Growling in anxiety, he jumped over the top of the cab just in time to give Tam another kick before she could wrestle an unconscious Evian from the car again.

Then, entirely on impulse, he scooped Evian's form into his arms and flapped his two great wings once, then again, and found himself fifty feet in the air.

He just kept flapping, floating above the trees and tried not to think about what might happen to Evian next.

CHAPTER 16
GLOBAL GENETIC MUTATION

VIVIAN DIDN'T KNOW whether or not the changes were over. What little she did know was that it was easier for her to hover than it was to stand straight up on her new legs. Her body required both her legs and arms for full support, and the twiggy mosquito-legs she now wore didn't help. Standing upright required twisting inside of her exoskeleton. Her probiscis tongue flicked out as a thought shivered through her body.

She had an exoskeleton.

And she was entirely alone.

The glass walls afforded her no privacy. She'd expected that. What she hadn't expected was to be treated like any other patient with a communicable disease. Vivian was one of the CDC experts. She'd been an analyst through SARS, COVID-19, and even Swine Flu, and she'd excelled at it. Vivian already knew that the disease didn't spread through the air, but her compatriots in the CDC wouldn't take her word for it. Hence, all conversation came through a tinny-sounding radio link embedded in the glass wall.

The bed they'd given her wasn't comfortable. The only way she could position herself to get any rest was to hunch over on all fours and let her wings droop over her back. Then, supported by the hinge joints of the exoskeleton, Vivian could sleep for thirty or forty minutes before she lost balance and fell on the floor.

She would persevere. And she would overcome. And, she knew this was special, she still had her mouth, tongue, and a small set of lungs if the scans were to be believed that supported her ability to talk.

As the following day ascended—something she could only tell by the arrival of well-rested people and their enviable sixteen-ounce coffees—she decided it was time to get some answers. They'd run enough tests by now to have figured *something* out, certainly.

"Carla," she shouted.

Carla looked up from her drink but didn't say anything. She looked right back down again.

"Carla, I know you can hear me through this thing. Come on, tell me. What have you learned?"

The skin on the woman's face turned bright pink, and she shuffled farther away from the glass than the break table that someone had installed by the room's only entrance.

"How are you, Viv?" came a voice she recognized. Vivian felt her blood go hot as she lifted her eyes to see who entered the door next.

"Neko," she hissed. "Get him out of here."

"We spent all night last night trying to find him," said Carla, who Vivian saw didn't bother to move as Neko pushed his way into the room. He rested a hand on Carla's shoulder before stepping around her chair as Carla continued. "There's no way we're letting him go. The last surviving member of the Biological Security Task Force? Not a chance."

"I'm a surviving member," she argued. "Me. He's a traitor. He left me to fend for myself, alone out there. Don't trust him."

"He told us what happened," Carla said. "I think you're being unfair. What would you have done? What did you *do*?"

The truth was that Vivian had run. Just like Neko, she'd sprinted away when Katie had changed into a spider. But Katie had become a fucking spider-woman and had killed Greg in less than a second without seeming to even think about it. "I didn't kill anyone, did I?"

Neko shook his head.

"N...no," said Neko, not looking at her.

"Well? What's the verdict?" Vivian asked. "What's wrong with me?"

She asked the question to Carla and not Neko, though Neko responded.

"Genes," he said, holding up a piece of paper that she could make out clearly from where she stood. He only held it for a second, but she committed the entire thing to memory as soon as she could recognize the figures on it. He didn't meet her eyes, keeping his face pointed toward the wall or floor, or anywhere but on her.

"Global genetic mutations?"

"Yeah," he said, as though he hadn't stranded her in the middle of nowhere. "You know about genetic drift, when a species mutates slowly over generations, taking on different changes that make that species more suited to the environment? It's like that, only it's all happening within you, and over a matter of hours, not decades."

"I'm not asking you," she said. "I'm asking her. Carla, what's all this mean?"

"You're right, Vivian. Global genetic mutations. So far, we think there's a bacterial vector delivering the changes, but we can't be sure. We've never seen this before."

"But can it be reverssssssed," she said, noticing for the first time that her "s" had become elongated and challenging to say.

"I mean, you're an anomaly," Carla continued. "Nine times out of ten, genetic mutations are dead ends. For your cells, over a thousand mutations are all working together. Something happened to you."

"Something intentional," Neko said, unprompted. Vivian glowered in response and considered if she had the strength to punch through the glass and strangle him. She decided against it for the moment. She still had questions; this was the only place to get answers.

"How's that posssssssssible? The woman—thing that did thissssss to me wassssss already changed. How could a genetic change propagate passssst its original ssssssource?"

"That's what we're trying to figure out," Carla said, her eyes gleaming in a way that Vivian recognized from when she'd first helped decode the genetic structure of the COVID-19 virus. The sense of adventure and wonder, at the violence and ingenuity of nature—all of that rolled up into a tiny nugget of emotion from deep within. Nothing about her new situation sparked such wonder in her this time.

Three billion base pairs, she thought. Three billion sugars all rolled together to create…whatever she'd become.

The glass box she was in was at least ten orders of magnitude brighter outside, and the lights left not so much as a shadow on the floor. She peered through the transparency toward Neko. His eyes drifted in her direction and then back down to study whatever spreadsheet or software they were using. She settled down and willed her eternally flitting wings to steady themselves.

"Mirror," she said. Both Neko and Carla jolted at the sound of her words. For a second, Carla stared on in a daze while Neko stared *near* her but not at her. She explained more slowly, "I need a mirror."

It was Carla who answered. Neko looked like someone had

trapped his cat in a meat grinder with a finger hovering over the "on" switch, not that Vivian would ever do anything to Furry Little Monster, even if its attitude about life matched the unfortunate name.

"No," was all Carla said at first. Then she ran a quick hand through her hair and turned her attention back to the spreadsheet.

"Even COVID patientssss get mirrorssss," Vivian reminded her. She knew the protocols and emotional health required mirrors to be available to reinforce a sense of self-identity within the patients they treated. She hadn't seen herself fully since the global mutations had begun.

"I mean, you don't want one. You don't look like yourself, Vivian. We're working on figuring out how to change that, but it might be better if you don't worry about it. For now."

"Mirror," she repeated. "Or no more tesssstssss. And get me a tablet."

Carla snapped her head back up from her work, sending her brown hair fluttering up and settling with strands landing in her eyes. She pushed them back as she gazed at Vivian and nodded. Carla then turned her head and nodded again at a thick, short man with a goatee.

"Okay," she said and directed her attention to one of the other members of what must have been the new Biological Security Task Force.

Wheels spun in Vivian's head as she thought it through. Of course, they were. Four of them, counting Neko, the "lone survivor." Pity him, and his poor girlfriend. The new task force held her under examination. Whatever their motivations, hers was higher. A standard-issue tablet held the modeling and simulation software she needed along with the genetic structure of her changes.

"Give me the work you've done up until now too," she said, careful to avoid "s" sounds.

"Do you think that's a good idea?" asked Neko.

"Nobody asssssked you," Vivian said, raising her voice. "It'ssss my body. I'm capable of doing thisssss work too."

"You are," Carla admitted. "And you're one of the best. We didn't think you'd be in a state to be able to help."

Carla passed on another nod to someone nearby. This was a woman with orange-gold hair and an anxious air that floated with her as she fled the room to retrieve the equipment that Vivian and asked for.

Twenty minutes later, the first task lackey shuffled back to the door, covered in a thick white suit with an attached helmet. The man pushed a body-length mirror on wheels in front of him, waited the obligatory five minutes as both he and the mirror were sprayed down with decontamination foam. He continued through the opening on the other side, exiting the man-trap into the chamber.

Vivian could see scared eyes peering out of a thin two-inch-high clear plastic patch on the helmet. She smiled at him. He stumbled and fell, shoving the mirror with his body. In an instant, she found herself next to the mirror. She caught it with her long claw-like fingers and held it in place. That had been too easy. In the last few seconds, she'd flitted across the room without even thinking. The man stayed where he fell for a second and then crawled, *crawled*, from the room as though she were a dangerous tiger or leopard and might yet decide to eat him.

In truth, Vivian hadn't decided on that point yet. Her stomach, or something stomach-like in her, churned at the overwhelming odor of his salty sweat. He seemed to glow with the heat of his panic, beckoning her to come to him. She felt her mouth open, and something protruded tongue-like between her teeth. An urge flooded through her: feed, feed, feed. But she was slow to act, and by the time she decided she was hungry enough to jettison what remained of her humanity, the man had crossed the threshold to the man-trap and slammed his hand on the button. Vivian scrambled toward him, forgetting she had wings, only to have the door slam in her face.

She stopped.

Vivian's extended, wiry fingers were too thin to cover her eyes, but she tried anyway. Vivian willed whatever it was that had come out through her mouth back in. It didn't work at first, as the memory of the man was etched into her brain, and all she saw was the glow around him, calling her to him. The man had feared her. Only terror would make a grown man crawl like that across the floor. His widened eyes betrayed everything she needed to know about his emotional state. He'd been terrified, and from the salty taste that flooded her mouth after the appendage pulled back between her teeth and the shuddering that it sent through her entire body, he was right to fear her.

Her eyes drifted to the pile of discarded Chinese food boxes in the corner, contents still inside. Her once-favorite food, which she had often shared with Neko snuggled on the couch watching old horror movies, had become no more appetizing to her than sandpaper. Her body shook with revulsion at the thought of forcing chicken-fried rice into her narrow mouth.

In a frenzy, she covered the ground toward the mirror. Sanitizing foam covered the entire surface and melted down it in trickles that cleared gaps. Using her claws and forearms, Vivian cleared away what she could of the foam.

Red eyes peeked back at her between two lonely rivulets. Vivian smeared more of the foam away to reveal a dome on her forehead. As she worked, she saw the crystal clarity of her claws before her, frantically wiping the mirror clean. Once it was finally clear enough to see, she stepped back and screamed so loudly that everyone in the lab stopped and turned to stare.

Her hair had turned flame-pink and floated back over her shoulders, having grown stiff and wiry and making her head look somewhat like the tip of a burning match. Two massive snake-like antennae poked out like elongated horns and floated around above her head just out of her peripheral vision. Two insect-like wings poked up over her shoulders, shielded by half-foot spikes from where her shoulder blades had been.

There wasn't anything left of her black field uniform except a part that clung around her neck like a collar. Vivian's face, aside from the glowing red eyes, looked like her from the nose down. But she hadn't imagined the appendage that forced its way through her mouth. Shaking, she slowly opened her mouth to peer inside. Her tongue was thinner than it had been before, almost snake-like. She flicked it out, and there, on the roof of her mouth, she saw something that looked like a collapsed telescope. Vivian snapped her mouth shut.

"The tablet is in the man-trap," Carla's voice interrupted, turned robotic by the speakers. Vivian didn't move. She wore no clothes, but her skin had turned solid and thick. As her clawed fingers moved along her belly, she felt nothing except pressure on the wide, hairless chitin surface. It was like pressing a pin against a fingernail. She saw that her chest was bright orange, and aside from her pointed blades of fingers, the backs of her arms and legs seemed covered in red tiger stripes. Her body had shrunken too, and the hunched posture she used to keep herself upright and balanced was more insect-like than human.

With another scream, she slammed her elbow into the mirror and shattered it. Splinters of glass fell to the floor beneath her hardened feet. Vivian paused to examine those feet, large with the toes extending out into claws. She collapsed to the ground as her stomach roiled in her chest. The fact that she was naked in a glass observation room, a state of which she'd only been vaguely aware before seeing the mirror, seemed less than consequential. Especially when, in the little mirror that clung to the bottom of the frame, every inch of her body was covered in chitin. Viv could hardly call herself a woman anymore.

CHAPTER 17

GOD HAD NOTHING TO DO WITH IT

DARKNESS SHROUDED the city by the time Margie, in all of her newfound power, discovered the strength within herself to leave the sewers and break out onto the streets above. The streets of Arlington, Virginia, were so quiet that for a moment, Margie nursed the frightening thought that she had somehow become the only being left on the entire planet. A yellow taxi zipped by along I-395, swamping her in yellow light as she pushed back into the shadows and away from view. After it passed, she carried herself down Campbell Avenue away from the highway.

The lights were out in all of the restaurants along one side of the street. The other side, where the later-opened bars were, still had some lights deep within, but not enough to illuminate the streets. She floated down the median between the two, gliding on her tentacles. The air smelled of stale meat that had been burned black and the faint after-aroma of cabbage. On her right, she passed Extra Virgin, sparking memories of her, Julep, and Thaddeus attending the after-hours jazz and drinking way too much wine. For a second, she paused before the building. She gazed through the glass, trying to ignore the monstrous reflection in the window, and imagined herself instead in her favorite cocktail dress, red with a high neck and a slit up the side that nearly made it to her ribcage. The *looks* she used to get in that.

A stray tentacle crashed into the glass, shattering it and setting off a screaming alarm that caused her to lurch away. Margie looked down at the raw opening in her abdomen from where the tentacles swarmed. If she had seen herself in the alley, she would have run screaming. Being the monster, that option had been stolen from her.

She shook her head as she crept up Randolph Street and approached the apartment building where Thaddeus and Julep lived. The narrow entryway forced her to lower herself to her legs and funnel the tentacles through before her as she padded across the thin tiled entryway.

So far, nobody. She was alone and probably the better for it.

Walking had become unnatural for her. The cold tile seemed to sap the energy from her feet, and the tentacles changed from her allies to her enemies as she struggled to keep them under control and from dragging across the floor. It was an awkward shuffling walk that carried her to the elevator door. She pushed the button and waited, tapping her foot as she did that fateful day that her sister had gone missing, waiting for the slow elevator while endless thoughts paraded through her mind.

The door slid open, and the first thing that Margie saw was a little head of blonde hair surrounding eyes as wide as golf balls. Margie smiled at the girl-child with her eyes as she stepped through, one bare foot slapping behind the other.

The child didn't smile back. She also didn't run screaming away.

"W...what floor?" the child asked as she stared unapologetically at Margie.

"Freessddd," Margie replied. Her lack of a mouth made it

difficult to form words. One angry tentacle tried to lash out toward the girl, making the girl a target for Margie's failings, but Margie stopped it inches from the girl's face. Margie redirected it toward the number pad and slammed it into the number four. The girl backed slowly toward the far wall of the elevator.

"Are you okay?"

Margie nodded affirmatively at the girl.

"That's an amazing costume," the girl said. "Do those hurt? How do you keep them on?"

Instead of answering, Margie turned toward the door and away from the girl, watching the lights flash by. One… two…three…

"Bye, miss," the girl said, finally relaxed enough to smile back.

Margie nodded back over her shoulder and stepped through the opening. She crossed the hall from the elevator to follow the hallway around in a giant circle before she came to the door of her lover's home. *Her* lover, she reminded herself. Not Julep's. Julep didn't know how to treat a man, and besides, *she* was the one carrying his child, not Julep. Mother's right made Thaddeus hers, no matter what Julep thought.

The ceiling was higher here in the hallway, so she gave up her awkward padding to the more comfortable silent floating, using her tentacles to suspend her in the air. When she arrived at the door, it only took one tap with one of her appendages to cave it in on itself. She pushed through the opening to find the couch folded over on its side and white stuff covering the furniture (feathers?). It was as though Thaddeus had gotten in a fight with a down pillow.

She tried to imagine the pain he'd felt losing her, his one true love. He must have been tortured. No longer. She would find him and take care of him. Together they would be a family.

"Who's there?"

It was his voice, only not his voice. It found its way into her head, but her ears detected nothing. She felt pain in it, deep pain, as though the bottom had fallen out of his soul.

"Me," she said with a thought, following the tug toward where the voice had originated. She passed the caved-in ceiling.

"Don't come in," he said to her. She detected fear mixed into his words.

"I'm here for you, lover," she responded. *"Our child, our beautiful child, will be born. He will need you."*

"He?"

She smiled inside as she crossed the room. Margie had no idea whether it was a boy or a girl, but she knew Thaddeus. A little boy would be precisely the thing to cement him back into her life.

"Don't," he repeated, causing her to stop short of the bedroom door. *"You need to understand—"*

She shoved the door open. There, lying on the floor, breathing shallow, thin breaths, lay her sister Julep. Rage built up inside of Margie as she scanned the room. First, she didn't see him. It may have been willful, but she'd looked right past him. Only after a second pass did her eyes and mind finally register the hulking snake-man before her.

"Where is Thaddeus?"

"Margie?"

She looked at his eyes, examining them closely, seeking him in there. She couldn't find him. All she saw were the cold yellow-gray eyes of a monster, which made her wonder what he saw her as at that moment. Did he see Margie, or did he only see a tentacled freak? One of her stray appendages bumped against her sister's form, and the tip immediately opened as its only ambition to feed brought it back to life. Margie barely felt the impulse in time to stop the wayward appendage from plunging into Julep and consuming her as she had the army of rodents.

She cursed herself for the decision. The world would surely be better off without Julep Hode. When Julep moaned, two of Margie's tentacles flew toward her, and this time Margie did nothing except await the blissful sweet flow of nutrients from one life force into her own.

Thaddeus stopped her. He threw his body between them, and Margie's assault fell impotently against the scaly armor of his broad shoulders. Then he squirmed uselessly against his bindings.

Bindings? Retracting her tentacles from their initial attack, she used two of them to lift him from her.

"*Get away from her,*" she hissed at him without speaking. She launched him across the room and into a far wall where the stucco shattered behind him. Broken pieces of the chair he'd been affixed to showered down to the floor, and she realized that in her fury, she'd set him free. With strands of tape and wire hanging down from him, Thaddeus rose on his (snake tail?). Margie cut her attack short. This wasn't her Thaddeus. How could she not have realized that?

"*Stop. You don't understand what's happening, Margie. We need to get a doctor.*"

"*Who are you?*"

"*This is me, Margie. And she used to be a monster like me too. But look at her now. She's human again. I did that. Me.*" While he was speaking, he peeled away pieces of severed duct tape off his spikes and from his tail. Then, he uncurled his tail and arched his back into a crackling stretch. "*I can do it for you too.*"

"*How?*"

The mop of fingerlike tentacles that hung from his lips like an eel-infested mustache lifted all at once. In response, she settled down on her rickety feet and then floated like a body halo around her, all aimed in one direction.

"With these," he said, stretching the tendrils on his face toward her. He was too far away to reach her. *"But that's not all they did. Her breathing is so faint, Margie. I'm afraid she might die, and I've been tied to that chair, forced to watch as Julep's life fades away. Thank God, you showed up."*

God had nothing to do with it. Margie's heart seized in her chest, and she felt her eyes—her pathetic still-human eyes—begin to moisten while the knowledge sunk in. Thaddeus had never had any intention of being with her. In the last five minutes of the conversation, he hadn't asked once about *her*. His only concern was for Julep, the soft mass of human flesh lying atop a mound of discarded feathers: feathers the same colors as the ones in the destroyed living room. Margie made the connection in her mind.

"She was a bird? She'd turned into a bird and fought you, didn't she?"

"Jealousy brought her to this, Margie. It wasn't her fault; it was mine. You too. I don't know how, but it must have been me that brought this upon us all. I should never have been with you."

Margie slipped two tentacles under Julep's unconscious form and lifted her by the arms into the air.

"This is what you wanted? This fragile thing?"

"She was strong enough to beat me."

Defending her. Of course, he was. He didn't have a real understanding of the cruelty that Julep had always heaped upon her. Sure, Margie had explained their lives together, how Julep's insistence on being the one who got the most attention had kept Margie locked into a lifetime of second places. Margie had told Thaddeus how Julep had perfected cruelty with a smile at Margie's expense. Hearing about it and living through it for nearly thirty years were two different things.

It was an unfortunate moment for the baby to kick.

The force of the kick teetered Margie backward on her unstable legs. Her arm clutched her abdomen, and she felt the rage mount again inside of her. This thing inside her was *his* child, his and hers, and for so long, she'd thought it a love child. No love had created this thing that was likely an abomination like her. This creature inside of her had been created from lust and lies, and self-deception. One of her tentacles balanced her before she fell, and she spiraled Julep's form to the left, neither toward Thaddeus nor away from him, but toward the bedroom window. Whether she could have Thaddeus or not, Margie would be free of Julep.

Stabbing pain pierced her gut as the body sailed from her grip. Margie bent over onto what would have been all fours had it not been for the tentacles that still held her aloft. She felt a clenching in her belly and a body-racking pain that started at her tailbone and spiked up her spinal column. For three seconds, she couldn't breathe at all. Then, slowly, the pain diminished, sapping with it her energy. Margie worked her way into an upright position on her tentacles. She was covered in sweat again, or whatever that oozing stuff was that leaked out of her pores when she was agitated. Her eyes skipped toward the window, which she'd expected to be shattered. Somewhere below, Julep's broken body would be on the sidewalk.

The window was still intact. Not so much as broken glass on the floor. She searched the room only to find her sister's body wrapped up in Thaddeus's tail. He'd saved her from being knocked through the window as Margie had intended. She hissed in anger.

Thaddeus's voice came into her head. *"Come to me, and I can turn you back. I know I can."*

And make her weak again. She knew better than to believe his motives. There was no concern for her in his heart. He had only room for one person, who was curled up in his snake tail for protection.

She could fix that. With a scream, Margie directed all of her tentacles that no longer supported her weight at Thaddeus. He couldn't possibly fight all of them at once, and she recognized her advantage. He slapped two of them away before she wedged one into his tail. The tip of this tentacle could sense her sister's body only inches away. Focusing all her energy, she forced it forward, flexing it against his powerful tail. She understood that she could crush him. When he discovered that he couldn't protect Julep, he would wither like the parasitic weed he was. She could almost taste the flesh, and her body quivered with excitement.

Another jolt of pain from her abdomen. She wrenched over, and every single one of her tentacles pulled back around her, forming something like a protective shroud. This time the pain held her for ten seconds, then twenty, then thirty before releasing. When the pain ebbed enough for her to see clearly again, she was alone in the apartment.

It didn't matter anymore. Thaddeus didn't matter, nor did her cruel sister. Margie knew what that pain was now, and something in her broke at the realization. The only pain so crippling yet that didn't kill had to be one thing; her child was ready to come into the world. This lifted her heart as she felt the sweat run. Her child would be fierce, like her, as he should be to come into a world so cruel as this one. And she would teach him the lesson she'd learned far too late, only the strong thrive. Her child would be the strongest.

The pain came again, so severe this time that it felt like her insides were ripping apart. Even her tentacles, in their defensive posture, couldn't maintain their makeshift shield. She collapsed to the ground with her appendages falling around her and a sickly smile scratched into her face.

Yes, her child would be *feared*.

CHAPTER 18
BAT MAN

ARISTIDE'S great wings pounded against the moonless night sky. Stars shone like floating dandelion seeds before an oil field on the horizon. Beneath, the highway wound like a snake through the foliage. The only movement he saw was a speck against the blacktop that skittered from one side of the road to another, from the cover of a fir tree to the broad top of an oak. He blinked and stared harder. To his amazement, Aristide's field of vision zoomed in, pulling the road up to him. Then, the movement again as something broke out of the brush. Aristide's jaw dropped open. He shifted Evian in his arms to move her straying hair from his view.

Down below, Tam sped along the highway on her arms and legs with the assistance of two other arms that jutted out of her side just behind her rib cage. The speed at which she traveled almost matched his airspeed. As he followed the road around, so did she. He turned left, and she followed left. He turned right, and she did the same. Aristide wasn't confused about that. Tam was tracking them like he'd tracked deer in the East Texas woods.

Suddenly, a horrified scream echoed out into the night.

Evian's body came to life, squirming so much that she almost wiggled free of his clutches.

"Hold on," he told her in a new voice that sounded more like a growl than speech. But she seemed to understand as she stopped struggling. "It's me, Evian. Aristide."

She immediately pushed against him again.

"Stop, Evian," he commanded. This time the difficult words formed as he over-annunciated to mold the growl into something useful. She stopped, and he took a handful of seconds to look down into her wide, wild eyes. "It's me."

"Aristide?"

With the realization, she wrapped her arms around his neck and her legs around his waist, holding tight to him, much to his relief. Flying wasn't so difficult; he'd learned that most of the work was gliding. Up a couple of wing beats, then coast, up then coast. Her limp form, however, had begun to tire his arms. As she relieved him of the work by holding onto him, he felt how tired they had become when a burning sensation spiked up his arm and ebbed.

"It's me, yeah," he said.

"You're not wearing any clothes."

Aristide laughed so hard that both of them nearly plummeted to their deaths. He beat his wings again and lifted them higher. Tears of joy streamed from his eyes along his cheeks. Damn, it felt so good to laugh in the face of all they'd just gone through. Aristide caught her eyes with his own and saw her smile. He had no idea what his face looked like after the change, but if he did look like a hideous freak, she didn't betray it in her endearing eyes. He squeezed his arms around her and pulled her more tightly into his embrace.

"We can stop at Neiman Marcus when we get to Shreveport," he said. The higher he went, the farther behind Tam seemed to fall and the farther ahead he could see. Aristide took a deep breath and lifted again, ascending another ten feet, before he noticed that Evian shook violently against him.

"Aristide." She exhaled in a thin gasp. "Can we go lower, please?"

He dropped again, ten feet, twenty, before she finally stopped shaking. They were too low. Tam had no trouble keeping up below them at this height.

"Are you okay?" he asked.

"I think," she said. "I couldn't breathe for a second. The air, it was like it didn't have enough air in it, if that makes sense. And it's so cold."

He hadn't even noticed. However high he ascended, it was all the same to him. The air seemed a perfect seventy-five degrees though he knew logically that wasn't the case. And his lungs had no problem securing what they needed from the thin atmosphere. His eyes dropped to the ground again, and sure enough, there was Tam, relentless in her pursuit.

"What?" Evian asked.

"Nothing."

"Don't say that. We're too close for that. I'm clinging to you while we're flying across the night sky after…well, I'm not exactly sure what happened, I guess. I remember being attacked by something gross."

"Tam," he said. "And since you asked, she's been tracking us along the highway. I can't seem to lose her. She's like a spider or a cockroach down there. I mean, if one of those could move at over a hundred miles an hour."

"But you can fly. Can't you leave the highway? She can't possibly move that fast in the woods."

She didn't seem surprised that Tam could keep up with their airspeed. Aristide chalked it up to all they'd experienced. If a banshee materialized on the horizon, neither of them would bat an eye. The impossible had suddenly become possible and even the likely.

"I don't know North Carolina well enough," he said. "Do you?"

"If I can just…"

She twisted in his arms, and he worked to let her, unsure what she was trying to do. Evian worked her legs from around his back.

"Don't let me fall," she whispered into his ear. He grunted and clasped his arms around her. She twisted her entire body around so that her back was to him. For a second, Aristide worried about her modesty as he clutched at her to secure her torso to him. He managed to pull one arm around her shoulder and another around her sternum and then wrapped his legs around her thighs to keep her close. She fished through her pocket with her left hand and pulled out a phone.

There she froze, with her right hand clutching his arm and her left holding her phone. He couldn't see her face, but he knew that she was likely seeing the ground for the first time. She twisted her head sideways.

"Don't let me fall," she reminded him. She dropped her right arm to hold the device in one hand while exploring her navigation app with another. Then, she pointed toward dense vegetation off the right of the highway.

"That way," she said. "Woods for a while, then there's a lake. If the woods don't slow her down, the lake will do it." She patted his forearm that held her shoulder. "Are you okay?"

The burn was back in his arm, but this time he was using his legs too. He wouldn't drop her.

"Yeah," he growled. "I'm fine."

The foliage passed beneath them. At first, Tam managed to keep up. The treetops swayed as she exited the road in the same direction and seemed to continue for some time. When they continued, the moving trees fell farther and farther behind until it was only the two of them and the clear night sky. As the intensity of their escape dissipated, Aristide found unpleasant thoughts flooding back through his mind. He grasped Evian tighter, his only link to humanity and the only person in the entire world who could see him still as Aristide.

"I'm thinking we must be going almost two hundred miles per hour up here," Evian said, still staring at the tiny dot on her screen as Aristide watched the horizon. "It'll take about four hours to get to Natchitoches from where we were on the highway, according to this navigation app."

"If there is a Natchitoches," Aristide commented, letting his despondency get the better of him.

"What do you think happened in Charlotte?"

"Besides Tam?"

He didn't imagine the shudder that went through her body.

"Besides Tam," she agreed. "Unless you think Tam was enough to kill all the power in the city?"

"She could have," Aristide said. "But she was trapped in the garage. And she didn't do that to herself."

"You think there was another one in the city?"

"Are you sure you want to know what I think?"

She swiped across the screen. A half-second later, she nodded.

"I think that there are hundreds of them in Charlotte. A little scratch is all it took to cause this, and it probably didn't take much more than that to infect Tam. From what we've seen, the mutations could be almost anything. So far, we've seen spider-woman, lizard-woman, and octopus-woman mutations."

"And batman," she said, tapping her fingers gently against his forearm. "Why so many more women than men?"

He shook his head.

"I'm not sure," he said. "It took a long time for me to change, though. Maybe it just takes longer for men to change."

"You're drifting," she told him. "It's more to the right."

Aristide changed direction following Evian's instructions.

"There. Perfect," she said.

"Natchitoches?" he asked. "Not sure what you mean by perfect. I heard the place was a fork in a river."

"It's more than a f…fork," Evian stuttered.

He pricked up his ears. A slight misspeak, that was all. It didn't have to mean that Tam's attack had poisoned Evian's blood as it had his. And even if it had, Evian hadn't been scratched. For all he knew, Tam's only real action had been as a catalyst to his already infected body. The words he used in his mind to convince himself fell short, especially when the question loomed unanswered still in his mind. Why so many more women than men? But he was a Marine, and Marines solved problems, not created them, and definitely didn't think too hard about them. So he kept his mouth shut on the inflictions that she pretended not to notice.

"Really?"

"A *big* fork," she said. "And one of the first major engineering projects of the Army's Corps of Engineers. Before the river diverted, all trade down to New Orleans used to flow through the Red River. My family's b…been there since before the eighteen hundreds. There's a lot of old money still hidden away in there from the plantations and the Metoyers."

She shrugged against his chest. It was less a shrug than a repositioning, a way to pull her injured shoulder away from where it pressed into his pectoral muscle. Aristide loosened his grip slightly.

"Did you think this would be where we would end up?" he asked, staring at the far horizon, trying to divine the future. "Really. What did you think when you saw me in the bus station in Triangle?"

"I thought you were cute," she admitted, settling into him. "I thought you were funny, and you're a Marine, so of course, I imagined what you'd look like in one of those uniforms."

He chuckled. Other Marines in his unit had less to say

about anything, even the ones who grew up where he did. She wasn't wrong that they'd let pretty much anyone in. Anyone who could shoot or run had a future in the USMC. That was part of the reason he was admitted.

"I failed out of college," he told her, taking a slow glide to ease his cramping wings. "Twice. Once at Texas A&M and once at the University of Texas. My dad thought I was going to end up living in the streets."

"And look at you now," she said.

"Yeah," he replied as he resumed flapping. "Look at me now."

An awkward silence lay between them for a few seconds.

"I didn't mean literally look at you," she said. "I mean, you're in the Marine Corps. You've saved my life, and from your stories, maybe a couple more. Oh, and that's twice you saved me, remember? I'd say you're doing all right for yourself."

"If you don't count the fact that now I'm a hideous bat-person."

She took a second and what must have been a painful twist of her neck to turn her face up toward him. He gazed back down at her as well. It was easier than looking off into the distance, and nothing new came into his mind.

"You're not hideous," she said. "Your face…I know you c… can't see it. You look pretty much like usual. Do you r… remember that show that was on for a few years in the nineties…what w…was it? *Gargoyles*? You look like that. Only you're not blue or red or orange. Mostly stone gray, I guess. The main difference is that you're about twice as big, and you now have wings which, under the circumstances, have been pretty damn convenient."

As he peered into her blue-green eyes, he found himself drawn in, speechless. Her cheeks flushed. Evian turned her face back down toward where the trees passed by.

"What about me?" she asked. "What did you th…think?"

The stuttering had noticeably worsened, and she hadn't so much as a lisp before. Whatever Tam had done to her was having some effect, even if her face and body didn't seem to show it yet. Things were changing under her skin. And the way her body tensed every time she stuttered told him that she knew more than she let on about what had happened to her.

"I thought you were pretty enough," he said.

"Pretty enough for what?"

"I mean, pretty enough to talk to. Your eyes, your hair… that was part of it. And…"

"Honesty, Aristide. Did you want to know me, or did you want an experience you could brag about to your Marine buddies? Remember, I'm an Army brat, and I know your type."

That cracked his lips into a smile.

"Maybe at first," he replied. "But you…something about you. You're just so…"

"Interesting?"

"Weird. I was going to say weird."

"And getting weirder," she said, trailing a long sigh afterward. "By the s…second."

Beneath them, the tree line broke, and the moon reflected up at them from the surface of still water. The trees stood in stoic silence. Aristide swung over the glassy tabletop close enough to spray both of them with his wingtips striking the water's surface. Evian laughed and pulled her arms up in front of her face. It was just them and the night, and none of the worries saturated the silence of the evening. But it only lasted a second.

"I'm changing, Aristide," she said in a low voice as she wiped spray from her forehead. "I can f…feel it. It's already taking my voice."

"I know," Aristide told her. "With any luck, we can get you

to Natchitoches before the change."

"I don't know if we should," Evian told him. "I know I argued with you earlier, but this change…there's so much to it. I can feel a hunger growing, something pulling me, something that I'm afraid if it continues…"

Her words trailed off into nothing. Another second passed before he felt something sharp digging into his chest. Aristide squeezed her even tighter and pulled back up into the sky to gain time, beating his wings hard enough to feel the heat of muscle pain in his back. Faster and higher, they climbed, and more and more, she pressed forward against his arms as the now multiple prongs dug into his chest. Aristide had no choice but to loosen his grip as her body began to contort and elongate.

"Breathe, Evian. You'll be okay."

"N…no, I won't," she replied. Dampness spattered against his forearm as they rose.

"We're so close now."

"You're a sweet m…man, Aristide," Evian replied. "A s… sweet man."

They hovered over the lake as she said it. Something about her words felt like a goodbye. Aristide clutched her harder, holding on to what seemed like less and less of her even as she grew heavier. Her chest shrank under his grasp, and she wriggled in a strange motion that worked through her entire body. The motion became increasingly violent until his grip finally slipped, and she plummeted from his arms.

Aristide dove after her, spinning and pressing his wings to his back to speed up to catch her, but he was far too slow. As she fell, he caught sight of her elongated body that trailed out and her still human torso as she connected with the water below. He thought for an instant that their eyes met, and in that moment, just before she broke the surface, she reached for him. Then, she was gone.

CHAPTER 19
SLIPPING AWAY

THE THIN TABLET became Vivian's bane. It thwarted her in two ways. The first was that the stretched rubbery spikes that her fingers had become were difficult for the glassy surface to detect. She found that she had to punch multiple times, which revealed the second problem: her strength had grown so much that on one occasion she skewered the tablet like a marshmallow. Obtaining a second tablet had taken a series of promises and three hours of her associates talking amongst themselves.

None other than Neko delivered the new device. From the wide eyes of the lookers-on, Vivian figured that he was the only one brave enough to do it, a stark reversal of his earlier cowardice. Sending him as their liaison was an interesting choice, as Vivian could think of no one else whose head she would rather separate from its body. To her great credit, she showed restraint, far more interested in the tablet and solving her own dilemma before the time passed by which she no longer could. He practically threw the thing at her and then bolted back out through the man-trap. His bravery only seemed to go so far.

She flitted across the room to catch the tablet midair and clenched her teeth as the tablet made a creaking sound in her clutches. Willing her grip to slacken, she placed the device on the bed so she could hover above it and view the screen. She punched in her passcode *carefully* and watched the loading screen bring up the genomic research app. The label on the bottom conveniently read "Name: Vivian Purnell, Age: 24, Sex: Female, Condition: Global Mutagenesis, Cause: Unknown."

It wasn't unknown. The cause was that she'd been scratched by a spider-woman. During that scratch, something had found its way into her bloodstream. That put the cause somewhere in the vicinity of insertional mutagenesis or possibly aflatoxin-induced mutations, unlikely in itself unless Katie's modified body had also changed the aflatoxins to amplify the mutation potential in the agent. Vivian thought she could rule out the various radiations, as that would have also affected Neko, and his stupid ass was perfectly fine. Whatever Vivian had been infected with would have had to reproduce within her body, and would have had to be timed to make mutations that wouldn't kill her, and that would all work together.

In other words, what had happened to her was completely impossible.

Although...as she thought it through, chemical reactions could produce clocks within cells with the waxing and waning of chemicals in various complementary reactions. That would make the reaction quite complex. Her wings buzzed in excitement as she considered the possibilities. The infection's first stage would be small, probably copying lysome structure or mimicking red-blood cells or something else so that it could travel through the body undetected. Each could operate like a miniature time bomb, counting down until they explode.

So she had some ideas. But she raised her eyes to look through the glass walls of her voluntary prison out at eight agents including Neko, some of the smartest people she knew and they had to have come to similar conclusions. Proving it was the hard part. Ideas were the easy part. Anyone could design a vector to insert genetic mutations into cells, she knew. But if there was one thing that she also knew from her premedical school bioinformatics courses it was that the likelihood of a single random mutation yielding a phenotypical expression that didn't kill the host was extremely low, let alone widespread mutations that completely altered the genetic structure of the host organism.

Which is what she was. A host organism whose body failed in fending off an intruding disease vector. The long way to solve her problem would involve researching various databases for potential phenotypes that correlated with the expressions she was seeing. Next, she could cross-check those against her DNA to see which held. Then, she could start working on a vector to reverse the effect. That was exactly what she expected her coworkers to be doing, as it was very methodical and likely to eventually yield results. In one to ten years, if she had to guess, they would likely be able to accurately categorize *some* of her mutations. Only then could they consider actually doing something about it, and with a strange situation like hers, the clock was probably already ticking. There might not be a Vivian anymore by then.

As if her body intended to drive home the point, pain climbed up from her back to her shoulders. A loud popping sound echoed from where the exoskeleton sections of her shoulders joined and then something thick and wet oozed down her back. Vivian convulsed over the floor and writhed as crippling pain stopped her wings and drew her downward. She was on borrowed time, and she was the only one who seemed to care.

She could sense that something was wrong. The mutations, the scattered way they occurred. She could feel her humanity being slowly replaced by the desire for fresh blood. Her thin legs and exoskeleton were things of an insect. They were mutations that couldn't happen. What she'd seen of the data told her that the samples of her blood included insect DNA, specifically that of a mosquito. She'd witnessed Katie take on the traits of a spider, and then there was the lizard woman. And then the octopus-woman on the bus was an entirely different mutation.

As she contemplated, with her grasp of the science slowly slipping away, she found herself arriving at a new conclusion: the vials, whatever had infected her, were more than just human DNA. They had to be; otherwise, the global mutations would have ended with extra arms or perhaps mutations consistent with human deformities. To get working collections of genes into her blood would have required, in whole or part, all of the DNA changes required to produce a working insect. And for that, the vials would have had to be more than merely the combination of human DNAs. Home Sweet Awakenings, or the parent company, would have to have mixed in something else. Perhaps the human DNA was less interesting a reaction than human DNA mixed with that of other creatures.

Her speculation ended there, as the pieces jumbled in her mind and no longer seemed to make sense. She had been so close, she thought. She almost had it, and then it slipped away again.

CHAPTER 20
THE BAIT

ARISTIDE TURNED to do another pass over the water. If Evian had survived the fall, she offered no sign. The mirror-like surface of the pond remained unbroken once the ripples faded. It was as though the last several hours had been nothing but a bad dream and really, he'd only had himself for company the entire time. The thought tugged at him, but he refused to believe that no matter how fuzzy his thinking became. She had been there, and he'd been with her, and she'd helped him to escape from Tam.

Mostly.

Tam burst through the trees at the shoreline. He could see perspiration over her face reflecting the moonlight. The mutation seemed to be spreading faster now, as her arms had grown longer and thinner. When she glared up at him, she wore a smile filled with sharp, incisor-like teeth clamped together. Otherwise, he thought she looked still more or less human. He could believe it from the front, though he knew firsthand that it was a façade, like a human-shaped mask that she wore to deceive. Behind it lay a network of wormlike appendages of which he felt he was out of range. Just to demonstrate the point, she shot a small flurry of darts up toward him that fell well short into the water.

But Evian didn't know she was there. So if Evian had survived the fall, and even swam for shore, she would find herself face-to-face with Tam, who'd been a challenge for him even in his massive new form. A disoriented Evian wouldn't stand a chance against her. He wasn't certain whether or not Tam would attack Evian, since she had undeniably changed into "one of them," but it was a chance he couldn't take. One last glance at the unbroken surface of the water, and he was convinced. He had to move. To stay here would be to admit that he'd lost Evian, and then Tam would search for her and potentially find her. He gambled on Tam's vision being still clouded by darkness and that she couldn't see whether or not it was him alone in the sky, and cut back over the water to head north again, all the while glancing over his shoulder at the undisturbed surface of the pond.

Tam took the bait. As soon as he let his shadow fall across her face, she turned and bolted back into the woods in the direction that he'd gone. Aristide glided a few more feet, then took a deep breath and let it out in a growl. He screamed into the night sky a mournful wail that carried with it the pain and stress and anger of the last twenty-four hours. Then, with slow, methodical beats of his oversized canvas wings, he began the trip back northward. The burning sensation in his wings spiked with every wingbeat, so he flew higher and then relied on glides more and more as he cut across the night sky. Down below, the trees shook as Tam followed.

CHAPTER 21
COMING UP HUMAN

KATIE'S human senses weren't up to the task of isolating a monster fleeing a massacre. The main problem that she had was that the destruction had been so horrific, and so devastating to so many, that even under the cover of darkness through which a mostly sated Katie crept, there were far too many people at the crash site to allow her full, unfettered access. Odors assaulted her as she circumvented the area in a wide fifty-foot arc, hidden behind deciduous trees.

Human, human, human. Everything came up human. The people had all seemed to aggregate on the top of the overpass, as though Red Dress Woman had to stick to the normal human conventions of roads. Until her transformation, Katie had thought the same way. She remembered in spotty flashes that she'd looked up and down the highway for potential exits, not thinking of the simplest fact that the trees here were wide and strong and the highway wasn't so high for her in her new form. For this reason, and the fact that she felt it was probably best to stay out of sight, she ducked beneath the overpass, where she stepped one right foot down into an air puddle that smelled of the ocean.

Heavy salt and rotting algae caused Katie to stop and draw her leg back up. That had to be Red Dress Woman. There was no ocean within a hundred miles of the intersection. Of course, she couldn't be certain. But it was the first interesting odor she'd detected, and it led away from the scene, so she crept along after it.

She scurried over the roadway, careful to stay in the shadows and to protect the parts of her that still hosted fragile human-seeming skin from the rigid outcroppings of stone and pavement overhead, ducking from shadow to shadow. The smell grew in one direction and diminished in another. Katie followed the smell from the overpass into a dense grove of trees where the only way through was to follow a barely detectable animal trail that wove between them. The odor grew as she continued along the trail, until it became unbearable. She struggled not to choke the closer she got to the source. Katie's legs stopped her as they refused to allow her to move in the direction.

That was something she'd not expected. The idea that Red Dress Woman might be unapproachable. Katie's mind reeled as her body swayed as though it were intoxicated. She stumbled once, then twice, pushing forward through a wall of something intangible that seemed to be sapping her energy away. Her eight legs trembled and she staggered backward. Ten, twenty feet backward almost all the way back to the highway, and her strength began to return.

Again, she pressed forward, with the same results. Every time she caught enough of the odor strongly enough to follow it to its source, she immediately lost most body control, as though her body itself wanted to flee. Whatever it was that she oozed into the air seemed to be toxic to Katie. The thought hadn't even crossed Katie's mind to be concerned about it. But she'd hit a wall so thick with it that she felt instinctively that to proceed farther would be to cause her own death. She was just about to turn back when she saw movement in a clearing not too far from where she'd stopped. Turning to face the darkness, her vision crystalized around the motion, and she knew she'd found what she sought, whether she liked it or not. And it was coming straight toward her. Like her, Red Dress Woman skulked in the shadows, moving from one to another. And also like her, Red Dress Woman's mutation stopped at her midsection, as though she'd had her torso ripped off of her human form and sewn atop a mammoth-sized octopus body.

She would have been impossible to miss. Even searching in the wrong direction for most of the day, someone must have stumbled into the tree grove and through the woods to find this clearing where the woman hid. As Katie backed away, in the opposite direction to Red Dress Woman's advance, she saw something that curled her stomach. Red Dress Woman didn't simply slide her form over the ground. Bits of white bone fragments scattered when she dropped each heavy arm onto the earth. The unmistakable sound of skeletal remains crushing beneath her weight made Katie's mouth draw into a thin line.

What have you done? she thought, examining the ground between them to cement the knowledge that no, Red Dress Woman hadn't gone undetected by others. At least, three skulls grinned up at Katie from the dirt, if she reconciled her multiple lines of sight correctly.

"*Nn…n…ooooo,*" a voice, not hers, pierced into her consciousness. "*Don't look at me.*"

Katie stopped moving. She hadn't mistaken the intruding voice in her head.

"*You can hear me?*"

"*Don't look at me. I can't help it. This wasn't my fault.*"

Except then Red Dress Woman mis-stepped, and her form slid down what looked like a veritable hill of bones. From her times working on endemics, Katie knew how many bodies were tucked into that mass behind the woman. At least thirty.

One or two mistakes, maybe. Even the bus, Katie had been willing to forgive. In her own awakening fugue state, she didn't know for herself who she might have hurt had she not been alone. But this…

"I can help you," Katie said, even though fear clutched at her. The odor grew more powerful by the second with each undulating step that one of Red Dress Woman's appendages took in her direction. If she let Red Dress Woman get too much closer, Katie would be the first giant spider-woman skeleton tossed onto the pile. She backed up to find herself pinned against a tree.

"It wasn't my fault," the voice that Katie now attributed to Red Dress Woman sang again in Katie's head, but the woman added nothing else. She only repeated the words over and over again, like a CD that got stuck on a single track. Katie felt dizzy with the odor wafting all around her, and then she swayed where she stood.

"Back up," she commanded. *"I can help you if you back up. Don't come any closer."*

"They died coming to me," Red Dress Woman finally said. *"They died. They were dead. You have to understand. And I…I was so hungry."*

Red Dress Woman wasn't slowing down. Katie finally understood. Many of the people who'd searched for survivors of the bus massacre must have ended up exactly where she was. And the stench, which now held the underpinnings of ammonia, had been as toxic to them as it was to her. They'd died on their own, and she could attest to the powerful drive to eat. Raw venison still coursed through her insides, something she'd never have considered in human form and hoped she could one day live to forget. This could be overlooked, could be explained. People could forgive this once they knew the story.

Except it hadn't happened that way. Katie felt herself

swaying more and more violently as even eight legs were no longer enough to guarantee her stability. Maybe the first two or three were like that. But twenty to thirty? No. Some of them had been sought out, found in their homes, maybe eating dinner, going to the movies, or enjoying a hike in the wilderness. And Red Dress Woman had approached just as she did now, knowing full well the power of her presence.

Katie clambered backward, pressing herself against the tree, unable to think clearly. The world became fuzzy around the edges. In a last attempt, she shot her web up the tree trunk as high as she could, then swung herself up after it, clutching with her eight legs and two human hands, pulling as quickly as she could to get clear of the stink.

"*Stay away,*" she said again. "*This is no accident. I'm so hungry,*" Red Dress Woman said, not slowing her approach.

Katie had no defense. Human lungs had controlled entryways, and she could have closed her nose and mouth and held her breath. But her legs, her spider legs, never stopped breathing. As she climbed, she found herself in pockets of cleaner air, though, and able to think more clearly as long as she stayed aloft. Even with all the power of her tentacles, Red Dress Woman was unable to climb after her, it seemed. But once Katie was up in the tree, all Red Dress Woman had to do was wait. Eventually, Katie would have to come down.

Or maybe she didn't.

Katie examined the nearby trees where the thin ends of branches intermingled. She couldn't jump them, not trying to coordinate multiple legs at once. But she could use them and bind them together with webbing. Trying to ignore the continuing sound of Red Dress Woman complaining in her mind, Katie began her work of spinning webbing, creating an impromptu dome-shaped topiary from the tops of the trees. Once she was safely out of range of the paralyzing odor, Katie peered through the webbing at the sobbing form below.

"I work with the CDC," she said, unsure if that was still technically true as the question of whether a giant spider-woman could be employed at all was definitely in the category of questions she'd never had a reason to ask. *"We can fix you."*

It was technically more of a goal than a tautology, but it seemed to get Red Dress Woman's attention.

"You can?" Red Dress Woman seemed to ponder this a moment. Then, she stretched tall on her eight thick tendrils, using them like legs, and straightened her back, craning to peer back through the branches up at Katie.

"I think so anyway. I was part of the Biological Security Task Force. We deal with threats that could affect national security. To do something like this, change our entire body without killing us, would be nearly impossible to occur naturally. Someone did this to us," she said without moving her lips. *"That means we might be able to undo it."*

Red Dress Woman's shoulders slackened, and her face fell toward the mass of bodies upon which Katie had found her. Katie followed her eyes to the pile and saw a blood-red sash sticking out from the pile that matched the one piece of Red Dress Woman's dress that clung cluttered around her neck. Red Dress Woman wasn't going to come with her, Katie realized. The pile of bodies and the lingering longing look like she was searching for something told half the story. The other half Katie had already seen. In her mind, she recalled the videos of the bathroom door ripping off and the blood-curdling screams as Red Dress Woman in monster form tore through both friends and strangers.

No. Red Dress Woman wasn't going to come on her own. Katie had seen it before during the SARs outbreak. A young man, an international traveler, brought the disease into the United States, infecting who knew how many people. Worse than that for him, though, he brought the virus to his family in New Jersey. Of his large family of over twenty people living in the same home, over half were hospitalized, and three died. The guilt had turned the man from a jet-setting trend maker into a muttering fool who wandered the streets of Jersey for months before he finally stepped in front of a train.

"There's nothing left to fix," Red Dress Woman said, just as Katie had known she would. Katie saw a red tear trickle down Red Dress Woman's cheek. *"Everyone I love is dead."*

"You couldn't help it," Katie argued, clinging vainly to the hope that she could still convince Red Dress Woman to make the trip in. *"But you can help make a difference. It doesn't stop with you. This is spreading, and millions will suffer. How many others will die because the mutations kill them?"*

But Red Dress Woman wasn't paying attention to her. Instead, the woman had climbed back atop her perch of skeletons and lay her heavy tentacles over the pile as though she were trying to hide what they both knew was underneath.

"Why did this happen? What did I ever do to deserve this?"

Katie had seen that before too. People always wanted a reason for things, like being a good person or a wrong person had anything to do with contagions. Justice was an intrinsic human desire. But there was a cause, wasn't there? And with her mind still intact, Katie couldn't waste the opportunity to interview someone who, as far as she knew, was one of the first victims. Katie had earned her transformation by being spit upon by a lizard-woman. But how had lizard-woman changed? She might never know that, but she might learn something about Red Dress Woman, so she changed the subject slightly.

"Do you remember when it happened?"

Katie waited patiently for the woman to decide whether to engage. Forcing the conversation would only make her close up, and Katie would have nothing then. She couldn't bring the woman to the CDC involuntarily. Just being close to the woman was death for anyone around her, and *that* trip would be nearly impossible to make for a spider and octopus. Someone would kill both of them before they made it to Triangle. Or if that didn't happen, Red Dress Woman would definitely kill people if only by accident. But when Red Dress Woman stared at Katie with those green-gray eyes, Katie knew that she would talk. The woman took on *a faraway listless look.*

"My friend's wedding was in the community center in Triangle. It was all they could afford," she said. *"I remember Stan…"* She stopped and took a deep breath. *"There was this little necklace thing in the wedding gifts. It was shaped like a teardrop and glowed yellow and green. It was beautiful like someone had captured a star."*

"It wasn't yours?"

The woman paused. Katie leaned forward in anticipation as a cold breeze blew across and shook her in her canopy perch. She clung more closely to the webbing as she swayed, listening. Red Dress Woman started again, shaking her head.

"Nobody seemed to notice when I took it. I wore it on the bus," Red Dress Woman said. *"I mean, that was all we could afford too. The bride and groom were in the rented limo. The rest of us wanted to celebrate together, and a bus trip just seemed…fun, I guess. But we didn't get very far before my boyfriend, Stan, saw it. He demanded to know who gave it to me. He said the necklace was some sort of declaration of love, like it was from a secret admirer."*

"Was it from your ex?"

Red Dress Woman shook her head, her eyes never wavering. *"I don't know who it was from, and it wasn't there for me. But I couldn't tell him I stole it, could I? He was so jealous."*

"Did you see anything in the bathroom? Like a spray bottle, or maybe a capsule of some kind?"

Red Dress Woman shook her head. *"No. Nothing like that. I remember crying for a while. I know it wasn't glamorous, riding a bus from the community center. But he ruined it with his attitude. I took it off because I didn't want this memory scarred by our fight. I was crying so hard I dropped it into the sink. It broke there, and that made me cry harder."*

"What happened next?"

Red Dress Woman motioned to her elongated torso riding atop squid-like tentacles. *"You know, don't you?"*

"I suppose."

Katie tried to piece together bits of the story she thought might be important. Whatever was in the vial was part of it, or at least Red Dress Woman seemed to think so.

"What did the liquid in the vial look like?"

"I told you. Green, blue, yellow. And it glowed and swirled around inside the teardrop. It was beautiful and serene."

Glowing liquids made Katie think of bioluminescent algae, especially being shades of green and blue. But Katie was used to cataloging and investigating diseases. She didn't have the knowledge it would take to discover whether there could be a connection to Red Dress Woman's squid form and the substance. She thought there might be, though, and it was worth trying to track down.

"Did you see a note or maybe something saying who left the gift?"

This question seemed to stump Red Dress Woman. She paced around in a wide circle, scattering bones and emaciated bodies around her. The activity released the pungent stench of decaying flesh from the mound. Katie felt as though she should gag in response, but her new body almost became intoxicated from the smell. Her legs wanted to carry her back down, and her stomach grumbled at the promise of undigested flesh. That must have been the hunger. The promise of food overpowered the contentment the single deer had brought to her. Katie's mouth watered despite the overlay of the toxic fumes that would spell her death. She very carefully crept farther up into the trees, spinning more webs just to be safe.

"Home Sweet Awakenings," Red Dress Woman said. "It was stamped on the bottom."

Along with the words came an image, a tiny tear-drop-shaped bottle on a silver chain. Inside the bottle, slow-spinning fluid worked its way up toward the cork and down toward the wider base. This triggered something in Katie's memory. She went back over the day to earlier, in Thaddeus's condo with the smashed bottle against the solid inner wall and the mostly person-shaped hole in the roof. She couldn't be absolutely sure, but she thought that the glass might have looked the same.

It was a start. Just as she was about to thank the troubled Red Dress Woman and move on, Katie noticed too late that the Red Dress Woman had fixed two of her powerful tentacles around the base of trees that were supporting Katie's impromptu refuge. With violent shakes, the trees swayed independently in different directions.

"Stop! What are you doing?"

"I'm so hungry," Red Dress Woman screamed up at her if thoughts could scream. *"I need to eat. Now!"*

The trees shook harder, ripping her webbings apart. Katie clung to one of the treetops as it swayed violently forward and backward, threatening to throw her off. She knew she couldn't survive being in the fumes again. And she wasn't able to do anything about the shaking. She was destined to find out just how long she would last crushed in Red Dress Woman's powerful grips.

There were other trees.

She looked around as she flew backward and forward with increasing velocity. A fir tree very close to her swung within reach and then back out again. On the opposite side, a wide, old oak stood almost by itself. Red Dress Woman couldn't possibly make that one shake, but if Katie managed to get to it, she didn't know if she would be able to ever escape. She might find herself treed until the slowly building hunger forced her to take her chances with the creature that Red Dress Woman had become. But another question loomed in her mind: how long would it be before Katie found herself reduced to a need for food, whatever the cost?

If she didn't act fast, she would never find out. A creaking sound began on the lower trunk. It was a sound that Katie understood to be the sound of wearing wood as the tree trunk fell victim to too much flexing. The next time the tree came down near the oak branches, Katie sprang on all eight of her legs into the sky and landed among the branches. She felt one stab her in the side and three of her legs found no purchase, but five did, and she lay gasping aloft under the stars. That choice was made, but as soon as it was, Red Dress Woman moved her attention to the oak.

"You don't have to do this," Katie argued.

"Yes, I do. I do. Yes, yes, yes," Red Dress Woman said, as her speech descended into little more than babbling with the occasional "yes" mixed in. Katie saw that Red Dress Woman's mind was out of reach now. To Katie's dismay, the oak tree to which she'd freed herself was only about twice as high as the fir tree canopy she'd created, and the toxic air found its way into her body. She did the last thing she could to protect herself, carefully winding a web around her in its highest branches. Nothing to do now but wait.

And watch the stars. They dazzled her with sparkling whites and yellows and reds…colors she knew that the stars couldn't actually be, yet there they were. And something else was up there too. She wasn't absolutely certain, and her reasoning mind still tried to connect the pieces together. There was only one word that would describe what she saw: batman.

She waved one of her spider legs up toward the sky, and the batman spun around where he was, forming a low-flying circle like a vulture over her head. Then he dropped toward her like a rock, to stop and hover fifteen feet over the top of the tree. Massive, muscled, and gorgeous with his dark black almost onyx skin. She smiled weakly at him as she swayed on her makeshift hammock under his flapping breeze.

"Katie?" the man growled down at her.

Katie recognized the voice inside of the growl. She knew that man, and she'd fled with that man before. She searched for a name in her memory, and then she locked onto it.

She'd attacked him. But she hadn't known it was him at the time. Katie had awoken confused and disoriented and lashed out. She'd scratched at him, and…probably turned him into the bat creature before her. Katie still didn't know enough to understand how it worked.

"Are you in there, Katie?" he growled. "Any of you in there reasonable enough to work with?"

Aristide. She knew it was him. Katie nodded her head slowly.

"Stay away from my food," the voice came, floating up from the ground and settling right into her brain. Aristide didn't seem to notice. Katie wondered about that. Why had her voice been stolen and she been given this weird ability to talk with Red Dress Woman and Aristide could still speak with actual words and a mouth? Katie had lungs, attested by her breathing with them. She struggled in her toxin-addled state to figure out how to communicate to him all that had happened. Aristide alighted on a branch beside her, and all she could do was point upward.

"You want me to carry you out of here?"

Better than anything she could have said. She nodded twice. Without even a second thought, Aristide scooped his arms under her and rose into the air. At exactly the same time, two trees on the far side of Red Dress Woman's lair split, and a woman came through, similar to Red Dress Woman in the back, but her entire front was so intact that it seemed like an overgrown sea anemone had been stapled onto her.

"*Dinner*," said Red Dress Woman.

"Shit, it's Tam," said Aristide. "Hold on."

He flapped his wings harder, lifting her even higher over the trees while the two monstrosities did battle below. The last time she looked down, Tam seemed to have the advantage, and Katie couldn't help wondering if Tam would simply replace Red Dress Woman and add an octopus skeleton to the throne of bones.

CHAPTER 22
NEKO - TO GO

SOME OF THE words spoken loudly enough to make it through the glass walls made sense to Vivian. She strained to understand what should have been, for her, basic knowledge. One of the orderlies mentioned global genetic mutation, which she knew meant a successful mutation. Most mutations were either inert or killed the host, depending on where they happened. For a mutation to succeed, it had to play well with phenotypes—a fancy word for how genes translated into things like arms, legs, eyes, and other traits. She knew that if an ear, for example, wasn't connected to an ear canal, then it wouldn't work. If a lung ended up outside the body, then the person would die.

At first, it had interested her too. How had it happened that all over her body, all at once, several mutations happened in a way that didn't kill her. But she wasn't at all sure she was ready to say that she hadn't been killed yet. There was still time, and she was still changing. It might have simply been the case that she was in reality slowly dying. Now, though, her interest had changed to only one thing: how could she be cured?

Slow death was exactly what her body was telling her she'd experience if she didn't eat soon, and what it craved terrified her. She clenched her teeth and squeezed her eyes shut, focusing on more of the conversation buzzing outside of her enclosure, picking out new words since her mind had stolen away so many from her.

"Antigen," she heard, something that creates an immune response and antibodies. That was promising. If they were far enough along to even think about producing antigens that would be globally effective, then that meant they were almost ready to trial some. It would also explain the large wall of cages with rodents in them across the workspace from her cage. A spark of hope inside of her desperately tried to turn into a flame as she doubled over with hunger, before the next word hit and sucked her pain away. It was similar to antigen, but not quite the same: antiviral.

That meant one thing, her struggling scientist mind tried to tell her. It meant that they were more worried about transfer, most likely, than undoing. It also meant that her mutations could have been caused by a viral vector, which meant that her body could be producing more of the same, which meant that the likelihood of her ever leaving the glass cage dwindled by the second. They might be close to producing an antigen for her condition, but she knew how it worked. Transmission was far worse than any one individual, and being their main and only source of the viral vectors, she wasn't going to get the antigen even if it was a hundred percent effective, until after they'd milked enough of the viral vectors from her blood to continue their tests without her. They hadn't even begun that part of the process yet.

She tried to pop her back and lay down on the only bed on her side, careful to let her wings fall over but not touch the floor. Vivian didn't want to get them dirty. She blinked once, then twice, then tried again to continue her sleeping. It was nearly impossible to gain comfort with her exoskeleton digging into her soft parts every time she turned. Eventually, however, she was able to sink into a deep, dreamless sleep.

When she awoke, the stifling pain in her back told Vivian that the mutations hadn't stopped. She'd morphed again, and this time in addition to the exoskeleton that had grown over in a way that kept her perpetually in a hunched position, she'd spawned an extra set of wings and an extra-sharp desire to suck human blood. She'd tried calling her impulse other things, but at some point, she had to be honest about it with herself. The longer she waited, the more the people beyond the glass looked like glowing balls of light, and the more the thing in her mouth tried to force its way out toward them. The last human contact she'd been offered had nearly cost the low-paid orderly his life.

Worse than that were the mental skips that her brain took when thinking through the genetics problem that lay before her. She'd begun talking to herself aloud to help her think through the pieces, while her companions seemed to see her more and more like a caged animal than a human being. She could hardly blame them since her words sounded less and less like human the more excitable her proboscis became.

"Spider-woman scratched me, and I changed," she said. "Lizard-woman attacked her, she changed. Condo-man didn't change. The woman in the red dress…"

Something was missing; she could sense it. A more human Vivian would have been able to see it. It was right there.

"Got it all mapped!" Neko's voice called out in exuberant celebration, as though that exclamation mattered.

The tablet that Vivian stared at, hunched over, sang with a notification: genome complete. She tapped it as gently as she could, but it was still almost too hard for the device. The crack in the tablet screen widened. The device did accommodate and brought up her genome sequence. It was as useless to her as the partial had been. She turned her head toward Neko, and for a second, their eyes met. Then he shoved his glasses up on his nose and tried to fix his comb-over, and she realized that he didn't see her at all. Somehow, the lighting had changed, and though she could see out, the external surface of her cell had turned into a mirror. In anger, she launched the tablet against the glass and felt a slight satisfaction at his jumping backward when it collided.

Then, she noticed the crack, and her mind had something else to work on. The thin split in the glass was practically unnoticeable, except she'd seen exactly where the tablet had hit. A centimeter-long split in the glass begged to be amplified. These rooms were made for the dead or dying. The idea that a giant insect-human hybrid would occupy them had likely never crossed anyone's mind. The entire thing would shatter around her if she put effort into it. Having stalled in her research due to steadily diminishing cognitive ability, Vivian had to do something that wasn't staring at four letters repeating in random complex ways.

No.

She stopped herself. The first thing she would do if she broke through that glass was give in to her craving. It would be a bloodbath, and she wasn't even sure how badly she would feel about standing over Neko's lifeless body. *That* terrified her and kept her motionless, staring at the crack but making no movement toward it. She needed a plan if she was going to put all those lives at risk, and she had nothing. Nothing would be gained from leaving the cell. In a very real way, she'd reached the limits of her understanding. From the wayward glances of her coworkers, she'd lost any support she could have expected the last time when she'd lashed out at one of the people tasked with bringing her the tools she needed to perform the evaluation.

Vivian screamed with her entire body. It didn't sound

human, even to her. Someone in the far back of the room dropped what sounded like a coffee cup that shattered on the slick tiles. All motion stopped except the swivel of eyes in her direction. Vivian clamped her claw over her mouth, which she instantly regretted as her fingers had grown even sharper and sliced her cheek above the cheekbone in the process. When the taste of her own blood dripped down into her mouth, any control over her proboscis evaporated into nothing. Her mouth shot open, and a long thin wire-like tongue flipped out between her teeth and hovered in the air before her.

From that moment, Vivian realized the truth of the matter. These people around her were no more able to solve her problem than she was. The difference was that they had networks to rely upon, and they still all had the trust of each other, while the more different she became, the less trust they had in her. And anyway, the process they were using would take forever, and at her rate of change, Vivian would be a full-on monster by the time they finished diagnosing her. Her dual set of wings buzzed and lifted her off the ground, a great relief to the thin twigs that her legs had become. She let them do their work as they bounced her from wall to wall, back and forth, while she thought. One perhaps naive, perhaps stupid, definitely desperate thought possessed the back of her mind. One of the many creatures could change her back.

Her rational mind knew desperation when it felt it, and the idea was exactly that. But also, there was some reason for it. Katie had been infected by someone who had already changed, so there was the ability of creatures such as her to cause effective global mutations. It was as if that trait was preserved for some reason. That meant all the tooling was still there, the sneaking of the genetic change into the body, chemical timers for releasing complementary changes in tandem, down to whatever accelerated the genetic changes to force phenotypical changes so quickly. All of that tooling was in place. The only thing that needed to change—in the naive and simplistic cry for help that was her idea—was that the target "design" would have to be her former self, of which she was confident that as long as she could still think, some of her old unmodified DNA had to be lingering in her body somewhere. If it were her decision, she would have searched in the fat cells, inert enough to potentially not be modified by the new DNA and bacteria.

The more she obsessed over the idea, the more she liked it, which she partially chalked up to being needy and partly to her being out of other timely options. Excitement coursed through her, speeding her flight path from one window to another and back. One window, to another, then back again. One window…

She hit it too hard. The crack she'd started with the tablet exploded outward into a pile of shards on the floor toward where Neko and his coworkers had gathered to discuss some sort of results. Vivian looked at Neko, her proboscis extended, waiting for a little taste of her enemy's blood. Vivian shook her head to clear it. It was too fast, and her antennae had trouble following. Her skull pounded as they flopped in the opposite direction of her turning skull. In a ball of pain and fury, she took the opening. Neko glowed like an ice cream cone with a halo.

Vivian grabbed him, even as he stabbed his hands at her to push her away. It was the CDC, so the only people with guns were the building guards, and none were in the room as she carried her prize through the doorway and down an open hall. Workers scattered, and folders dropped to the floor as screams followed her through the building. Ground zero, in her mind, was Arlington, and that was where she would go—the man with the wife who'd disappeared through a hole in the ceiling. If there was a potential for reversal, she unreasonably thought earlier mutations might be the solution. If anything, it was a self-delusion, but one she was fully invested in because she was running out of time. Her mind was atrophying away, and the sad truth was that finding others was the last possible solution she would ever come up with.

With Neko screaming in her talons, his comb-over flapping in the breeze, at least she had a snack for the trip.

CHAPTER 23
BABIES ARE BLESSINGS

JULEP'S EYES OPENED A SLIT, just wide enough for light to make it past her thick black eyelashes into her retinas. What she saw made her immediately squeeze them shut again. As long as she kept her eyes shut, she could pretend that whatever had happened over the last several days had been only a dream, a perturbation of the natural that had only occurred within the confines of her tired mind. Cool air flowed over her, and her body shivered in its wake. *Her body.* She opened her eyes once more to see the trashed bedroom that she shared with what she'd thought was the love of her life. Only to find…

Her mind brought back flashes of what she'd learned. Her sister, the bane of her existence, the woman who always seemed to think they were in competition, had taken their rivalry to an entirely new level by fucking her husband. Julep clenched her teeth as she half-grinned through a grimace at her featherless skin. Her fingertips brushed over it, dry and a bit flaky in spots, slick with some sort of gel in others, but her skin was her own, and no feathers were present except in a pile on the floor beneath her making a nest that might have been comfortable except for the chill in the air and the two creatures she'd seen when her eyes had been open for half a millisecond.

Julep's eyes shot open again. Spiked shoulders and the tentacles that hung down in front of her dripped with what she knew to be *her blood*. Those belonged to Thaddeus, including the snake tail that swirled around between them. The way he looked at her held a tenderness that contrasted sharply against his recent attacks. Her hand went to her neck where prongs had violated her skin. No wounds, not even bumps. Aside from the groaning growl of her empty stomach, Julep was remarkably whole.

Something moved behind her. Julep pulled herself to her bare feet and turned quickly, but the skittering motion continued just beyond her gaze. As she followed with her eyes, she made a point to step backward so that she could continue to keep Thaddeus in her sight. Her hands immediately covered her body as she felt an embarrassment that she'd somehow not experienced as a half-human bird-woman with her boobs hanging out for all to see. Strange the bits of her that had died when she'd changed. It was as though the empathy and humility had all been drained out of her and all that had remained was the rage. Julep remembered the rage, how when her humanity had been stripped away, the only thing that mattered was Thaddeus's infidelity.

Something hard and plastic jutted into her back. Julep whipped around quickly to see that she'd collided with her closet door. She pushed her way quickly inside while she tried to ignore the quiet shuffling just out of sight. She pulled the door shut behind her and then slipped on a black sweater and some thick jeans, not about to make the hazardous trip to her dresser for any undergarments. Julep pulled tennis shoes over her bare feet, feet with toes instead of claws, and she squeaked in excitement. Her hand shot to her mouth as she realized that she hadn't said anything since the change. Dry lips creaked apart. Something that resembled a dying crow began in her chest and worked its way through her lips and into the world. It morphed into an unintelligible scream and finally into her own name.

"Julep," she shouted then clamped her mouth shut. "Julep," she whispered to herself. "I am Julep Hode of the New England Hodes. I am a human being."

The joyous sounds of her own voice, slightly deeper than it had been before her transformation and maybe a little chirpy, made her eyes water. She took a deep breath and pushed the closet door open again. She vaguely remembered a battle or something, Thaddeus versus her sister, Margie. Julep scanned the room quickly and saw little in the darkness. The skittering noise waxed and waned before her but she saw nothing. Thaddeus's eyes followed in the same direction as hers, so she knew she hadn't imagined the sound.

"Where is she?" Julep asked, standing as straight as she could and trying to intimidate the monstrosity before her with a furrowed eyebrows and an unblinking stare. She didn't believe how well it worked. Thaddeus shrank from her and only pointed to the far corner by the entrance to the master bathroom. "In there?"

He didn't say anything else. On the opposite end of the room was the door that led out into the main chamber and from there out into the condominium hallway. She could escape. She could make her way out into the night and…then only worry forever about being pursued by her sister. She couldn't live like that. Julep noticed that Thaddeus didn't move, and then she remembered why. She'd wrapped him in a rat's nest of bindings, and some still probably held. One thing she knew was that she couldn't handle her sister alone.

"If I let you out," she told Thaddeus, "you have to promise not to eat me."

He nodded, but what else would he do? Still, she did recall

that he'd saved her, so at least she could be reasonably sure that he wouldn't kill her, whatever else he had in mind. She tried to ignore the skittering noise as she worked on his bonds, wishing she hadn't been quite so thorough. Most had broken during the fighting, but the ones that held seemed firm when she'd tried before. Her finger control as a monster had been clumsy though, and the big knots were more easily worked out by her human dexterity. In seconds, he was free, and she now had two problems.

"We're not together," she told him, just in case. "This is a partnership of necessity. She's in there, right?" Julep pointed to the bathroom.

Thaddeus nodded.

"We have to kill her," she said.

Thaddeus shook his head. Typical.

"Restrain her? Surely *that's* okay for your little harlot."

He nodded, and he motioned with his hands to his facial appendages and pointed to the bathroom. She got it now. He wanted to turn her back. Thaddeus thought he was responsible for freeing Julep from her bird-monster body, and now he had a messiah complex.

"We don't know if it was you, Thaddeus. It might just have been time," she said. "After cheating on me, you want to *save* her? No. We *kill* her, Thaddeus. Nobody will care. A monster, self-defense, she attacked first."

And that spawn that she carried. There would be no more evidence of Thaddeus's betrayal. Then, maybe, Julep might let Thaddeus live, a grotesque disfigured being alone with no place in society.

Thaddeus didn't nod or make any movement that signified that he agreed with her about what should happen to Margie. Julep decided not to press the issue. Soon enough, if she remembered her sister's rage, the choice would be out of their hands anyway. Margie would attack, and then she would have to accidentally die. Then, she remembered Thaddeus kept a gun safe…but what was the code?

The sound of a giant rat scurrying caught her attention. Whatever it was, she would have to kill that too. Julep ducked back into the closet and reached up to the top shelf where the gun safe lay atop a pile of clothes. She pulled it down and ran her thumb over the scanner. Nothing happened, because of course she'd never wanted the thing in her house, and Thaddeus must have thought he was being clever by hiding it away without telling her he had it. He was a constant liar. She couldn't wait to be rid of him too.

"What's the number?" she called out over her shoulder. She waited a second for him to answer, then yelled again. "What's the number, Thaddeus? Yes, I know about your gun safe. How do I get in?"

Still nothing. Her heart pounded, and her head hurt behind her eyes. Rage filled her. Julep turned to reprimand Thaddeus for yet again disappointing her when she saw the tendrils near his lips fluttering wildly as though he were trying to speak. So he tried, at least. This subdued some of her rage. She pulled down the gunmetal black gun safe that was about the size of a breadbox and carried it to him.

That scurrying sound again.

Julep turned toward it, hoping to catch sight of whatever it was. In her mind, it was a rodent, and whatever lingered in her birdbrain secretly longed for it. That would have been dinner for her at one time. Julep bit back her sickness at the memory of gorging herself on the city's rat problem. This wasn't that. She could tell from the sound that whatever made it was larger than she'd thought. Whatever it was, it was about the size of an Australian Labradoodle. Once she had the gun, maybe she could shoot it.

He wouldn't give her the code. With his poor pantomime, Julep thought he might be saying that he didn't want Margie to die. At least, that was what she guessed from the frantic waving motions of his arms. She scolded him with her eyes.

"If you want me around after this mess, you need to get over her," Julep said. "Her and that bastard you put in her belly. She dies, or good riddance to both of you, Thaddeus. Nobody should have to go through what I've gone through. And she's a goddamn monster, Thaddeus. What's on the outside finally matches what was on the inside. We kill her. Now."

Thaddeus finally pressed the numbers into the side of the box to open it. As she approached to retrieve the box again, the tentacles hanging from his face rose and drifted toward her. She yanked the box from his hands and stepped quickly back with it before any of them could touch her. Julep pulled the Glock-19 pistol out and slid the magazine of hollow points in. In a single motion, she cocked it and held it, pointing toward the ground. Thaddeus stared at her with wide eyes.

"I didn't say I don't know how to use a gun, Thaddeus. I only said I didn't want one in the house. Follow me."

The skittering sound passed quickly from behind the dresser out to the bathroom door and in. That made her life easier, as now Julep could kill both creatures in one spot. It occurred to her that the sound could be from the chubby cat from next door. Whatever it was, she resolved to kill it. There would be no time for figuring out a friend from a foe once they got close. She would have to shoot at whatever she saw and be okay with it.

What if it's a child that somehow snuck in here while all the chaos was happening? she wondered.

"Shit," she said. Even she couldn't kill a child, and it would take time to tell the difference between a child and a monster. It was time that she didn't have. But she realized that she didn't have to figure it out herself. If she sent in Thaddeus, it was a good chance that he'd been compromised enough to eat whatever it was first accidentally. Julep knew how tenuous it was when the hunger took hold.

"You go first," she told him.

Thaddeus unwound his great snake tail and slid on it, albeit unnaturally. He seemed to have the basics of slithering as he wiggled his tail with slow undulations that moved his body. His spike-studded torso sticking up above it made the movements less graceful, and the phallus that was so much more generous than anything God had given him seemed to get in the way as it was positioned just beneath his torso and sometimes dragged against the ground like a giant slug that had latched onto where his privates might have been. It was a horrendous sight watching him cross the room and duck his broad shoulders into the doorway.

Julep heard a scream, blood-curdling and loud enough to shatter at least one window, and she thought possibly her eardrum. Then the sounds of fighting and two of Margie's tentacles punched through the wall, almost connecting with Julep's head. She ducked, and they sailed over her. Julep pulled the weapon up and aimed in the direction that the tentacles retreated and fired twice. Two large holes erupted in the plaster-covered brick, but she was positive that the bullets hadn't made it all the way through.

"Fucking hollow points," she declared. She'd need a clear line of sight to use those bullets. Julep rolled to the left as another tentacle punched through. If she played this game long enough, the roof collapsing on them all was a definite possibility. Her neighbors would hate that.

The thought of her elderly neighbor standing in the doorway of a destroyed apartment, slowly stroking that annoying lard-assed white cat of hers, made Julep laugh as she slid her back against the wall. Sobriety hit as another thud echoed through the apartment. The fighting was still going on, so if there was a chance that she could get her sister, this was it.

She summoned up her willpower and regained her feet. Julep stepped around the edge of the door, gun at the ready. The lights had been destroyed and her eyes slowly adjusted. Only then did she register that the sounds of fighting had died down. At first, she thought someone had won. But it wasn't that. There was still movement and too much movement at that. And that annoying skittering sound kept moving from one side of the blackness to another.

Julep squeezed her eyes shut, trying to force her eyes to adjust better to the black. When she opened them, her stomach wretched, and she forced down her sickness for the second time in as few minutes. The fighting had died, probably, but what was happening now wasn't feeding. Julep realized that she'd only been thinking about her sister in the abstract. She had the vague recollection that Margie had turned into a monster of some sort and that there may have been tentacles involved. Julep hadn't expected to see a woman's body suspended in the air hovering on tentacles that extended out from the woman's stomach as though something was attempting to pull itself out of a human chrysalis. And she *really* hadn't expected to see a snake tail wrapped around the levitating creature's atrophied legs. It might have been an attack, except that look…that look on Margie's face, especially when those wild, roaming eyes peeked out through the frills of the slimy mound of fibers that the woman's hair had become. There was joy in those eyes, and if she wasn't wrong, something that looked like ecstasy. What they were doing definitely wasn't fighting.

Julep raised the weapon. Margie's eyes went wider as Julep squeezed the trigger back and exhaled. Margie's head erupted into a red mist as three bullets connected. Then her body went limp. Thaddeus's snake tail found Julep then and the narrow end wrapped itself around her legs before yanking her toward the mass. Another scream, this time from behind her, and the skittering sound magnified, but she was too preoccupied to look for its source. The tail tightened as Margie's carcass dropped to the carpet with a thud.

Julep's eyes found Thaddeus's. He looked back at her with a guilty glance. Thaddeus seemed to change his mind about whatever he'd had in store for Julep, now that she was incapacitated. He lowered himself over Margie and let Julep go. Margie's body twitched, and her tentacles still moved. Julep planted another shot into one of the larger stomach tentacles as she saw Margie's blood-covered face appear.

Even Julep could tell the wound was superficial. She might as well have missed Margie completely. Julep lifted her arm to fire again when something the size of a small dog hurled itself over her shoulder and wrapped eight legs around her hand with the weapon in it. On instinct, Julep jerked her hand back and then kicked the thing across the room, only to realize that the thing, whatever it was, had absconded with her weapon.

The creature sidled toward Thaddeus, who held out a hand for it. Then, it climbed onto his arm and up to his shoulder. Thaddeus turned his face toward Margie as though she had said something, then paused while, Julep guessed, she responded. Julep stayed immobile, well aware that she was too far from the door to make it out amid these bloodthirsty creatures. Her advantage had melted away, and all she could do was watch. Thaddeus turned his face toward the creature, and his chin tendrils flashed out at once and embedded themselves into the creature's sides. Bliss was portrayed by the look on Thaddeus's face, and that must have been what he looked like when he fed on Julep earlier. A shiver went up her spine as she watched. The clawed arms and spider-like legs shrank and drew together, and the greenish tint of the tiny creature's skin changed, replaced slowly by a pinkish glow. A piece of exoskeleton peeled away, revealing more pink flesh beneath. Fifteen minutes later, the new pink body of a newborn baby contrasted against Thaddeus's gray-black skin.

Margie said something else. Thaddeus nodded and held the child out to Julep, with two perfect little arms flailing out toward her. He motioned for her to take the child—a boy, Julep saw. Not in a position to say no, Julep stood and accepted the child into her arms. He looked exactly like Thaddeus, and bitter anger and hostility rose within her as she realized why she was getting the boy. They had other plans. The two of them were going to run off together and leave her stranded to raise this thing she held. She carefully placed the unconscious baby on the floor between her and the monsters, trying to forget the image she'd seen earlier of…monster sex? She shook her head.

"No. It's your baby. You raise it," she said, resisting the urge to punt the boy right at the couple, who had so far not wholly disentangled themselves. Thaddeus nodded as though he understood, and Margie seemed to notice something was happening. Her octopus arms pulled back from Thaddeus as though he carried some disease, but she wasn't fast enough. He turned his face toward hers and, in less than a second, embedded all of his face tendrils into the sides of her neck. She went limp in his arms.

Julep could only watch as the tentacles detached and withered on the floor. Margie's belly closed up, forming back into the overexercised abs of a single woman dedicated to body maintenance. The tint faded from her skin, and her flesh tone turned back to the pinkish brown she'd been for her entire life. Her hair tendrils thinned back into hair. The transformation stopped with her hair, though, now damp and clingy and *black* instead of the dark brown her hair had been before. Besides the slight discoloration and the snake man holding her aloft, the Margie of her repulsive memories slowly emerged. Thaddeus dropped her body to the floor in a limp mass as soon as the transformation was complete. He let out a deep sigh and flexed his back. Julep pushed with her feet, sliding herself closer to the door. With luck, she could make it into the hallway before he realized that he was now the undeniably most powerful being still standing. As she slid, he turned his gaze upon her, making her freeze in her tracks.

He wasn't done. And that baby wasn't going to survive his hunger. Gritting her teeth, she scooped the baby up and locked eyes with Thaddeus.

CHAPTER 24
EVIAN ALMIGHTY

ARISTIDE STAYED HIGH. With Katie hanging down beneath him, strapped to him by webbing her body had produced and that he didn't want to think too deeply about, Aristide had no trouble gaining altitude. Unlike Evian, ascending higher into the stratosphere didn't seem to bother Katie at all. And, despite her earlier attacks, she seemed remarkably docile and focused as they traveled together.

Traveling might have not been the correct word. Aristide was careful to stay in a figure eight pattern, albeit a large one, somewhere above the unnamed lake that he'd lost Evian in. With two sets of eyes focused on every movement, he was hopeful that they would find Evian soon. Though part of him, a somber part, knew that from as the height he'd dropped her the likelihood of her survival was minimal. Katie must have known it too, even if she said nothing about it. Instead, she spread her great legs out in a wide circle to help ease the flight, which gave her a surprising amount of lift.

"There?" he asked, pointing down to where three concentric circles moved outward as though someone had just tossed a pebble into the brackish water.

"No. That's only a fish. Look at how it's moving."

Sure enough, more circles started and then more as the fish moved along beneath the water's surface. He stared at the circles still, though. Something bothered him. At first, he couldn't place it, but then it caught him and he nearly laughed.

"That's got to be her," he said. "Or a fish the size of a truck."

The circles were inches apart from their height, and even smaller in diameter. But he'd gained so much elevation that in reality, they were closer to eight feet in diameter, and nearly twenty feet apart. He could think of no fish that might be in any lake that got big enough to move like that.

"Going down," he said.

"No sign of Tam," she remarked. "I think we've lost her for good this time."

"Where she was, was good eating," he said. "Your CDC friends can do something about that, I'm sure. But in the meantime, she might just have decided to stay put for now."

"Either way, it makes it easier to find your friend," Katie said. "Are we going down?"

He nodded, even though she couldn't necessarily see him from her vantage point below. Aristide looked for a good tree close to the bubbles in which to deposit Katie. It was easy enough, as the trees crowded around the edge of the lake like children watching a bubble show. The early winter air smelled of rotting leaves and dead fish as they neared the water, even as high up as they were. It took three minutes for Katie to detach herself from him, most of that time using her still-human arms, though they were getting a little scalier looking as time passed. She nodded at him as he leapt from the branches and sailed down toward the water. He had time to glance back once before he hit the frigid surface and saw that she'd already busied herself making an ornate web. Then, he touched the water and slid beneath its surface.

Darkness. Whatever improved vision he'd gotten from his transformation was useless beneath the water's surface. He heard, however, something large moving toward him.

"Are you there?" he asked, only to have the words turn into a garbled salad as they left his mouth and died in the water.

"You shouldn't have come."

The words materialized in his mind, as Katie's had. Katie's voice had gone silent when he was two-dozen feet away from her. Which meant, if he did the math, that whoever was talking to him was at least as close as half a semi-trailer. He felt around with his arms as best he could, but water kept filling his wings, keeping his movement constrained to the area just around where his dive had landed him.

Aristide couldn't breathe. And he couldn't swim with his misshapen body. It only took about fifteen seconds for him to start feeling lightheaded. The worst was that he couldn't respond to the voice, which he knew, *he knew*, had to be Evian, and she was probably as confused and dangerous as Katie had been in the trailer "office" before. At the current rate, he had at least the consolation of knowing that the water would claim him first. Something slick brushed by his left wing and made him recoil.

"But since you're here," he heard the voice again, then a pain in his ankle as something sharp sank into it and dragged him down even farther beneath the waves. He kicked at it with his free leg to no avail. He couldn't stop his lungs from slowly filling with the black water. Aristide could hear his drill instructor laughing in his head, chortling and telling him that jumping into that lake with no plan was the stupidest thing he'd ever in his life. Aristide could think of several stupider moments, but his internal-drill instructor had a point. It wasn't like Aristide to take such reckless chances. Where Evian was concerned, Aristide had trouble focusing or he'd have at least had a strategy for escaping. There had been no forethought, so

when his descent came to an abrupt halt, he strained to see in the water what had stopped him.

Aristide felt it before he saw it. Beneath his arms and around his waist were the remnants of the harness that he'd been using to carry Katie. It had pulled tight and now held him up, despite the increasing pain in his left leg. He splashed around uselessly in the water until he found a thick, wiry rope that he guessed was a spider web. Defeated and soaked, he grabbed hold and Katie pulled him inch-by-inch out up into the treetops.

———

"She might be dead already," Katie offered as she worked to disentangle Aristide's wings from her webbing. Aristide tried not to wonder if the hunger that seemed to saturate his entire body was the same for her. Everything that moved looked edible, and he'd spent a lot of energy dancing in the sky before.

"She's not dead," he replied.

"Well, she's not here."

"I heard her down there," Aristide said. "Same as I hear you right now. It was her, but it wasn't her. I think she's the one who bit me."

"Bit you?"

"Yeah," he said, pulling his left leg up to show her. Just above the claw was a raised welt in the shape of teeth, only with half the circumference of a basketball.

"That's new," Katie said, as she reached out and touched the area with her fingertips. In the blackness of night, her body concealed itself too well inside the branches of the tree. She looked like a human torso suspended in the night sky, and had it not been for several of her spider legs working on the webbing that he'd confounded himself in, he wouldn't have known there was more to her.

"New in what way?"

"Her head would have to be as large as the front part of an SUV," Katie replied. "What must the rest of her body be like?"

Aristide tried to think back on whether or not he'd seen her change. Partly, he had. He'd seen her legs rip through her pants and mold together on the way down, stretching almost comically into what looked like the back of an eel. But he didn't remember what had happened to the rest of her. She could have turned into a school of piranha for all Aristide knew. He examined the bite mark again.

"Maybe a motorcycle tire. Not an SUV," he said. It was smaller than she saw it, which was an interesting fact that he filed away.

"Either way, if her body is proportional to those toothmarks, then she's at least as large as a small bus."

As if to answer their unasked question of how large Evian had become, the water's surface rippled. Circles pushed out from the center of the lake toward its edges. The moon reflected from the ripples like a flashing light as Aristide looked on. A second later, the water relinquished something massive. It was difficult for Aristide to make out at first because it happened so quickly. One second, there was only the smooth surface of the pond. A second later, ripples. A second after that, it looked like a mountain was pushing its way up from the water. On instinct, Aristide pushed his way back into the branches. He noticed that Katie backed down too, although he didn't like the way she looked at him. Aristide could only guess how quickly she could wrap him up like a stuck housefly, so even while watching the water, he kept Katie in his sight.

Though it was hard to resist gawking, Katie certainly didn't seem to hold back, even though she was a giant spider-woman. Following her gaze, Aristide knew why. As the water fell away, two giant wings expanded outward that dwarfed his by at least ten times. There was no other way to describe her than the word he desperately didn't want to use, dragon. Evian had all the markings of a dragon, down to the flickering red scales that covered every inch of her elongated and distorted body. No humanity was left in her that he could see, save perhaps the eyes, which were now the size of saucers but still held in their centers the blue-greens he'd grown so used to. Aristide wiped spray from his face as she shot up into the air. He tried to fly after her, but the webbing was too sticky and he'd still not worked himself completely free from it.

"Hold still," Katie demanded. He stopped struggling and watched Katie's legs carefully as they worked the webbing. Evian flew higher and higher into the sky. From her trajectory and their recent flight, Aristide knew where she was flying, Natchitoches, Louisiana.

"Evian, stop!" he yelled as the last bit of webbing fell from his legs. He pushed out of the tree and toppled left as his waterlogged wings failed him. Aristide plummeted through the treetops, falling and falling farther toward the cold water below. He flapped again and still nothing. His wings caught air a third time, though his flight pattern was rickety, and he almost fell back into the water.

As the moving air dried his wings, his flying improved until he lifted up and over the treetops, chasing after Katie. Then something sticky struck him, and his flight became jittery again. He looked down to see Katie hitching a ride with her web wrapped around his midsection. Two powerful thrusts and he cleared the trees high enough so that even with her in tow, there was no longer danger of collision. All he saw before him was a bright spot on the horizon where the moon reflected from Evian's scales. Aristide pounded the air behind him and set course in the same direction. A direction which, if he wasn't mistaken, was the exact opposite of the direction she should have been going.

CHAPTER 25
RULES MATTER

THE WIND FLOWED over Evian's thick scales, caressing her leathery wings with the gentleness of a lover. She was nearly water-free from the impromptu blow-dry. She glanced back over her shoulders that she still couldn't believe were hers. Each was larger than a desk and the power that went through them buzzed like a thousand bees. Somewhere behind her, Aristide was in pursuit. But she'd seen the spider-woman hitch a ride. There was no way that Aristide could catch her carrying such a burden.

And she didn't want to be caught.

She didn't have the craving that Aristide had told her about: that bloodlust that lurked just below his skin. In fact, her mind didn't feel different at all. Evian recalled everything with perfect clarity save the time that she hit the water's surface and then emerged again. That was a massive black hole in her memories, but otherwise, she was only Evian, the same girl who'd ridden the bus with her head on Aristide's lap.

She ran from Aristide for the reason that women had been hiding from men they love for centuries; she didn't want him to see her like this. The closeness she had felt and the safety of his presence were at risk if he did because nobody could care for a massive beast with scales that smelled of rotting fish. He wouldn't be able to handle it. He would try, she knew he would, but it was beyond anyone to do.

And she couldn't go home. Aristide had been right about that. Nobody on the Red River would be willing to accept such a monstrosity into their homes (as if she'd fit anyway).

She pondered what she was. Was she a dragon? She had the wings and the scales, but did she have the fire? How did a dragon go about breathing fire? Maybe she was just a giant lizard with wings.

It was a strange mental journey to go on. Evian tried vainly to shoot fire from her mouth. After all, looking like a dragon should come with all the dragon perks. She pursed her dragon mouth into an "oh" shape and blew. Nothing. She tried a guttural approach, a kind of mix between a forced burp and a growl. That did nothing either. Finally, she gave up and let her broad wings bring her to a coasting altitude far above the highway. She was much higher than Aristide could go with his weak wings and thin skin. Evian was a dragon, and she thought she could reach the moon if she really wanted to.

That was not what she planned to do. She planned to go back to Fredericksburg. She planned to do some clean-up. The monsters that she'd seen so far were nothing compared to her size and her strength. The lizard-woman was already dead, but somewhere there was an octopus thing that had almost killed her and Aristide both, and she intended to return the favor. And then…maybe hide. Find a nice abandoned sewer or perhaps slither down into Luray Caverns somewhere and build a lair there to live out the rest of her life in solitude.

Evian realized that *that* compulsion wasn't hers, and it wasn't at all what she really wanted. What she really wanted was to turn back. Her eyes watered thinking about Aristide before the bus trip that started all this. It'd been obvious to her that he was a Marine from the start, and not just because of his hair. The way he acted and the way he carried himself upright and without fear had attracted her to him.

Evian's eyesight sharpened as she flew. Darkness or light merged to become one and the same. To her, there was no difference between the abandoned town of Charleston and the vibrant city of Washington, D.C. that she could see in the far distance. Both were as clear as broad daylight to her. At her higher altitude and with more powerful wings, Evian took only about thirty minutes to cover the same distance that it had taken the two of them together several hours to traverse. It had been easier too because from her altitude she could see the roads laid out exactly like a map, so it was easy to pick the direction to travel in. She descended on the city of Fredericks-burg under the cloak of night and landed on the abandoned home of Greg and his poor lizard-woman wife.

She sniffed and rooted through around the brush, looking for some hint of the woman. Evian observed that she had come to the wrong place. But she picked up something new here. As her olfactory senses continued to sharpen, she caught the distinct trace of Aristide and her former self. Katie's odor was there too, from before and after the transformation. Then, there was something else. Female, she guessed, based on how much more similar the smell was to Katie and her than to Aristide. But whatever it was, the trail was slight and seemed to come to an abrupt stop where the truck had been in the driveway. She settled into the trailer to get a better sample of the aroma. Her claws wrapped around it and squeezed in the sides under the pressure of her weight. Evian could have carried the trailer off like a falcon with a fish.

The truck was gone.

Evian could see the tracks and could smell the woman. The vehicle had pulled from the lot and turned north. Splotches of scent still remained that Evian picked up on as she trotted down the highway on all fours. The occasional truck or car spun off the road as it approached her. Evian ignored them, focused on her prey. Her mouth watered, and her senses were at high alert, and Evian felt so very alive. A taxicab driver dared to try to pass her in the high-occupancy lane.

Fire leapt from her mouth before she knew she was doing it. The funnel of flames connected her mouth to the taxi, which exploded immediately. There were no screams. However hot the fire had burned, it had melted the frame of the car, and the man must have died so quickly that he probably didn't feel a thing. He might not even have known he died. All the better for her.

Evian stopped.

She was close to the city of Arlington now. She could tell because of what the signs on the road told her. Her mind was still mostly hers, and she was glad for that little kindness at least. Evian settled down beside the car and ripped the door out. The tantalizing smell of roasting meat made her mouth water. Yes, she'd lost control. Yes, someone had died. But now, that someone was well done, and it would be a shame to waste him. She lowered her mouth to the car and supported it with one claw while she ripped the roof off. Then, Evian found the man with her mouth and yanked him free, lifting him into the air. She lifted her head and opened wide to snatch him from the arc in which she'd tossed him. One gulp later, and he was gone.

She was still fine. No guilt, no pain, and she didn't necessarily crave more like Aristide had seemed to imply she would.

Turning northward again on the highway, she stared at a wall of headlights. It seemed that this close to Washington D.C., traffic moved every day of the year. Her actions had stopped the three lanes her massive body covered that went northbound, as well as the four lanes on the other side, including the HOV lane, in which some of the cars had done a full-on reversal and sped the opposite direction.

It wasn't her fault the taxi driver had broken the rules. He deserved to be eaten.

She saw others ahead of her, also alone in their vehicles beneath the clearly-marked signs that indicated HOV-2, meaning *two or more people per transport*. It was as though nobody had respect for the laws any longer. One quick flash and three cars burst into flames. One held a family, but they'd been flanked by lone riders, so she called it justified. And once dead, of course, they were all prepared for a good snack. She popped the lids of the cars open like oyster shells and slurped up their contents.

CHAPTER 26
THE GREAT ESCAPE

THADDEUS BLOCKED the door with his lengthy serpentine tail. Margie lay on the floor, her breaths coming in thin whispers as her naked shoulders rose and fell in the night's cold air. She would die of exposure if Julep wasn't allowed to at least put some clothes on her. She tried to lunge for her sister, thinking perhaps at the very least she could share body heat, but Thaddeus jumped forward to block her. She wouldn't make it to Margie before Thaddeus stopped her. It was that part that stayed Julep. She didn't know what stopping her meant. That, and the fact that she was conflicted about saving Margie and what that would mean for the rest of Julep's life, more pain and suffering.

"She's going to die," Julep explained, not so much because she cared but because he seemed to. After all that she'd seen, her goal had changed to getting the fuck out of the building. Thaddeus raised his hands toward the tentacles on his face and made a motion so similar to eating that Julep hung her head down. He was hungry and wanted to eat, and so far, all she'd seen him munch on were her and Margie and the baby. Thaddeus unwrapped his snake tail and extended it so that it not only blocked the door but trailed across the room behind her. She could go nowhere else except toward him, but he wasn't focused on her. His eyes were on Margie's unconscious body lying on the floor, probably staining Julep's carpet. She could see the struggle in his mannerisms: to eat or not to eat.

Julep prodded him on. "Go for it," she said. "Kill the bitch. I don't care."

Only she did care. Because she would be the next meal. She clutched the baby tightly to her chest.

Thaddeus didn't move. Julep barely dared to breathe as she watched the spikes on his shoulders rise and fall with every breath. Something was percolating in his brain, and she couldn't get in there to find out. Would he go after Margie? Would he decide that Julep would make a better snack? There was one thing that Julep knew for sure: sitting in terrified silence wouldn't get her free. She cleared her throat.

"You might as well do it, Thaddeus. We both know you can't resist forever and the sooner you're fed, the better we can talk this out."

He stared at her. The tendrils on his face waved at her like the arms of an air dancer. She cringed in disgust.

"She wasn't important anyway, lover. Margie was in the way of our happiness. It's okay if you kill her for what she's done to us."

Julep's only option was to keep talking, even if she couldn't tell whether the words were having any impact. A half-second later, just as she was about to embark on a soliloquy about how immature and irresponsible Margie had always been, and how she probably stuck a pin in his condoms to make sure she got pregnant (precisely the sort of thing her sister would do), Margie stirred. It wasn't much, just an arm flail that thudded onto the floor. It was enough to recapture the interest of Thaddeus's face tentacles. Julep breathed a sigh of relief that they weren't pointed toward her any longer. She resumed inching her way toward the door, keeping one eye on Thaddeus, who kept both of his on Margie. He began to close the distance to her sister's unconscious body.

For half a second, Julep felt a twinge of remorse somewhere deep within her body. Within that second, she got flashes of the life she and Margie had shared. This brief parade of memories captured the times when they were younger, and alone, and playing those children's games that always seemed so important. Hide-and-seek among the rafters of their not-quite-finished childhood home, an ambition of their father's and perhaps his only ambition. The two of them were motherless before they began to compete for all things, starting with his limited attention.

As soon as Thaddeus, in his enraptured trance, moved his tail from blocking the door, sliding forever forward toward Margie, her nostalgia waned. Julep blinked out two tears and lunged for the door handle. In one motion, she flung the door open wide and hurled herself through, landing and sliding painfully on her back across the coarse hallway carpet, baby on her chest and somehow miraculously still silent. Thaddeus's tail seemed more aware than he was about her escape, as the rattle-like tip flared up and chased after her. She twisted around and panicked as she misjudged the distance between her and the rapidly approaching tail. Thaddeus let out a scream that reverberated through the opening and down the hallway. Julep launched herself back toward the room, grabbed the door handle, and slammed the thing shut behind her. Then, she turned and sprinted down the hallway.

Doors cracked open, and Julep could see an occasional eye in the gaps, but nobody came to help a screaming woman sprinting down the hallway. She wouldn't have stopped anyway, though, as she didn't believe that any of those doors could keep Thaddeus at bay for very long. Her plan was to get out of the building and then…she slid to a stop.

To her right, the doors slammed shut almost immediately. On her left, one person was too slow swinging theirs closed, and Julep launched her body at the opening, crashing through and landing on top of her scrawny neighbor, who, until this day, she'd never even had an occasion to talk to.

"You can't come in here."

"I'm already in," she said. "Shut the door. Quick!"

He didn't move fast enough, so she pivoted, slammed the door, and then twisted the deadbolt. The man stood there and just stared at her. He seemed confused and disoriented, and slightly lecherous.

Julep sprinted past him. She heard the sick crunching sound of wood and metal come from behind her as she ran. Then, she heard the guttural scream of the man whose only contribution to her well-being was being overly curious and slow to shut his door. A trickle of schadenfreude worked through her chest, even as the scream abruptly stopped. Then she felt guilty, but not guilty enough to stop her dead sprint into the back bedroom. She slammed the bedroom door and bolted to the closet, opened the door, and closed it behind her.

Julep paused to listen in the darkness. Nothing. It was possible that after Margie and the apartment man, Thaddeus's appetite was sated enough to gain her reprieve.

Julep worked her hand into the closet door crack and pushed it open an inch. The room was still empty from what she could see, and the door seemed intact from where she crouched. If this condo was like hers, then the living room had a sliding glass door that opened to a balcony with an adjacent emergency exit. It would be wet and cold, but she could manage it even with the baby.

The child cooed.

Julep froze. She patted the baby's forehead, and that seemed to calm him. Scrunched eyes showed movement beneath the eyelids and impossibly small fingers clutched at the air. Deciding that he would stay silent for at least a second or two, she rose from her crouch and slid the door open farther. She ducked down, grabbed the baby, then crept forward and immediately tripped on something that she couldn't see, slamming her face into the floor though she managed to hold the baby aloft on bruised elbows. She stayed there immobile, lip throbbing and probably bleeding.

Getting to the living room, and then to the sliding door, would take her a total of about fifteen seconds, she guessed. Julep reclaimed her feet, sprinted to the door, and pressed her ear against it. No sounds on the opposite side. She pushed it open a crack and peered in. No movement at all. The door hung from one hinge, and she could barely make out the silhouette of a man against a white couch.

Julep took a deep breath and sprinted across the room toward the door. So far, so good. About halfway there, she crossed in front of the man's silhouette and found herself unable to move. The man's emaciated face looked as though someone had liquified his insides and sucked them out through a straw. Leathery skin clung to the sunken cheeks on the man's face. Is this what happened when Thaddeus attacked someone who hadn't mutated as she had? Julep wasn't going to wait and find out.

"Move," she muttered to herself. Her legs wouldn't listen, so she tried again. "Move."

Nothing still. She sucked in some air. The baby screamed, no doubt sensing the tension that worked through her own body. Something moved in the hallway behind her. She turned and saw something zip by, and it wasn't Thaddeus. Then, she heard a buzzing noise like a tiny helicopter or a drone. It got louder second by second. Whatever was buzzing was approaching the door, which had now captured her attention.

"Move!"

Her legs unlocked, and she sprinted toward where the

sliding glass door should have been. The buzzing sound grew louder and louder until it was unbearably loud, repeatedly pounding against her eardrums. She threw back the curtain and breathed a very quick sigh of relief before kicking out the doorstop and flinging the door back. Then, she jumped out on the balcony and slammed the glass door behind her. She turned in time to see something massive with giant mosquito-like wings slam into the door. Not Thaddeus. She turned to head down the fire escape and clenched her teeth as she stared down the empty alleyway and hoped the thing hadn't seen her.

CHAPTER 27
PIECES OF VIVIAN

HUNGER. *Hunger. Hunger.*

Vivian slammed into the glass again and again, driven by the pain in her abdomen that kept gnawing at her insides. It was unrelenting and growing second by second. On the other side of the glass was her trapped prey. There was nowhere for it to go, and she would have it, except…except…

The thoughts wouldn't come. She knew that the thing before her opened somehow, and she'd seen it happen seconds before, but her mind couldn't get past the hunger. Vivian threw herself at the glass, smashing at it with elbows and knees and her uncontrollable proboscis which had a mind of its own and stayed plastered to the glass. Vivian slammed into the glass again, this time with her head, but the entrance wouldn't open. Beyond it, her prey stared back at her with huge black irises and a frumpy pair of jeans in a sweater that was varying shades of gray with the words "Merry Christmas" plastered across the front. Vivian could read the words, but her mind wouldn't connect the words with any meaning.

Alarms went off as something moved behind her. She turned quickly, but it wasn't fast enough. Something thick as a tree trunk had already worked to encircle her and before she could lift off on her wings again, the trap closed. Vivian was trapped and whatever it was squeezed her tighter and tighter.

Her heat detection "saw" it first. Vivian experienced an undeniable wall of heat coming toward her in vivid relief. Orange and red flared up in her visual field like bubbles forming in a wall of lava. Before the wall could reach her, she felt a sensation like a handful of ice-cutters stabbing her face and neck, and then her body went limp. The last thing she remembered before she fell was the sound of slurping and the distinct sensation of some part of her leaving her body.

CHAPTER 28
WAITING IS FOR THE DEAD

THE WOMAN on the floor had a wide nose and skinny lips, exactly the opposite of what passed for beautiful in Julep's mind. She had a skinny body too, like she had some aversion to eating actual food. The only aesthetic that she had going for her was that her bust size was definitely larger than Julep's by at least a cup, maybe two. These were petty and strange things to be thinking, but Julep liked that she could be petty, for what little joy it brought. Her stray thoughts were a welcome diversion and something better to focus on than the fact that the wall behind the woman had just erupted into flames, prompting Thaddeus to drop whoever it was and slither away into the darkness like a cockroach fleeing the light.

Julep could feel the heat from where she was on the opposite side of the glass, so she knew that the room had to be at least a hundred degrees and climbing. She gritted her teeth, tightened her lips, and yanked the door open. A sudden gust of air passed her and seemed to call the fire forward. Julep ducked as a tendril of flame shot past her and up into the sky. With luck, she could make it past the woman and into the hallway, and then possibly to the next room so she could get out on the fire escape. It only took her four feet into the room to change her mind. The wall of flame burned mercilessly before her, and there was no way she would be able to get past it.

A small part of her tugged her mind toward the woman on the floor. Whether it was guilt for letting Margie die or if it was some tie to humanity being restored, Julep didn't know. She left the infant on the floor of the balcony and braved the searing heat to crawl across the living room. She grabbed the unconscious woman, now almost completely changed back except for the two sets of limp wings extending from her back. Julep grabbed a leg and began to pull and crawl her way back toward the surprisingly quiet infant.

It took the better part of twenty minutes to get the woman out onto the balcony. Once there, Julep's problems didn't exactly disappear. She was stuck on a balcony with a strange naked woman. From the sounds of sirens, soon, an entire police department would arrive. The woman began to stir slowly, muttering something about a "niko".

"You're okay," Julep told her, right before the woman retched out a fountain of what looked like blood.

"Neko," the woman said, more clearly this time. The woman opened tired eyes but otherwise didn't move. A tear traced from the corner of her sunken eyelids down her ear and splashed into the puddle of reddish-pink fluid that she'd vomited onto the balcony. "Neko…"

"Do those things work?" Julep asked, pointing to her wings. "We have to go."

Her eyes kept turning back toward the flame that worked its way across the condo ceiling. Eventually, they would be out of options. As an answer to her question, the woman's wings flapped once feebly. Then they flexed out and expanded to their full breadth and length, but the woman didn't move. She just kept muttering the same word.

"I don't know what that means," Julep said, trying to

wrestle the woman to sitting. The woman's red-lined eyes opened, and she seemed to be focused on Julep.

"Who?" she said. "Neko is…was…my boyfriend."

Julep thought back to the atrophied body in the condo, and it clicked what the woman was saying. Whoever Neko was, the hunger had gotten to the woman. She was uselessly ruminating, and Julep needed focus or neither of them would live through the next couple of hours.

"What's your name?" Julep asked.

"V…Vivian," the woman replied.

"Vivian, we have I'd say five minutes before that fire makes it out here. That's the fire escape."

Julep pointed across to the balcony next door, over twenty feet away. "So when I'm asking if your wings work, I mean can you get us there?"

"I don't know," Vivian said, then stared off into the distance. "Neko…"

"…won't be the only dead person if we don't hurry."

Vivian nodded at Julep and wiped from her mouth to her chin, then each side of her face, clearing away the tears that had flowed there. She nodded again. "Yes. You're right."

Just then, the alleyway was awash in blue and red lights. Vivian picked that exact moment to suddenly become bashful. She struck Julep's familiar pose, a pose from which she could definitely not fly, but could conceal most of her nakedness.

"Look, you're going to have to get over it," Julep said, running her hand through the tangles and getting snagged twice. "It's embarrassment or death, Vivian. We have to go."

That seemed to do it. Vivian stood, hands still clutched in front of her chest.

"Here, you carry me, and I can hide you," Julep said. Vivian's wings spread out behind her. Each was easily twice Vivian's body height, much more expansive than they'd seemed tucked behind her and limp.

"Under the arms," Julep instructed, unwilling to leave anything up to chance. She turned and faced Vivian, wrapping her own arms under Vivian's as well. She held the child between them. Then, as Vivian's wings beat faster, lifting them a few inches into the air, Julep wrapped her legs around Vivian's midsection. Julep took a deep breath and ducked her head up, pressing her forehead against Vivian's collarbone.

"Now," Julep said. "I'm ready."

Vivian's body trembled in the air, and for a second, Julep thought the only direction they would be going was straight down. She dug her fingertips into Vivian's shoulder blades until Vivian shrugged her back.

"Sorry," Julep whispered. "Just nervous. Can you get us there?"

"I...I don't know," Vivian said. "I've never just had wings before. It took practice to fly with them."

How many times had Julep crashed into the sides of buildings when learning to use her own wings? She counted north of twenty, and even once she figured out how to avoid that, she had much more to learn for motor control. But she knew one thing. Vivian shouldn't have to flap much. Between here and the other balcony attached to the fire escape, there were only twenty feet. It should have been simple enough to jump, flap, and land. Julep could have done it.

"You've got this," she said. "You can do i—"

Before she could finish, they were airborne. Exactly as she'd feared, as soon as they crossed the balcony rail, both of them plummeted rocket-speed toward the police cars below. She saw on the way down that they were in a kind of semicircle around the building.

Oh, that's interesting, was all she had time to think before their descent was abruptly interrupted. Something sticky caught onto Julep's back, keeping her fixed in place. Only

Vivian's leg was caught by it. With some work, the two of them managed to free her.

Her wings were powerful enough only for one, as they'd just proven. At first, a disoriented Julep thought that they'd landed on a police or fireman's net. But when she realized they were still at least two stories above the ground, her heart beat quickly in her chest. She struggled to get her back free, even while considering what might happen when she did. Vivian's eyes shot wide as she hovered before Julep like a life-sized fairy. Then, Vivian shot fifty feet straight into the air and hung there, hovering, her wings buzzing like a drone once again. Julep turned to try to see exactly what had freaked Vivian out. She half-expected Thaddeus to have made it out of the building.

It wasn't Thaddeus. Nor was it Margie, who Julep was pretty sure had to be dead by now, God rest her little soul. No, this was another creepy-crawly. Half-woman, half-spider, the woman vibrated the web with each step. Only the woman wasn't looking at her. Julep knew the hunger well enough to believe that it had to be driving the woman mad, but still, instead of focusing on her prey in what was now so very clear to Julep, a spider web slung between two sides of the alley. A spotlight shot up from below, bathing Julep in its warm heat.

"Let her go, Katie," hovering Vivian said.

The web bounced once, and Julep's head snapped back. The sticky rope caught Julep's head and held it at an angle that prevented Julep from seeing spider-woman in full any longer. She only caught glimpses of a leg here or there out of her peripheral vision. Julep heard nothing from Katie the spider-woman, but she did hear Vivian speak again. The baby boy didn't seem bothered as she held him aloft from the webbing along her right arm, teetering on dropping him yet somehow holding her grip without crushing the child. The conversation around her continued.

"I don't care how long it's been, Katie. Listen…I can change you back. You can be you again. You just have to listen to me."

Another spot of silence, during which Julep guessed that Katie and Vivian engaged in the same telepathic conversations that she remembered having with Thaddeus before she changed back. She worked at her stuck left arm, pulling it against the webbing. It was no use. Whatever adhesive clung to her wouldn't let go. It was as though she'd been superglued in place.

"But you don't have to be this way anymore. You can change. You were right to come here."

Julep watched Vivian hovering. She couldn't see Vivian any longer in the glow formed by the spotlight reflecting from her rapidly beating wings. Vivian looked like an angel hovering and glowing from within, wrapped in almost living black shadows.

"Yes," Vivian said. "Yes, that's right. Patient zero. He's *inside*, Katie. We have to get him out intact. We have to… capture him and get him to change others."

Another pause.

"I don't know about the wings. I guess when we were interrupted by a firebomb in the hallway…"

The legs in the corners of Julep's vision disappeared. From the bouncing of the web, Julep could tell that the Katie was moving away from her. The bouncing was less and less, until finally the only movement was Julep swaying gently in the wind and the rapid patter of rain vibrating the ropes to which she was affixed. Vivian's glow came closer until Julep could make out something of her figure against the halo of her wings. Finally, Vivian was close enough for Julep to see her eyes, and what she saw there scared her more than anything she'd seen until that very moment.

Terror.

There was no other word for it.

"What?" Julep asked. "What did you tell her that made her leave like that?"

"You heard me about the firebomb?"

"Yeah," Julep said, forgetting for a second that she was trapped as she strained her neck to try to nod in futility. "I heard. That's what happened."

"That's not what happened," Vivian whispered as she took Julep's hand.

Vivian's wings seemed to have gotten stronger, like she'd finally remembered how to use them properly. She pulled, and Julep screamed at the pain of her arm being yanked upward. Just before Julep was certain her bones would break, her hand ripped free of the webbing. It was a small start, but if one part could come undone, then others could too.

Vivian hovered to her other arm. "Do you believe in dragons?"

The web suddenly snapped free of the building she'd fled from just as Vivian caught Julep's left arm. The baby screamed as it teetered in her freed right arm, cradled along her forearm like a football. Julep shot up into the air with enough force that she ripped free of the webbing and sailed up above the building just before the entire web erupted into flames. As she soared upward, she brought her left had around to secure the baby and clutched him into her chest.

"I do now," Julep said, staring directly into a green eye the size of an SUV cab window. "Fly. Fast."

It was a redundant command, as Vivian had already shot up another twenty feet into the sky. A trail of flame sparked after Julep, singeing her clothes enough to send tendrils of smoke up into her eyes. They'd only touched the edge of the flame, so she hadn't caught fire. Though she felt that some parts of her had already burned even under her clothing.

"Faster," Julep said again. "Higher."

"I'm trying," Vivian said, hauling them up into the clouds.

The dragon didn't follow. It perched on top of the condominium building as though it were posing for a photo shoot. Its long tail wrapped around the fire escape where they might have been had they made the flight they initially wanted. The dragon's torso rested atop the building and it glared down into the spotlight. Then a gunshot rang out, bouncing off the buildings, followed by another and another. Vivian and Julep kept rising until the gunshots sounded like popcorn. The spotlight didn't follow, now that there was a large problem to deal with. Julep looked down in time to see the entire alley burst into flames. Three seconds passed with the dragon looking on, and then in a second, the dragon descended into the street, scooping flaming and screaming spectators into its massive jaws. Julep had to look away.

The pair of them settled onto the rooftop park above a Macy's department store. There, only eight blocks away from the human roast, it seemed peaceful and quiet. The glow from the alley beyond looked like little more than a block party.

"Come on," Vivian said, hitting the ground running. "Clothes, then we need to get back over there. We need to get back before that dragon eats your man."

"He's not my man," Julep said.

"That's not what he told me," Vivian said. "But you'd know better. Either way, so far, he's the only antidote we have. Faster."

She grabbed a bench and launched it through the window. The alarm sounded, but Julep knew that the police were likely too preoccupied to fuss with a simple looting. She followed Vivian into the women's section, still holding the baby. Julep dumped the contents of a shoebox and placed the newborn into the soft, crumpled paper. His cat-like wailing ceased, and he stuck his tongue out between his lips. She grinned back before she shoved him under a nearby sales counter. He would be alone, but he was safer there than in front of a dragon. Julep walked away, doing her best to ignore the boy who finally seemed to understand that she intended to leave him. Her heart seemed to cramp with every wail, but she told herself it was only temporary, and he was safer there.

With his wailing in the background, Julep rubbed her eyes, then helped herself to some support in the form a solid black sports bra, matching crop tank, leggings, and shoes that fit. She then helped Vivian wiggle into a marled gray sports bra and red-cobra leggings.

There's no accounting for taste, she decided, and giving a lecture on appropriate dragon-fighting attire seemed a little out of place. When Vivian finished pulling on her workout boots, she definitely looked like she could outfight Julep anyway, but that may have been the wings that Julep lacked.

"Come on," Vivian said, sprinting back in the direction they'd just flown from.

Julep's eyes fell to the baby boy sleeping in a cardboard box.

"No weapons?" she asked as he plugged his thumb into his mouth.

"What weapon do you want to use to fight a dragon?"

Julep looked around at the pantsuits and blazers, then farther toward the shoe section, near where expensive perfumes lined the counter of the cosmetics section.

"Yeah. Good point. So what's the plan?"

"Sneak in, and capture your boyfriend," Vivian said.

"Husband," Julep corrected her then shook her head at the knee-jerk response. "Or he was until he fucked my sister."

"Ouch," Vivian said without slowing down. "Well, your ex-fiancé then. We need to get him back to the CDC so that they can figure out how he works."

"And you think you and I can do that?" Julep asked, slowing her sprint to a walk. Vivian slowed as well, her wings drooping down her back.

"We don't have to do much," Vivian said. "Katie's going to capture him. We need to get there before she tries to eat him."

"And Katie is the big spider-lady?"

"Now you're catching on," Vivian said. "Then…"

Vivian stopped running altogether. "She won't be able to forgive herself if she eats him," Vivian said. "She'll regret it for the rest of her life."

Julep could almost hear her whisper Neko's name, but it would have been Julep's imagination filling in the blanks for her. Whoever Neko was, he'd been important to Vivian, and Julep's guess was that Vivian hadn't been able to control the hunger. That wasn't a surprise, as Julep had eaten her fair share of rats and even a cat or two while she'd learned to deal with her change. She'd even considered a woman pushing a stroller and her fat, juicy-looking baby. She spared a glance for the boy in the box. The memory still unjustly made her mouth water at the same time that it repulsed her. An echo of the hunger still lingered in her blood somewhere.

"It wasn't your fault," she said.

"Doesn't matter right now," Vivian told her. "I'll take my emotional breakdown later. Now we have to save your man."

Vivian began to sprint again. When she got to the far end of the department store, they could see the flames through the glass window. Julep smiled again at the sleeping baby, and then left him to sprint after her. She hoped to be back later. If not, there might not be any way to save him. Julep helped Vivian throw several heavy microwave ovens through the window and, holding hands, they jumped into the night sky.

CHAPTER 29
THE THING ABOUT DRAGONS

ARISTIDE HAD TROUBLE FOCUSING. He'd had to drop Katie because she kept trying to take bites of him, and that had been a couple of blocks back. He knew she wasn't herself because he knew that he wasn't himself. All he could think about was Evian and food, and by food, the strangest ideas floated around in his brain. For instance, the people running around below looked like meals on legs. His stomach rumbled, and the thought of sinking his teeth into one of them had increased significantly during his long flight.

There was an entire city to search, though Evian was almost as large as a skyscraper so finding her should have been simple. In the darkness, his eyes saw everything as clear as daytime, yet still she managed to hide from him somehow.

When the spotlight pierced the clouds, he had a notion that she was involved. He turned toward the spotlight, almost ten blocks in the opposite direction. But as he flew, it only took him five minutes to get to it. He arrived just in time to see Katie scurry off into a building that was so engulfed in flames that looked as though it might explode. And he saw Vivian *flying* up into the sky carrying someone he couldn't make out.

They soared up into the sky. As his eyes followed their ascent, the entire alleyway caught fire.

Evian, he thought. He left his perch at the top of Russell Tower and soared toward the flames. Closer and closer he came to the strange-looking building that seemed to writhe and dance in the firelight. As he descended to land on it, the top of the building detached and fell like a leaf down into the alley. Spectators screamed as they ran for cover, though most were already aflame and wouldn't make it very far.

"*Evian,*" he thought again, reaching out with his mind and trying desperately to connect. He'd felt her before and knew he could do it again. Whether she would talk to him or try to eat him, he didn't actually know.

"*Aristide?*"

Her voice. In his head, she sounded exactly as she had sounded in person. Was it her or his imagination?

"*Evian, what are you doing?*"

"*They broke the rules, Aristide. Jaywalkers, every single one of them,*" she replied.

It was her, so definitely her. And he could feel the pain in her voice.

"*Stay away, Aristide. I've got this. Don't worry.*"

"*You have to stop,*" he said. "*They're going to kill you, Evian.*"

The laughter was unexpected and didn't sound like Evian at all. Two voices mingled together to form something demonic-sounding.

"*They can't kill me, Aristide.*"

It was a truth. He could tell from the lack of effect that it was, and that made him shake from head to toe. When the volley of gunshots opened up, not a single bullet seemed to make a difference. She swallowed down flaming body after flaming body, flinging her head back like a reptile.

"*You have to stop,*" he said. "*You're eating the police. What did they do?*"

"What did they not do, Aristide, don't you mean? Why am I the only one trying to keep order here? You're a Marine. You need to help me clean up this city."

This entire time they communicated with each other, she never slowed. Body after flaming body launched into the air and came down, shoved down by her massive throat undulating and flexing.

She stopped for almost five seconds and stared up into the sky directly toward where he hovered. *"Look, with both of us, this would go much faster. You could handle the do-nothing police while I get the lawbreakers. We could finish in half an hour and move on to D.C. next."*

Her eyes that told him what he needed to do. The eyes were still hers, mostly. Except, these eyes had irises like a cat, straight up and down. The color was right, and the tragedy in them was right. Even in her gold and green scale-covered dog-like dragon face, Aristide could see her pain. A screaming spectator sprinted toward her, probably not knowing where he was going as he was covered in flames. Evian dipped her head downward and scooped the man up, then gulped him down between her teeth. Aristide thought he saw a tear glistening in her eye, then it was gone. She turned her attention to the other screaming spectators, one after the other.

"What about Louisiana? What about your family?"

No answer. There wasn't so much as a whisper of thought from her anymore. Whatever happened next would be up to him, and he didn't have options.

Rather he didn't have any good options.

Aristide ran his tongue along his razor-sharp teeth. The hunger rose up in him; this time, he didn't contain it. His eyes watered, and he wanted to stop, but he was a Marine and had to do the right thing. The right thing was stopping this creature, who he could have loved, he realized, more than he'd been willing to admit. He dropped fast through the air. Cold wind whipped past him as he descended and sounded like a rocket in his ears. Aristide opened his mouth wide, and then to his surprise, his jaw dislocated and dropped nearly to his chest as he fell. He steered toward her, falling faster and faster, until he collided with her back just behind the shoulder blades. With a tear-filled scream into the empty sky, he sank his teeth into her neck.

At first, she didn't seem to notice him. She flicked people into her mouth and swallowed, still intent on continuing her feast on the unruly crowd. By the time she noticed he was there, she'd already begun to stagger. He drained her life force. Blood gushed between his teeth. Most of it dripped down his clothes in orange-red streaks. Some went into his mouth and filled his longing belly. For the first time in hours, his stomach pain had lifted and it seemed that this organ could almost absorb endless supplies. The dragon staggered into one building then another, then collapsed into a heap on the ground.

His body knew when it was time to stop. Aristide wanted to forget that this moment had ever happened. And if he couldn't, then he wanted to die with her. He stayed on top of her shoulders until they stopped moving. Every nerve in his body was telling him to flee. He couldn't bring himself to do it. A few seconds passed, and Aristide started to feel a rumble. The fire had nowhere else to go, he realized, now that she was dead. He lifted off of her just as she exploded into flames, propelling him into the sky.

CHAPTER 30
THE HUNGER

KATIE WANDERED through darkened hallways just small enough that she had to crouch to gain entrance. She stayed as far from the fire as she could. Something about the flames triggered an almost atavistic flight response, she guessed by the intensity of her aversion to it. She chewed her bottom lip as she crept, slinking along from shadow to shadow with eight black legs. She'd lost control. To not admit it was to let it happen again. It had taken her twenty-seven minutes to build the web in the alleyway, all on autopilot. Her animal instincts had taken over, and she almost tried to eat Aristide, Vivian, and some poor bystander.

There was hope. Somewhere within this labyrinth of a building hid the snakelike creature that had the power to change her back. The catch was she couldn't actually defeat the creature if she changed back first, so she had to capture it before it could catch her. She searched the dark corridors of the north side of the building while the flames ate away the south side. With any luck, he'd fled the fire as they all had, and she would stumble upon him soon.

Scampering from one shadow to another, Katie stumbled

across something slimy and two of her legs folded beneath her. The rest of her legs caught her and she ran quickly, circling up the wall and onto the ceiling, then she fixed all of her eye lenses on the area where she'd tripped. A long undulating tentacled arm zipped toward her. It took her a second to realize that there were leechlike teeth on the end, and she slipped to the side and let it fly past. Then she saw something horrific, even more startling than the beast she'd become. A woman's body hovered mid-height in the alley, suspended by tentacles that seemed to come from a rip between her lower body and torso. The woman said nothing and only sent another tentacle toward her.

"*What are you doing?*" Katie asked, communicating the only way she could.

"*You won't take him away from me,*" the woman said. Katie only wondered who for less than a second before she realized that she was talking about the man she sought.

"*Thaddeus?*" she asked.

"*How do you love my creation?*" his voice came into her head, gravelly and masculine. Wherever he was, he was close, but the problem with telepathy was that the voice could have come from anywhere. "*Behind you.*"

She didn't turn anywhere near quickly enough. As she did, she realized the massive mistake of taking her eyes off of her current attacker. Thaddeus was behind her, but all the way down at the end of the hallway. The creature that was trying to eat her was right there and had already sent two other tentacles her way. One slammed into her clavicle and wrenched her backward by the shoulder. The other bounced uselessly off of her armored abdomen. She could feel the creature scream in pain, but she felt even more pain in her shoulder as the creature yanked on her, pulling her over to the floor. It felt like the creature was making a concerted effort to rip her torso from her body.

Katie felt Thaddeus's approach before she heard him. The sliding of his snakelike tail across the floor sounded like sand pouring toward her. She turned her head to face him.

"Who is this?"

"Margie," Thaddeus said and then let out a low chuckle. "At least it used to be. It turns out my ability works both ways."

"Both ways?"

"I can bring you back," he said. "Or I can make you more of a monster. Isn't that right, Margie?"

The silent woman grinned eerily from ear to ear and then looked at Katie like she was a prime-rib sandwich. Katie saw no humanity left in her eyes.

"You have to know this is wrong," Katie said, then grunted as another tentacle stabbed her in the lower back.

"You think that now," he said. "Wait until I'm done with you. You'll see things my way."

He was gone too.

Whatever Katie had to do, she had to do, and she knew what that was. The hunger that she struggled to keep at bay and the animal instincts that came with it, they could save her. She could easily defeat even two of these creatures with her command of three-dimensional space. But she couldn't do it by thinking. Her movements wouldn't be fast enough. She hoped against all hope that she could return from what she was about to do. Katie took a deep breath...and let go of all self-control.

CHAPTER 31
GONE

FUCKING NEKO.

He had to be such a jerk, and she had to lose control because of his constant chiding and whining. "Put me down" and "You're a monster" and "I never loved you."

It was the last one that had caused her to eat him.

Tears had streamed down her cheeks as her proboscis had stabbed through his head as his eyes went dead. She'd wept while she sucked her fill of his insides. The memory made her want to lurch, but nobody had time for such banalities. Vivian focused on what she could change, and all she could do now was try to right some wrongs and hope that one day she could forgive herself.

They landed on the south roof of the condominium building. Flames danced on the north roof, and she guessed that over half of the building had been consumed already. Eventually, enough support would be gutted by the flames that the building might collapse, and then there would be no capturing anyone.

"Stairs?" Vivian asked.

"If we can open the door, yeah," Julep said. "Keep your eyes out. He's a sneaky bastard. Trust me."

Vivian pulled the door open and stepped through into the darkness of the roof access stairwell. The steps, fortunately, were standard spacing so running down them in the dark didn't turn out to be terribly difficult, especially since she kept a death grip on the handrail. The pair reached a landing in ten seconds. Vivian heard something that sounded like a muffled sigh in the darkness. She stopped and held up her hand.

"Stop," she said. "There's got to be someone down there."

"Where?"

"Ahead. I heard something," Vivian said. "Is there a light switch in these halls?"

She answered the question for herself. Yes, there was a light switch. It was right next to her hand on the rail. No, it didn't work because the entire building was on fire; therefore, the electricity in any given part of it was hit or miss. This stairwell was a miss. Night vision would have been extremely handy.

"Viv?" a shallow whisper floated up. "Is that you?"

Vivian's heart leapt, and her body did too at the sound of Katie's voice. Her wings flitted and, after bumping her head against the landing above, she lowered herself down, landing in total darkness. That was before she remembered that Katie had turned into some sort of spider monster. Before she could lift off again, she felt a hand close around her ankle.

"I can't move well, Viv," she said. "They're in here. Two of them, Thaddeus and an octopus woman he called Margie. Is that Margaret Hode?"

Julep snarled somewhere in the darkness.

"Wh…how? She was changed back, like me," the woman asked. Vivian could imagine her eyes going wide at the same realization that she was making herself. Perhaps this change was only a temporary reprieve.

"No. No, it's not," Katie said. "He's figured out how to

make the process go both ways. He turned Margie back into that thing, only I'm pretty sure that now there's no Margie left anymore."

Vivian tried to pull her leg free. To her surprise, Katie's body lifted off the ground easily. That shouldn't have been possible with the massive spider abdomen. And there was that little clue that she was talking.

"What happened to you, Katie?"

"I failed," she said. "They trapped me, and he did the whole cure-me thing. I think he needs to reset to human in order to go back the other way. They were going to make me one of them. But I…"

She coughed softly. Vivian would have given anything for a light then.

"Help me," she said to Julep. "Let's get her out of here."

"And what about Thaddeus?"

"Let's get Katie to safety first, and then we'll go back." Somewhere down the stairwell, something clanked. "I think we'd better do it quickly."

The pair dragged Katie up the stairs and back out onto the rooftop. The fire had spread to other buildings in the city and now lit up the entire area like it was daylight. The first thing Vivian noticed about Katie were the round bitemarks on her back and shoulder. The second was a patch of hairy prongs that stuck out just above each thigh. Sticky webbing oozed uncontrolled from one of them.

"They didn't get me," Katie said. "They tried, but I managed to cut off one of Margie's tentacles with my teeth." Katie chuckled then coughed. "She thrashed around like a dying fish, and that distracted Thaddeus enough for me to make it to the stairwell. Then whatever that thing he does started to hit, and I couldn't tell which way was up. I just ran until I couldn't run any longer."

"You're not…"

"Not all the way changed back. I know." Katie paused. "They're monsters, Viv. You and I...we're just misunderstood. I'm not even sure...I'm not sure that we *should* bring them back."

"He can change people back, Katie," Vivian said. "And he could put CDC ahead by eight months or more in developing an antitoxin for whatever this is."

"I'm not sure it's worth the eight months," Katie said. "How would we know that he's changing people back and not creating more monsters? CDC can find the antitoxin with you and me if we get there fast enough. I say we leave them to die here and get out while we can."

That could have been just the fear talking. But of all them, Katie was the least likely to work from a place of fear. That was why she was in charge because while Vivian was freaking out, Katie held firm. If Katie thought they should let Thaddeus die when the building collapsed, Vivian could get behind that. But could Julep? Vivian looked toward Julep, who watched the fire as though she wanted some marshmallows to roast over it.

"I'm fine," Julep said, unprompted. "The sooner we get out of here, the finer I'll be."

"I can only lift one of you," Vivian said. "And the other..."

"I can help," came a voice from overhead. Vivian looked up to see a live gargoyle flapping in the sky overhead. "I'll take you, Katie."

"My hero," Katie said weakly as she lifted her arm. "Thank you, Aristide."

"Aristide? Like the bus?"

He nodded as he lifted Katie into his arms.

"Where's Evian?" Vivian asked, looking around confused. A roar sounded in the background, and Aristide shook his head slowly.

"Gone," was all he said. He lifted into the sky. Vivian grabbed Julep and followed.

"We have to make a stop first. I need to pick something up," Julep said.

Ten minutes later, the group lifted away from the sport clothing store as the baby screamed in the night in Julep's arms. In the distance, the massive building that used to be a condominium unit belched a ball of flame and crumbled in on itself.

CHAPTER 32
THE NEW TASK FORCE

SIX MONTHS LATER, and Katie Villin and Vivian Purnell sat atop the roof of a single-family home of at the end of a private drive in Alexandria, Virginia. Katie looked at the skylight, then back at Vivian, who nodded.

"This is the place," Vivian whispered. "Home Sweet Awakening provided the contract. This is the address that Chaitlain gave them as their lab headquarters."

"But nothing looks strange. If anything happened here, shouldn't there be another hole in the roof or something?"

"You didn't notice the pile of mail stacked against the front door?"

Katie shrugged. Skeptical as usual, a stack of main didn't mean to her what it meant to Vivian. Despite that fact that the analysts assured them both that this was where they'd most likely find the research notes to what they were calling UHS-26450j for now, the original formulation for the vial-contained substances that had initiated the first identified changes. If they could find the research, they might be able to prove the anti-agent safe for people like them, with non-life-threatening mutations only.

The opening was too narrow for Vivian's wings so Katie reached down to her midsection and pulled open two flaps in her cargos just above her thighs. Thick conical protrusions extended out from the openings. Two spinnerets the size of fists, set just above her hipbones, were the only non-life-threatening mutations that remained from her time as a spider-woman. Thick fibrous webbing shot out of the hairy structures and affixed itself to the roof just beside the skylight.

"Do you think we'll find it in there?" Vivian asked, tapping her head just behind her eyes, adjusting the night vision mask that covered her eyes.

"Probably," Katie replied. "It's not like he knew we were coming."

Katie used her spinnerets and slowly released webbing to lower herself through the skylight opening. She tested it by bouncing with her legs against the underside of the opening. When she thought it was strong enough, she nodded to Vivian. Vivian then stepped through and straddled her chest while Katie lowered both of them. The air smelled of rot and decay.

Once through the opening, Vivian took flight, hovering near the top and surveying the room. Bodies lay scattered around what looked like it had at one time been a bathroom. It looked like bites had been taken out of each, and entrails hung over the shower as blood congealed in the sinks.

"It's gross in here," she said. "This has to be the guy."

"All right," Katie told her. "I'm going down." She lowered herself more quickly until she reached the floor, then took a deep breath and pinched off the webbing by contracting her spinnerets. That part hurt every time but less lately as she'd gotten better at it. She lay supine and examined the room, keeping her ears alert for anything. As far as she could tell, they were alone except for the bodies surrounding them. One she recognized from the CDC debrief.

"Chaitin Russell," she said as she closed the flaps back over her spinnerets. She could have gotten rid of them with the new CDC treatment, but doing so seemed like a denial of the change she'd experienced. The spinnerets and the bright silver-streak in her hair were a testament to the person she'd been who was strong enough to experience all that she'd been through and come out the other side. This *was* her. And when Vivian refused to give up what she called her "fairy wings," it also gave Katie the strength to say no. She would keep her scars.

Katie rolled over onto her belly and slid forward. She was certain the room was empty. The door creaked slowly open, and all Katie could think to do was wait and watch. What she saw made her heart stop. Fingers—or she thought they were fingers—nearly six inches long and growing, pushed their way through the opening. But when they cleared the doorway, she could see from the moonlight trickling in that they weren't fingers at all, but claws. And attached to those claws were arms.

"Are you seeing this?" Katie whispered. Her earpiece buzzed and crackled. Then Aristide's voice came piercing through.

"Are you ready for us?"

"No, stand down, Aristide…for now. We don't know—"

A hand she hadn't been watching closed around her ankle. A second later, she was airborne. Vivian was faster than Katie had ever thought possible and caught Katie midair, but that brought both of them down and made Vivian an easy target. The claws retracted and shot forward, thudding solidly into Vivian's chest and pushing her into the wall. Katie heard little more than an "uhf" in her earpiece and then Vivian went limp.

Katie twisted while she fell to land on her knees and one hand. She raised her eyes to see the creature before her. The creature looked like someone had taken Victor Hart, the arguable mad scientist who accidentally invented the monster virus, and stretched all of his appendages, then filed them down into points. His fingertips were razor sharp, as Katie's bleeding ankle could attest. Her knees and elbows and shoulders all looked similar. Even his face had been contorted into a silent-hill version of himself, complete with gnarled teeth that, through some miracle, still opened.

"You die now," he said in an emotionless statement. He lifted one of his long arms to strike.

"N…now," Katie whispered into the night. "Aristide, now. Now!"

Five grenades at once crashed into the room. Katie dove to protect Vivian as the monster tried to eat one of the grenades. It exploded in his mouth, sending a shower of teeth over her where Katie's back was exposed. She gritted her teeth as some of the teeth penetrated through her Kevlar vest.

Vivian moved.

"Good girl," Katie said. "Stay with me."

"It's not as bad as that," Vivian said, gasping. "Just got the wind knocked out. Need…to…breathe."

"Aristide's coming in," Katie said.

Vivian looked at her. "Are you sure that's a good idea?"

"What else are we going to do? Look at that thing."

It wasn't just Aristide. Katie had succeeded in convincing the CDC that the Biological Security Task Force needed actual, legitimate military strength. They'd caved to her demands almost immediately because even a month after they'd figured out how to turn people back from monsters into humans, North Carolina was still dark. For some reason, North Carolina had turned into a cesspool of monsters, and Katie guessed from Aristide's descriptions that Tamitha Vega was a significant part of that situation. So far, they hadn't found Tam, but Katie felt that she was still out there somewhere. Nor had they discovered Julep's former lover Thaddeus and her sister, neither of whom did Julep express much remorse about. Both were most likely dead. Katie had instructed her team to count them in the more than twenty people presumed dead in the condo collapse.

Katie recruited Aristide as the first member of her militant group because he had first-hand knowledge of what they were dealing with. And now, as former Marines followed the grenades through the skylights and windows, she was glad she did. It took a handful of minutes for Aristide and his crew to neutralize the area. Katie didn't like how two of Aristide's men stared at Vivian's wings, but they didn't say anything. Once the room was secured and the lights restored, a tall man approached and removed his gunmetal helmet.

"Aristide," she said.

"Katie. Vivian," he replied. His eyes were cold, not like when she'd first met him. Any emotions in them had died the night Evian had. In his way, even with the reversal of the mutation, he'd stayed a monster. His forces were efficient, effective, and lethal.

"Thank you," she said.

"You should have sent us in first to clear the place. You could find what you needed after."

"Then, you'd have to have searched the entire building. We found him quickly and would have gotten what we were looking for."

"Did you find it?"

"Over there," Vivian said, pointing through the doorway into the hallway. It took Katie a minute to realize she was talking about the room on the other side, through a crack in the door, and then on the far side. There was a blinking green light that indicated the man's research laptop. Katie wasted no time in retrieving it. She settled in beside it at the desk where it lay. The thing was fortunately unlocked. She guessed that Victor had set it that way once the biometric stopped working and his mind began to unravel. She scrolled through the folders until she found one marked Borderline Cosmetics. It looked like he'd saved it from an email at some point.

"According to this, Borderline Cosmetics bought their patented antiaging process and decided to use it as a romantic luxury gift. For several thousand dollars, you can buy a vial and get your and your romantic partner's unique DNA signature."

"Is that the stuff that's causing all of the trouble?"

Katie nodded. "According to the analysts, yeah."

It was a strange thing to say since she wasn't an analyst any longer. She was now a perpetual field agent, at least until they got the outbreak under control. North Carolina was next on her list of hot spots.

Aristide looked confused. "So what does that mean?"

"This stuff is designed to offset aging. That guy," she said, pointing to the now motionless body of Victor Hart, "designed it to be a crème. He also designed it to get through the skin's defenses and affect genetic change at a microcellular level. The mixing process that the cosmetic company used added different DNA from different animals to increase the uniqueness of each vial. When Julep broke her vial because she hurled it at her cheating whore of a husband, she got some of it on her skin, and it reacted, changing her into that bird creature."

"Sir," one of Aristide's new joins approached him, pulling his attention away from her. "Perimeter is clear."

"Good," Aristide said. "Tell the team we got what we came for. We'll be leaving soon."

The man snapped to attention and saluted, but Aristide only nodded. The man waited for a second, then turned and left.

"You'll disappoint them if you don't return the salutes," Katie said, nodding toward the man's exit.

"Look at this," Vivian exclaimed and spun the laptop around. "This explains the secondary mutations."

"What am I looking at?" asked Aristide.

"Viral vectors," Katie replied, and Vivian nodded. "Specifically, mutation rates for viral vectors. They're not supposed to replicate in the body, but look at sample 1.2a there." She pointed to the screen. "That one mutates outside of replication. It wouldn't have taken much to trip it over. That's probably what happened to the lizard-woman and Tam. They still carried a massive load of viral these in their blood. So the spit and the projectiles were essentially just infected mediums for carrying the virus into new hosts. Remarkable."

"I guess," Aristide said. "I was scratched. What about that?"

"You were scratched with a claw that had already tangled with an infected host," Vivian said. "That transferred the viral load to you."

Aristide just nodded and turned back to his work. His curiosity, Katie knew, only went so far. The information he gathered largely was along the lines of what he could use to kill the creatures. She remembered the conversation she'd had with him while he was recovering.

"If something could turn Evian so evil, then it will turn anyone."

That was what he'd said. And she hadn't agreed then and still didn't. Aristide, Julep, Katie herself...these were all evidence that the serum could be overcome. Vivian, Evian, the Red Dress Woman, and even Thaddeus were evidence that it couldn't. In a nutshell, it was less likely someone could overcome the hunger. At night, sometimes, even Katie still awoke with that longing in her gut, the craving for the warm smoothie that dissolved animal wrapped in spider silk. In the mornings, she awoke disgusted with herself, and the lingering craving never fully went away. But she dealt with it and guessed that Vivian had her demons and Aristide too.

There was no going back after a transformation like they'd

experienced. "Katie stuck one finger in the air and spun it in a circle, the universal signal for "Let's go." Aristide, Vivian, and tens of soldiers, all part of the new and improved Biological Security Task Force, ran from the building. Demolition came in next and leveled the entire place.

It was the only way to be certain.

Katie, Aristide, and Vivian piled into a black SUV. Katie pushed the button to bring on the engine, and the engine roared to life. Katie turned to Aristide in her passenger seat.

"Ready for North Carolina?"

His lip went into a straight line, and he nodded without saying anything.

"Dinner first?" Vivian asked. "This work makes me hungry."

"I bet," Katie said. "I guess. Where to?"

"Morton's Steakhouse," Aristide chimed in.

"Oooh, I like that," Vivian said.

Katie imagined biting into a raw, bloody steak, barely at room temperature. It wasn't an animal slushie but would scratch the itch for a while. She felt herself salivating at the thought. Katie wondered if they would think she was weird if she asked the chef to put the steak through a blender.

Perhaps that was something she'd be better off trying in her own home. Katie nodded to Aristide.

"Okay, Morton's," she said. "I'm buying. Tell the team?"

She thought she caught the slight trace of a smile.

"You're buying for all of them?" he asked.

"Might as well," she said, smiling back at him. Then she bit her lip and looked at him as she shifted into drive. "This one went well. Not sure how North Carolina's going to go. Let's let them eat up while they can."

CHAPTER 33
SEBASTIAN

AT THE DEAD end of a dirt road in the vicinity of Spotsylvania, Virginia, Julep Hode poured lukewarm water into the baby bath seat insert in the upstairs bathroom. In the wheeled bassinette that she'd brought from the master bedroom, an infant with green hair and matching bright green irises stared up at her with so much unconditional love and trust that she couldn't help smiling when she was ready to place him into the tub. Just to be sure, she ran her hand under the pouring faucet one more time.

"Well, Sebastian, the water certainly seems ready for you," she said, as she turned toward the bassinette. Four distinct beeps alerted her to a call. Julep sighed briefly as she turned from the furniture to where she'd left her phone on the nightstand. A glance at who it was told her that the new Bioengineering Task Force right-hand apparently had nothing better to do with her time than check in with Julep.

"Vivian?" she asked when she clicked the button to connect.

"Hi, Julep," Vivian's voice rang out. "How are you and Sebastian?"

"He's doing well. Eating like a horse and growing like a weed."

"Is he showing any signs?"

Vivian asked the question as though she actually believed that Julep might tell her about Sebastian's little *abnormalities*.

"Nope. Just a pleasant, plump little boy."

She heard what she thought was a sigh of relief on the other end of the line.

"Good. Any sign of Thaddeus or Margie?"

Julep shook her head when she answered. "Nope. I doubt they'd come looking for me anyway, even if they made it out of the fire."

"Yeah, maybe. Keep an eye out just in case though, and let me know if you see them?"

"Sure."

"One more thing. That reversal process the CDC has worked out…it hasn't been tested on those of us who've been reversed by Thaddeus. There aren't enough of us to make a sample size, so even if it was, there wouldn't be enough data to make a determining factor."

"I'm all the way changed, Vivian."

"None of us are. Why do you think I keep checking in?" Vivian paused. "Anyway, don't take it. And don't take Sebastian either. Not unless he starts showing signs of…unusual body changes. Okay?"

Not that Julep had intended to do so anyway. She bit her lip to keep from laughing out loud. Both she and Sebastian were as perfect as perfect could be. A hint of a giggle escaped her mouth.

"I'm serious, Julep."

"I know," she said. Sebastian's call sounded in the background. "Look, I have to go. Anything else?"

"Just be careful, I guess. And call me sometime. It's weird that I always have to call you to figure out how you are."

"I will, Vivian. I promise."

"Okay then."

She hung up the phone. Sebastian sounded again, and Julep worked her way back to the side of his bassinette. Her nephew croaked with delight while shoving a plastic toy frog into his mouth. She reached in to retrieve him. As she did, a tiny spark of fear flowed through her veins when his lizard tongue poked out between his elongated incisors. The tongue only licked at her fingertips as she lifted him out and placed him in the seat where water ran over his delicate child-downy hair. She was efficient at the bath, and equally efficient at the bottle, though distractions still caused her head to pivot uncontrolled sometimes. Occasionally, she made herself feel stupid trying to lift off the ground on muscles that had reverted back to spinal support, causing a painful cramp when she mistakenly tried to fly.

As she pulled him from the bath, she saw a giant wolf spider creeping toward her across the far end of the counter. Instinctually, she opened her mouth, and a tiny dart flew from the tiny proboscis tongue that usually concealed itself under a flap of skin. On target, as usual, the unsuspecting spider met an early death.

"There," she said. "All clean and beautiful. Are we ready to see Mom and Dad, all shiny now?"

The child cooed.

"Very well," she said. "Looking only, though. No touching 'til you're older."

He cooed again, long, low and sweet, like a whippoorwill. His smile lit the room as he clawed at her with tiny fingers. She swaddled up the child and plucked the spider from the counter, unpinning it in the process. Then she handed it to him, and it immediately made its way through his sharp teeth to rest against his tongue for only a second until the sickly sweet crunch of its exoskeleton sounded out in the room. Julep's instincts had long since reverted to normal, so she found the spider revolting and a little terrifying, but little Sebastian loved them as a snack. That would be useful when he was older, so she fed him what she could, and this one had been too large to let go to waste. She put him over her shoulder and slapped him on the back until he let out a massive belch that brought with it a bit of spider guts onto her shoulder, which she wiped clean with a burp cloth.

"There, there," she said. "Better now?"

She carried her nephew with her down two flights of stairs to a giant metal door that had been locked with three deadbolts. Each one she slid open in turn before stepping down onto the first stair and flicking the light switch. She took great care not to slip on the metal stairs as she descended into the twilight-darkness. Near the bottom, she pushed open yet another door, and gave herself a moment to adjust. Before her in the black, two terrifying forms materialized. One of them lurched forward, trying the chains that held them in place. She smiled a wide grin and turned the baby to look.

"That's your father, Thaddeus," she said, motioning to the snake-creature chained in place with iron. "He's kind of a dick, but it's better for you to have a man in your life I suppose. And over there, that's Mommy. She can't really take care of you right now. No, no. Don't cry. She'd probably try to eat you, anyway."

She turned the child toward what was left of her sister, also chained to the wall in the opposite corner of the room. The creature there glared at her and licked its lips. The carcasses of rats that had been unfortunate enough to wander close lined the floor around her. Her tentacles, all except one, rose into the air and shot toward the two of them, falling well short of the mark. Julep smiled again.

"Nice try, sis," she said. "But as you can see, I've got your man, and I've got your son. And you've completely lost your mind. In the grand scheme of things, I guess that means I win, doesn't it?"

Her eyes drifted back to Thaddeus.

"I do have you, don't I?" she asked, staring into his eyes, seeking recognition. The piles of rats near him were smaller, as though he'd put in some small effort at least not to eat them. That was promising. But it wasn't his condition for freedom. His condition was that he do to himself what he'd done to her. Revert himself to something close to normal so that she could control him better.

She hadn't believed her luck when she'd found them in the rubble before the rapid response crews had come. Both were wrapped up in each other's arms like lovers, and both were unconscious. Neither had burned. Mainly because, from what Julep could tell, Thaddeus didn't burn with that thick hide of his, and he'd covered Margie with his body to protect her. Even thinking about that filled her with rage. Julep stared remorselessly at Thaddeus, whose face tentacles waved toward her as though she would be their next snack. In response, she opened her mouth, shot three of them with darts, and stormed with the child back up the stairs, ignoring the otherworldly screams that issued from whatever Thaddeus had instead of vocal cords. He should never have crossed her in the first place.

But he had. And her sister had for decades. She locked the deadbolts behind her as she carried Sebastian up through the kitchen and out onto the wide front porch. She placed him in his swing, and he cooed at her. He then bounced and played with spinning wheels that were perfect for brain development. Julep sat herself in her rocker and sipped at a lemonade that she'd left for herself. The next generation would grow into something beautiful, and she would see to it that Sebastian carved out his place in the world. She couldn't help smiling at the possibilities.

CHAPTER 34

AFTERWORD

KATIE SAT ALONE in her budget hotel room in Danville, Virginia, just across the border from North Carolina. She pulled out the hotel stationery and sat at what passed for a writing desk.

"Dear Mom," she wrote, starting a letter she should have sent years before. "I miss you. I'm in Danville, Virginia, at a Budget Friend Motel, if you can believe it. You'll never guess what I've been doing lately…"

~ THE END ~

If you loved this novel, don't forget to leave a review at https://www.amazon.com/review/create-review/?ie=UTF8&channel=glance-detail&asin=B0C99ML5GS. Every review helps!

GLOSSARY

One of my early readers suggested that having a glossary for those with less exposure to genetic mutations and bioengineering concepts would be useful. Thank you for your suggestion, and as promised, here's your glossary!

antigen - suppresses how a gene is interpreted or expressed, in this case, slightly misused to mean reversal as well

drift - in this case, a reference to 'genetic drift' but somewhat misused, though gene editing is very much happening

global mutation - mutation happening simultaneously all over the body

inert - resistant to change, dormant

phenotype - how genes show up in perceivable ways (like eye color, for example)

proboscis - a sort of tongue a butterfly uses to get nectar from a flower

transmission - how a disease travels within a community

vector - in bio-engineering, how genetic 'programs' are delivered into hosts, and a *viral vector means* using a virus to transmit genetic code

If you'd like me to add to this list, email me, and I'll update: andrew@andrewsweetbooks.com